Frederick Greenwood

The lover's lexicon

Frederick Greenwood

The lover's lexicon

ISBN/EAN: 9783337220211

Hergestellt in Europa, USA, Kanada, Australien, Japan

Cover: Foto ©Andreas Hilbeck / pixelio.de

Weitere Bücher finden Sie auf **www.hansebooks.com**

The
Lover's Lexicon

A Handbook

For Novelists, Playwrights, Philosophers,
and Minor Poets ; but Especially
for the Enamoured

By FREDERICK GREENWOOD

London
MACMILLAN AND CO.
AND NEW YORK
1893

CONTENTS

ABHORRENCE

WHEN love began, no one could have thought of dictionary-making, since there was not a word of material for the purpose; nor was anybody scientific enough to bring a sigh within orthoepic rules. Darwin has doubts on the subject; but that love had an established existence, with all-sufficing means of communication, impartation, discourse, long before words were invented, is evident from two familiar observations. Not only is love preferentially mute, it is most eloquent in that condition; as all its poets declare, and as we know of ourselves. And it is to be observed that the language of love as known to grammarians has an extremely meagre vocabulary, which could hardly have happened had it not perfected a speech of its own in pre-lingual times. Invention is the child of Necessity. Already provided in other ways, love had little need to share in the invention of words when that business began, finding it enough to draw here and there from the fund of common speech for mechanic uses. Many a trade of fifty years' growth could furnish a fuller word-

manual appropriate to itself than one of the oldest
and most inspiring of the passions.   This comes of
a long-derived superfluity of eloquence in muteness.
But had language been foreknown, or rather had
dictionary-making been foreseen in the caves and
woodlands of primeval happiness, the word that
stands at the head of the preceding page would never
have begun with the first and second letters of any
alphabet.   That would have been provided for.   Even
then there were cynics and persons given to joking.
We may therefore safely believe that if, in fore-
casting the future, vocabularies had been included in
the speculations of primeval man, care would have
been taken to coin no word and to frame no grammar
that could place syllables expressive of disgust in
the first line of a Lover's Dictionary.   However,
there could be no such prescience at a time so many,
many thousands of years before the dawn of lexico-
graphy ; and therefore, and also as an unforeseen
consequence of Roman conquest, " Abhorrence "
must stand where it meets the startled gaze in the
forefront of this undertaking.

   " It is better to begin with a little aversion."
The truth in this saying is only partial, and its
applications pertain to matrimony rather than to
love.   The whole truth is, that it is better to begin
with a little aversion unless your happier fate is to
begin with the headlong clash and embracement of
" love at first sight."   When that happens to reasonable young persons the best happens ; for in their
case love at first sight is love with second sight :
they know each other at once.   But when this magic
faculty of vision is absent, then indeed it is well to

start with its only substitute — study. There is nothing like a little aversion to make inquiry into any person's character effective and complete.

Aversion, however, is not abhorrence, with its strangely close relations to the passion of love. Not that those relations are always strange. It is natural to love, and a proof of its " beauty of holiness," that no sooner does it take possession than abhorrences of the fiercest kind start up in its train ; for they are all abhorrences of things unseemly or unclean. Nor are they so very strange, the abhorrences of a most unheavenly sort which attend upon a much less heavenly love ; as when a woman, being carried away by a wild irruption of outlawed passions, will forthwith abhor her rightful house-mate, traduce his very virtues in her heart, and even hate her children. By such extreme perversions we may know that if love lifts to heaven and takes its light, it also descends to hell and there makes evil its good.

The abhorrence that *is* strange is one that women are overcome by much oftener than men. It is an abhorrence akin to love, and violently preceding it : or sometimes accompanying its first stroke, which is then felt less like a kiss than a blow. Long before societies were formed to explore the interior mysteries of psychology, many unhappy men and still greater numbers of unhappy women could tell of a magnetic effluence of repulsion which yet holds its subject trembling within its range. A week, a month of agitation in suspense, and then the victim is caught in a return-current of irresistible attraction. When the unfortunate is a man, look to the lady for a certain *beauté du diable*, with other fascinations of the same. When it is a woman, there may be a kind of formal beauty in her fascinator, but, as a rule, look for no beauty of any sort that a man would acknowledge. Look rather for ugliness— ugliness carried to the extreme where it becomes a mystery.

It is believed that marriage contracted under this strange glamour is rarely as happy as women, in their kindness, are willing to imagine it. According to common observation, when a young wife so married does not walk as one who bears a guilty secret in her breast (as she often does, though nobody can guess what the secret may be), jealousy, of all things, is her constant torment.

ABSENCE

A word which, etymologically, is the same as *absentia*, being away ; but its signification to lovers is identical with "bereavement," or, more frequently, "bi-section." In fact and practice, absence is the discipline of love, its prime medicament and its probation. Only the last of these qualities is acknowledged by lovers, though by some the first is suspected and the other is well known. In theory absence is torture ; and no lover that ever lived would call it by a softer name, or confess to any infusion of sweetness in it. But the nature of love is such that its pains and its pleasures are often in embrace ; and of all the many distresses to which it is exposed there is but one without some joy in it, and that one is not the misery of absence. This

Juliet would have said, alone on her balcony, and
Eleanor, walking darkly in Rosamund's garden.
Absence is privation ; and the sense of it—such is
the unity of our nature—precisely tallies with the
corporeal feeling of hunger. Therefore with a little
imagination and adequate effort, the huntsman or
the alderman may understandingly participate in the
emotions of parted lovers though quite unacquainted
with the celestial passion. Longing the hungry man
knows, with its bitter-sweet mingling of joys remembered with joys to come ; and, as a stage beyond
that, yearning he knows ; and then, accompanied by
vivid intermittent visions of the desired object, there
is the fainting sickness nearer to eight o'clock which
an alderman really in love might be puzzled to
ascribe with certainty to the one privation or the
other.

Absence and hunger have other resemblances
which poets and young lovers will be less inclined
to spurn. Hunger is a good and wholesome thing
if it last not too long. If it last not too long the
body of this flesh thrives by it ; and love thrives
by absence in like manner and through corresponding processes. That it does so thrive is a matter of
instinctive apprehension with lovers of both sexes ;
but less with men than with women, who combine
a more natural understanding of the salubrity of
absence with greater endurance under its infliction
for limited periods. But it may also be enjoyment.
Some there are who, being possessed of a treasure,
do not willingly keep it in sight for long, to be
viewed in any casual mood or trifling moment, but
hide it away, sending their hearts out to it many

times before they will go to look on it again, and so
renew the sudden joy of "It is thine!" So you
may see the new-made wife, after flashing the fourth
part of a glance on her wedding-ring—tilting up the
fingers that hang by her side—fling the amazingly
glorified hand quite behind her. Considering their
nature, maidens there may be who contrive little
spells of absence from their sweethearts in precisely
the same spirit; it is a likely though an unavowed
practice. It is known, however, that absence is
planned for various conscious or half - conscious
reasons, though rarely by true lovers of the blunter
sex. Women will do so even for the pleasure of the
pain. Incapable of such refinements, men are too
rude, or perhaps too robust, to court pain for the
pleasure of it, though it may be done by the feeble
sort of youth which seeks a reputation for soul by
means of self-effemination. And again, women in
love, or hanging on the verge of it, will contrive
absences to prove the constancy or test the ardour
of their lovers. Even the most unknowing maid will
do this; and do it with no more artifice than plots
in the bosom of the rose when it droops in the stare
of her lord the sun. With a similar motive, women
will shelter themselves in absence when they doubt
the reality of the love in their own breasts or feel
uncertain whether it be well rooted or no; but that
is not so much the way with men, who are more
often impatient to test their love by looking on the
object of it than patient to endure the touch of
absence. Yet, being richer in love-lore (of which
they have a long inbred inheritance from the
maternal side), maids are more sensitive than men

to the risks of absence when it is carried beyond a
certain point ; and there are reasons for believing
that even without communication of any kind with
the evaded or the banished man they are able to
ascertain within themselves when the hunger of his
privation begins to sink from craving to a dangerous
point of lassitude. This valuable gift, like others of
a similar kind, is doubtless the growth of the many
ages that have elapsed since marriage by seizure
died out, courtship began, and barter became less
common.

In general the privations of absence differ in
effect from physical hunger in being worst at first.
Here, however, we must be careful to distinguish the
agony of parting from the pain of absence. That is
another matter, properly separate, and to be treated
in its own place. Absence begins when parting is
past ; but though, philosophically considered, no
share of the agony of sundering enters into them,
the pangs of separation are sharpest in the beginning. The dolours of the first hours of parting
are like the griefs that rise with the shadows of
twilight in homes bereaved—griefs that wrench and
wring. Afterwards they deepen into the melancholy
of night, at first starless and then pierced with stars.
And then for happy lovers—as most are through all
their dear miseries and sweet tormentings—morning
again, meeting again ; a new day, a new birth. Love
is renewed in the rencontre just as in its first dawn,
which is not like the dawning of the astronomical day
with its one-sided flood of light. For here embracing
beams shoot from west to east, from east to west,
at the same moment—meeting in the zenith with

the voiceless cry, " Thine ! Mine ! " No less glorious
is the clashing glance of lovers meeting.

It should have been said before that absence
reveals another difference in love. There is a
generally true saying that the absent are always to
blame ; but it is not so with parted lovers, whatever
the tiff, miff, or misunderstanding that clouded their
parting. In love, the absent are always in the
right ; which is one of the numerous proofs of its
heavenly character.

ACCEPTANCE

In essentials, love-making, taking, breaking, are
the same in all civilised countries ; but there are
differences of conception and idea, of custom and
method, in the different classes of every nation.
For some enjoy more freedom than others, and it
is the lower classes that have the larger liberty.
They come and go in the outer courts and choosing-
grounds of marriage with a freedom which their
betters have denied themselves ; and yet (though
this will hardly be believed), it is a freedom which
has none of the effects of licence. Amongst them
no bond is fast till they come to the marriage-bond.
Acceptance, engagement—the one means as much
as the other, and both mean that a certain young
man and a certain willing maid have agreed to go
a-maying in blithe fields with a church in the
distance. The church is there certainly, and eyes are
cast upon it from time to time as its spire rises over
a hill, or peeps through the trees at some far meadow

end. But the blithe fields **give a** nearer invitation, **and** there **is no** immediate design of going beyond them. **To** go about and about in them in free companionship, with random kisses at every **flowering** bush, is firstly an enjoyment of youth, and secondly, test, trial ; a finding out of the accord which should take **them** on to the sacred edifice, or the discord and insufficiency which bid them fling asunder **with** a parting smack and no harm done.

Think no scorn of **Susan** Housemaid **for such** excursions : she **is** but **the Amaryllis of a faded day.** The **true view of the** case **is a dissolving view, in** which Susan with her plumy brush **melts** into Clorinda with a flower-adorned crook. To **take** such views is what the magic lantern of imagination is intended for. So employ it ; reflecting, with **a** further generosity, that but for a difference **of** glamour between the shepherd who tended his flock on thymy hills of old, and the butcher's **assistant** who kills young lambs in June, there would be no vulgarity here but an idyll. On **a** bright summer morn, before the donkey-boys come out, there is little to choose between Hampstead Heath and Hymettus ; while as for certain unseemliness **in** Susan's way of courtship, it is all in the seeming.

And yet it can never be the way with people of fashion, or even of the upper middle classes. With them engagements are a serious matter, one that is not **to be** lightly thrown off even if subsequent promenades on the borders of familiarity bring doubt to Edwin's, doubt to Angelina's **breast.** But even where **the** proprieties are **most severe** there is or ought to be **an** understood interval between acceptance and engagement. The "Yes" in answer to an offer of heart and hand is no vow. The fair way to look at it is not as acceptance, but as impulse to acceptance. This every generous man must feel; going away with his answer, and coming again after an interval of not less than twenty-four hours for ratification of acceptance. The meanwhile may be sweetly employed on his part in the agony that lovers can always make for themselves when they are sure, but not *very* sure; while, as for her, the interval of a day and a night unpledged by her "Yes" should be allowed not merely as a free dreaming-space, but as a possible need.

For a maiden's mind has many mysteries; and it has happened before now that her own utterance of her own "Yes" has opened the door to a swarm of little doubts that harboured behind it unperceived, and amongst them a stinging verity or two which seek out to kill what now seem like illusions. The illusions promised that at the utterance of the word an inflight of joys would follow. But an hour passes, and there are none; another, and not a wing stirs. "It is too soon," she thinks. "I shall wake in the night, and then ——!" and so to her pillow in a maze of disappointment and surprise. She wakes, and the heart which by that time was to be a cage of singing-birds is more like a nest deserted. It is a sad case, and if it be not common, is yet more common than confessed. For how "un-maidenly" it would be to take back the "Yes," with the proper explanation! But it might be wise to take it back, as all who may be concerned are hereby advised; as well as that it is lawful to do so for the good and **sufficient** reason above described. **Not till** she has said "**Yes**" does **many** a **damsel** quite know her own mind. **The word reveals her** to herself, **either as** a happier woman than **she** thought **or** by unfulfilled expectations of joy; which is the more trustworthy portent of the two.

Be it always remembered, however, that the **free** interval between acceptance and engagement is but brief. Its just limits are confined within the parting of yesterday and the meeting of to-morrow.

ADDRESSES

According to the Venerable Archdeacon Smith, the **verb "address"** means **to** move in the straight line towards another. Thus should addresses ever **move** in courtship, certainly; though there **they** hardly ever do move in the straight line. **They are** more than advances (which often precede them), **and** would **be** more correctly described **as** the zigzag approaches and preliminaries to courtship, which yet they may **never pass into. They may** never pass into that warm and irretrievable phase for any one of three reasons : the first, that the forces of attraction may fail on nearer approach, in **which case the** advancing one **gently swerves away; the second, that** nearer approach may be repelled, when, coming **to a stand,** he staggers, trembles, and then shoots **backward on** the path by which he came ; the third reason **is** that the permitted lover may never proceed beyond addresses, either from constitutional incapa-**city** or the restraints of formal taste.

As civilisation proceeds, these restraints upon fervour become more common with the one sex, though they can never be quite approved by the other. In their hearts, women are easily convinced that some of Nature's wildings may be over-cultivated, lose their old sweet grace, run to formality, and take the lack of meaning which is so painfully obvious in wired bouquets. While conforming to those restraints, they can never heartily assent to them ; and yet there are thousands of girls who, after admitting the addresses of an admirer, have never known the courtship of a lover. Contrary to tradition, contrary to expectation (for who at eighteen believes the world so worn that there is no romance for her ?), the affair never went beyond addresses, punctiliously as these may have been continued to the marriage-morn and even after. This is a deep and most natural disappointment, and none the more easy to bear because any expression of it would be considered improper. Not a word can be said against anything that testifies to the advance of refinement or conduces to a gentlemanly reserve. That is universally understood ; but it should be also understood that reserve is carried to unkind excess, and even trenches on the fraudulent, when it leads a young maid to matrimony through a course of polite and passionless addresses.

ADMIRATION

Admiration is not love, nor even akin to it as pity is. A form of homage (which, like love itself, is a compulsory sentiment), it is always worth having.

Honestly earned and modestly enjoyed, it is both adornment and inspiration. When coupled with respect it may even lead to marriage; yet it is not love, but something essentially different. For it is possible to admire without any wish for reciprocation ; as is sadly known to many a maid whose heart was first set beating under a radiance of regard that had all the look of love at its beginnings, and yet was no such morning light, but only admiration beaming at the full. And it is equally well known to many a poor man who, when his hopes were at the highest, had the difference brought home to him by the object of his dreams.

Yet Love has no stouter comrade than Admiration when they do go together, which is very often ; and when the more sober of the two can also be called Trust, Pride, it is the most complete establisher of love, its confirmation and heart of courage. Therefore it behoves all enamoured persons to enquire within themselves whether the upspringing and growth of their love is accompanied by an admiration of this kind. The question should be answered hand on heart, remembering that no verdict can be trusted that is not prompt. A slow and hesitating " Ay " is little better than a "No." Comes the answer pat, swift and joyful, then all is well ; but if draggingly the case is bad. For, strange as it would seem but for so many proofs to the contrary, love is possible without any such companionship. It may even live and flourish where the companionship of Truth, Pride, Honour, or any other vindicating glory is quite impossible. Just as admiration may exist without respect, so may love without either. It is the fate of some to fall into a way of loving, and that beyond recall, where all is either false delight or conscious shame ; so unworthy is the object of devotion.

By this we may see that if there be a heaven of love there is a corresponding hell. That, indeed, many lovers have said, but not always with sufficient knowledge of the subject. The hell of love is not jealousy, nor scornful rejection : bad as they may be, these are but torments of the upper air. To find it, look to the unhappy souls that are filled with an uncontrollable passion by fascinations half satanic—beauty skin deep, with naught but baseness and the brute below. These wretched ones are of both sexes, but there is this difference between them : the men suffer most in degradation, the women in pain. Both take comfort from a sense of fatality : it is their doom, they say. Yet were they free to choose, most of them would prefer the turbulent passion of their lives, with all its penalties, to the peace of such a love as may spring up amidst tranquil breadths of trustful admiration, like a fountain in a green pasture.

ADMIRER

Any one gifted with taste, discretion or finesse may admire of course ; but Admirers are a genus apart. Haunting the court of the Great Goddess, they lounge in its purlieus and never enter in. Admirers belong to comedy, and love is a serious passion. When it is most joyous it is farthest from comedy. Thus it is that young people are rarely Admirers themselves, or inclined to take much account of others who are. There is not heart enough in the matter for them, whether as admirers or admired. In the May-day rovings of youth, their free affections may hover for a moment here and there on the poise of admiration ; but—like butterflies when they discover no effluence of what they seek—away they fly again. Young maids know not what to do with Admirers, nor what to think of them except as footmen and forerunners of the true prince in the golden coach. Indeed, that is what they are generally taken for, with a glad welcome as such ; though with the welcome there is an end of them. But should the true prince never appear, then Admirers take a higher value. They now become a solace, an amusement, an adorning environment. And though no Admirer can make of life a romance, he can bring romance into a life with very pretty feigning, such as actors acquaint us with who are capable of being all Romeo, all Juliet, for hours together.

But this is not a common gift, and it is much less cultivated than it used to be. Even where it exists it begins to decline with the approach of middle age, of which period most Admirers are ; and moreover, they can hardly be perfect in the character unless they be men of the world. Not romance but comedy is for them ; and, by the same token, none are safely or successfully cast for it whom ruffles and a long waistcoat would not grace, who have not in them the right tie-wig courtliness, whose compliments do not suggest the backward making of a leg, and who do not play their part as admirers of themselves. In the last-named qualification there is an essential grace that would instantly

be missed, and it is their own main security. As
for the fairer sex, they may profitably remember—
and indeed should never forget—that "dangler" is
another name for Admirer.

ADORATION

The great Doctor Johnson, himself so much of a
lover that his constancy under trying circumstances
has been imputed to defective eyesight, has the following definitions of adoration : " 1, The external homage
paid to the divinity, and distinct from mental reverence ; 2, homage to persons in high place or esteem."
It will be observed that in the second definition there
is no inclusion of the loved one, whom "esteem"
cannot be intended to apply to ; and that in the first
"the divinity" is not a general term, to which any
he or she may be allowed admittance. And in defin-
ing "adorer" Johnson showed his own pious understanding of the matter yet more plainly. "Adorer,"
he says, "is he that adores ; a term generally used
in a low sense, as by lovers and admirers."

By a "low sense" the stern lexicographer and
tender spouse may possibly have intended to insinuate
a meaning of vulgarity. It is more likely, however,
that his meaning of "low" is the broader one which
is opposed to "lofty" ; but as in this connection that
signifies the Highest, the good Doctor's use of the
word is a groan that may be understood without
explanation. No doubt it occurred to his pious mind
that the profanation that pained him is most common
in Christian countries, where young lovers are so per-

suaded of their dear one's divinity that they would
still adore though a wilderness of lexicographers
reproved them. Nor are matters mended if there
really be something of the nature of religion in this
adoring sentiment ; as perhaps there is. There is little
evidence of its existence in heathen times. Were it
confined to Catholic countries, Protestants might
explain it by the corrupting influences of Mariolatry ;
but it is not so confined. On the other hand, it may
be advanced by Catholics in defensive illustration of
the worship which Protestantism decries ; their argument being supported by the very fact that Jews,
Mahommedans, and indeed all the infidel except those
which belong to Christian-bred races, are void of the
feeling that distressed Dr. Johnson. Orientals are
not only incapable of adoring their sweethearts (of
whom they have few) or their wives (of whom they
have many), but would be shocked at the imputation
of adoring them were they able to understand it.

And even amongst ourselves there may be some
mistake. Though there can be no doubt that many
Christian lovers (not being Asian or Asiatic converts
from idolatry) do adore each other, it is probable
that in most cases the feeling is misnamed. It is
really nothing more than love in sublimation,
borrowing its language from the troubadours and
our own sweetly-passionate lyrists. The true sentiment, with its steady service and duteous flame, is
only known, perhaps, amongst a certain number of
wives. Here, indeed, unflagging adoration may be
found ; accompanied by the mystic fact that it is
frequently bestowed on stocks and stones, and sometimes resembles the worship of malignant spirits.

Husbands are worshipped for their goodness, certainly; and even when they are not too good. But they are as much adored, if not for their coldness, hardness, arrogance, contemptuousness, then despite these qualities; and, as if in travesty of the law that couples heat and motion, it is often found that beaten wives do most warmly adore.

Like the fascination of repulsiveness (see art. "Abhorrence") this is one of the mysteries of a mysterious subject: as also is the fact, of which it is probably a counterpart, that husbands the most tender, faithful, and devoted do not adore. In this point they are converted to Mahommedanism by the marriage sacrament; though it must be allowed that the effect is insensible, and that its operation is seldom immediate. Theirs is another sentiment, as different from adoration as the daisied meadow from the soaring mountain-top, which yet they may have descended from to lead their sweethearts to the altar. As lovers they may begin with adoration, and lovers they may remain; but with no worshipping of divinities far into wedlock: whereas the most adoring women—yea, such as are despised—will begin to worship when the wedding-day is in the dust of last year's almanack.

ADVANCES

To make advances is to come forward; and yet the phrase is almost as commonly employed in speaking of a woman as of a man. No doubt there are cases where it is so used with propriety; but a just discrimination would declare "advances" more appropriate to the offers, overtures, and preludings of the hardier sex when inviting the affections of the other. Unhappily, however, the right word (for there is a right word) cannot be employed where the guileless of the other sex are concerned ; for if "advances" wrongs them "allurement" would be a greater injury, so long has that word been clothed with sinister meanings. In itself it is as good a word as could be wished ; and it is just the one that is needed to mark a difference which philosophy is interested in and of which justice demands the acknowledgment. Attraction and coming forward are not the same things ; and to confound the one with the other is to bring confusion into the idea of "the eternal feminine" ; which is attraction, in all its various embodiments and manifestations.

But although the word exactly describes the peepings and effusions of the spirit of love, drawn from its hiding-place and willing to bring near to it what attracts itself, many a maid would perish rather than hear of her "allurements" ; unless, indeed "sweet" went before the word, or "unconscious," or "innocent," or some other shame-dispelling adjective. And it will be said that good girls have nothing to do with advances, allurements, or anything of the kind. Such arts being permitted to widows, widows avail themselves of the privilege, no doubt : and seeing that they seek no entanglements of the heart, but rather an honourable contract than anything else, they may do so without blame or self-reproach. But (it will be urged) they are arts which are never practised by guileless young women. And all this

is perfectly true, with a difference which the word
"practised" defines.   However it may be with the
Becky Sharps and Blanche Amorys, traffickers in
what they hardly understand, they are no concern of ours; while as for the good girls, the
simplest of whom know more of love than those
others, of course there is no practice of allurement
or machination of advances about them.   They would
sooner pick pockets for the man they love than gain
him by considered wiles or the betrayal of a begging
passion.   Many, indeed, are so close and punctilious
that they would rather jeopardise all their happiness
than hoist the love-light from heart to eyes till the
dear one brings his own to look for it, and does
so with sufficient indications of anxious purpose and
resolved intent.

Yes, and some have suffered to their lives' end in
consequence, and (what was never intended) so has
the dear one too; for a man is not always to know
where his haven lies if the hearth-fire shine not on
him from the windows.   A thousand vivats for
maidenly pride!—but here, too, the fatal over-much
is possible, though perhaps it is wiser to say so in a
whisper.   But love, as it will spring up against all
suppression, so will it speak out at most times.
Don't we remember that it had its own language,
formed of wordless communications and silent
subtleties, long before a single alphabet was invented?
Need we talk of deliberate advances, allurements
palpable, when the chance encounter of two hands
will set up a clamour of meaning louder than all the
bells of Bruges, and more convincing than everything
that has yet been heard in the other schools of

divinity? There may be betrayal in a dropping voice, avowal in a footfall, beckonings in a turning away, wishes breathed in the rustling of a gown; and all with no more design than the reeds repent them of when they answer to the kisses of the wind.

And (taking all the young men and maidens and all the breezes and bulrushes in the world together) with no more harm. Not only is it becoming, it is in the nature of things, harmonious with eternal laws, orderly as music itself, that the necessary overtures should proceed from Strephon; but when Dorinda knows that the advances are there, though hardly venturing as yet beyond a tremulous beginning, what if she do smile them forth when he comes again that way? It is but a little fault, or no fault at all. Yet it becomes her to be careful. For the young and ardent lover has eyes which are ever on the watch for tokens of familiarity with love-affairs, or indicative of a born genius for them; the which he trembles at as she would not if she detected them in him.

ADVENTURE

In relation to the ordinary pursuits of life—as enterprise in search of wealth, the rewards of ambition, the excitements of sport and the like—the saying that "adventures are to the adventurous" cannot be mended. But when applied to enterprise in love-affairs the saying fails in accuracy. It should run "Adventures are to the impudent"; a version in which there is a sacrifice of epigram, no doubt, but a gain of precision where precision is a matter of importance. Yet innocent adventures are not uncommon, or guileless surprises and concatenations that are called adventures; and it is also true that many homely persons are indebted to such undesigned and transient imbroglios for gleams of insight, glints of discovery and warning, that might never have fallen to them otherwise. How much they are the happier for it is another thing; for here we are in a region where knowledge is often loss and revelation pain.

A longing for adventure is not confined to the wilder and weaker of the daughters of men. It is no infrequent visitor where evil thoughts are never permitted to survive the discovery of their presence. Indeed, Eve as she roamed in Paradise before the Fall, Eve as Heaven made her, had just such longings; and inasmuch as they are immanent in her daughters, what is that but the perpetuation of her story—the tale of the Tree of Knowledge in a thousand editions and millions of copies? And thereby hangs a moral; for just as someone in a certain book exclaims, "Adam? I am Adam!" so every woman may say in the days of her youth, "Eve? I am Eve!" And that she is; and should give due heed to all that is included in the mystery.

AFFECTION

Affection, a word of general application to the various passions and movements of the mind apart from reasoning (see the Judicious Hooker, who speaks of "affections as joy, grief, fear, anger"), has now become a name for one alone. Drawn by degrees into a single meaning, "affection" has been invested at every step with fresh graces and sweetnesses, till it may almost compare with "peace" and "home" as a compendium of lovely significances. As "home" is a word of lowliness, so is "affection"; and their lowliness, their lowliness in sweetness and security is the charm of both.

Many gentle souls are not only incapable of the grand passion,—they fear it, and would shun its whirling implications. Children of the valley, they look up and dread its soaring heights and the wild spirits whose voices descend from it. When all the poets have said their say, these gentle ones remain unpersuaded of the simplicity of love—the simplicity which they would liken to water from the spring. They suspect in it high mysteries like those that mingle in the ambrosia which the monks of Chartreuse make, and which is madness when taken from a mug. The ecstasies of love? They know that ecstasy is shot with pain, and the pain puts the delight in doubt, clouding its origin. Withheld by a complication of shynesses, they shrink from uttering the name of love, preferring to speak of their affection, as others speak of "my cottage" who would not choose to live in a palace and yet do not dwell in farm-huts either. To them love has meanings of romance, and therefore of instability. Its associations are with the dreamy, the visionary, the rapturous excessive: such things as will not hold or are too bright to last. For them, affection; and truly may we say (without detracting from that which can make of almost any man poet, prophet, conqueror for weeks at a stretch, and Aurora of any woman for periods quite as long) that very good it is. If it has no aspiring loftiness, it has breadths and depths enough, and they most comfortable : the breadths as of rolling clover-fields, the depths as of downy beds. It compares with everything that is snug, sweet, smiling, secure. You may call it the Three per Cents of the tender passion. Or you may liken it to a garland of violets, primroses, and the briar-rose—ever clinging, never fading. Or to a garden in a cathedral close, with its lofty old walls and its pretty old walks (ten to a square acre), and its cottage-flowers under tall hedges of yew. Or you may think of affection as the Goddess turned quaker, loveliest of the Society of Friends. When the lark rises of a June morning, shatters the joy that chokes his tiny throat, and flings its sparkling fragments up to heaven and down to earth—that is love. His mate, listening where she nests, her breast on her brood and her heart overfull of content—that is affection.

In short, a great deal can be said for it, as it may be hoped the daughters of exhaustingly-civilised man will soon make out for themselves. For the frosts of age have not so chilled perception in observant grandsires but that they see this : just as there is an end of chivalry and no more cabbage-roses, the hour is at hand when the heroic passion that Helen knew, that the Nut-brown Maid did share, and that, coming down to the days of Jock o' Hazeldean, if not later, suffered the shock of travesty in those of Lord Byron, will be extinguished in

these parts.   Gather all that remains even now, and
it would probably be found an insufficient outfit for
a single ballad.   One or two generations more, and
the maid who would view it and prove it (and there
will still be many such scattered up and down in
Western Europe) will have to fly to the banks of the
Bangweolo or stray where tribes are growing into
nations on the shores of Lake Tchad.   Here we have
an analogue to the anticipated cooling of the earth
which has hitherto been concealed from philosophy.
The peoples of the earth are cooling like the sun
(itself in course of reduction to civilisation and order),
and in the same way—the failing combustion of
elemental matter.   Therefore it may be expected
that before long the more heroic passions will only
be found in the yet untamed regions of the Equator,
to which all life must in aftertimes retire.

It is well, then, that affection should flourish
amongst us meanwhile ; well that it should take new
meanings, new associations, new graces, and be more
widely preferred.   There *are* points in its favour.
Wounded, it suffers less than love ; and not from
inferior sensibility, perhaps, but from a dwindled
egotism.   Less egotistic, it inflicts less pain while
it suffers less.   Though not so ardent, it is more
zealous ; and more zealous because its temperate,
unfevered, outward-beaming eyes have a clearer
vision for little things.   Affection is never without
a warmth of good-will which, interchanged between
man and wife on an automatic supply system of
spontaneous origin, corresponds to a total exclusion
of draughts.   Affection is a half-and-half of love at
its softest, benevolence at its sweetest ; and he who

drinks thereof to his daily bread may be counted as one that does very well.

Amongst women the difference between love and affection is—in the general—not so great as amongst men : that is to say, there is more of love in their affection. And if, being married, they remain childless, the difference is likely to be maintained. But baby draws all to a level in such cases ; which is no wonder, considering that he often brings down an adoring love from the topmost heaven where it circled with papa, transforms it, and makes of it a glory for his own exclusive self. Any way, as time goes on, it is to affection that the most constant, most fervid, most exalted love comes at last. It is always the same thing as love, minus its spontaneity, its exaltations, its visions, its rapture ; and they are much. Not to have known them is to be as the little fishes that dwell all their lives in cave-pools under ground. And happiest of all is the love which, beginning in youth with such delights, descends to long years of tranquil affection.

AFFIANCE

Though all words, like all men, spring from the same humble beginnings, they rise to different degrees of distinction, and share the mutations that befal the various families of the human race. Here also the accident of birth operates with extreme partiality ; giving to some words an eminence denied to others of equal worth when all is known. To extraction alone they owe a dignity and pride of place

which the most numerous, laborious, and useful
words in the whole dictionary are powerless to dis-
pute. On the other hand, words the most privileged
fall into decay from time to time : and while some
of highest birth and loftiest association disappear
with the Bigods and Mauleverers, others that were
unknown till the other day rise from the gutter to
dwell on the lips of princes.

"Affiance" belongs to the more fortunate order.
It is of a family which from the beginning of modern
civilisation, and, what is more, from the rise of Latin
Christianity, has been associated with the loftiest
embodiments of State and the profoundest tenets of
Religion. It is a word of chivalry, majesty, solemnity ; a most august word ; and in the particular
application to which it becomes more and more
limited, cannot be used by everybody. Emperors
are affianced ; kings are affianced ; dukes, marquesses
and earls (though here we come upon dubious
ground, from which nobles of recent creation are
certainly excluded) may also claim to engross their
engagements to marry under the same head. For
them it is a seemly word, and with them it should
rest ; remaining unchallenged and ungrudged by
persons of inferior condition, and such as are not
entitled to put their coachmen into wigs on week-
days as well as Sundays. No one that lives upon
or below that delicate line of demarcation—and
many ladies and gentlemen would have been saved
from a long course of inglorious pretentiousness had
they once asked themselves the question "Am I
entitled to powder James's head ?"—can assume to
be affianced with any propriety. Nor should the

disallowance grieve them.   They have privileges in
this respect which crowned heads do not share.
They may say "my dear" without going behind a
door to do so, and think, speak, write of their chosen
ones by the primrose-name of "sweetheart"; which
monarchs can no more do than call for periwinkles
at a public feast.

> The sweeter words of love and home are all of low degree,
> There is not one that well accords with prideful dignity.

Yet there is no pretty synonym of "affiance" in
the English tongue; which is a pity.   "Handfast-
ing" is good, and still obtains in some parts of rural
England; but even there it is thought too clownish
and countrified, and no citizen could endure to use
it, and still less the citizen's daughter.   "Betrothal"
is of good, sound, native origin; it is a word of long-
standing, and has had every chance of making its
way with English folk, both gentle and simple; but
since it was never a poet's word nor sweet to the
ballad-maker, we may suppose that it has lost little
favour now that it is altogether shunned.   It is,
perhaps, too much of a word.   Haply it went very
well on lips that welcomed mead, metheglin, and
such-like honey-drinks full and heady; but something lighter is now required, and no small beer
serves better than "engagement."   Yet engagement
is a poor word, quite without soul, and with nothing
to commend it but a modest whisper and dulcet
susurration of sound.   To bring out this merit, and
at the same time to mark the difference between one
kind of engagements and another, lovers are counselled
to linger melodiously on the second syllable.

AFFINITY

That we each have our "affinity" in the person of some precise counterpart of the opposite sex is the belief of all happy lovers ; who see their own dear other selves advance to them at every meeting, and are never so pleased with their pangs at parting as when they remember to explain those agonies by the infraction of a natural law. Save for this, their longing to be near and nearer to each other might be suspected of triviality even by themselves ; but that cannot be a mere weakness which, no less than the gushings of the water-springs or the turning of the sunflower to the sun, is obedience to the pre-determinations of Divine Order. This they instinct-ively feel ; and indeed they were the first discoverers of the law of "affinity." Philosophic speculation is a much later light than the divinations of love ; and though the ancient sages devised theories of an original oneness of man and woman, since disparted —(some telling of the absolute union of the two, others teaching that every soul as it descends from the creative hand separates on its approach to earth into a male and a female part, to be reunited by marriage here or after death)—it is not that the sages taught this doctrine to lovers : those simple ones taught it to the sages. It was from them that the idea was derived. As with astronomy, so in this higher field of celestial phenomena : its first observations, its first divinations, were made where shepherds feed their flocks and by the shepherds themselves. "He is mine ! I am his !" "This is

he [she] for whom my heart longed while yet I knew
him [her] not at all." "Thou art my life"—"And
you the very soul of me." Such cries as these, as
well as the equivalents of "surely we were born for
each other," and "marriages are made in heaven,"
were heard in many a field and grove ages before
the sages ; who of course found no more difficulty in
taking them up and working them into metaphysic
webs than did the late Emmanuel Swedenborg. But
they do not improve in any such loom ; where, indeed,
they achieve the double disadvantage of becoming
less sweet and less intelligible. They are best in
the old simplicities of meaning,—best as the poesies
and garlandings of a passion so conscious of divinity
that it must needs bring heaven down to it, though
it is never willing to ascend to heaven.

It is evident that the saying "Marriages are
made in heaven" was not intended to apply to all
unions so called ; unless its author believed them
a dispensation of trial, discipline, punishment, or
sometimes reward. But though it would bear that
interpretation very well, the simpler though less
religious meaning of the adage has always been
put upon it. And the difficulty of accepting it
disappears at once when we remember that the
originator of the saying may have drawn a distinction between marriages that are marriages, and the
partnerships, the arrangements, the junctions of con-
trivance, the fortuitous confluxions, the accidental
hankings, the confused implications and entanglements, which are variously called by that name. He
would explain that, contrary to the general idea, he
intended a wider sweep of negation than assertion.

He would say that to bring out the true savour of
his meaning particular emphasis should be thrown
upon the first word in speaking, while in print it
should be marked by italic letters. " *Marriages* are
made in heaven ": not the common tie, so often
ventured on nothing more than a bright complexion or a silken beard, but those true unions of
accordant souls which bring to each its counterpart,
supplying the complement of every wish, every need,
every unperfected joy in each.

No doubt in so saying he would seem to adopt
the Kabbalistic teaching, with his union of counter-
parts ; and, in truth, no lower doctrine is accepted
by the only substantial authorities on the subject.
Wherever happy lovers are, and whether you find
them in the first outrush and embracement of their
affections, or in the joy of the honeymoon, or in the
security of equal love after years of housekeeping
together, they have but one explanation of their
happiness, and that entirely transcendental.

The secret is, they hold, that one life was parted
till they met, and flowed together at their meeting.
Chance looks revealed it ; it was known by con-
sentaneous thoughts and dreams ; it flashed from
each to each in a fortuitous touching of hands ; and
it burst into a blaze of ascertainment with the first
kiss. They know it by a thousand intimations of
body and spirit, tested as often and ever renewed.
This they say, and there is no contradicting them.
Few are philosophers enough to enquire, all are
too happy to care, whether they came from heaven
one soul, separating on the downward way and then
seeking and finding re-union on earth, or whether

they were born into this world incomplete beings, to
lose or find completion in the only true counterpart
made and provided for each. Questions of that
kind sink into a matter of detail with mortal lovers
when compared with the momentous outcome ; but
wherever the second of these two theories is held
we come close upon the doctrine of "affinities."
Male and female, we have each our "affinity" some-
where in the world. Upon the discovery of that
affinity depends the contentment of our affections,
the completion of our very selves ; but yet the only
guides of affinity to affinity in this wide and wandering world are certain mysterious yearnings to an
ideal, and a faculty of instant recognition when the
longed-for unknown comes into sight. To find the
unknown, by help of whatever promptings of an
inner spirit you may be gifted with, that is the
difficulty ; and it was ever great. The conditions
being what they are, there must needs be multitudes
of failures ; and their number is less surprising if it
be true, as some of the later *illuminati* announce,
that a man's only true affinity may have died a
married woman in the fifteenth century, or may not
be destined to appear on earth for a hundred years
to come. But perhaps this is only one of the refinements of speculation which superior intellects raise
upon all theory. To entertain it is not obligatory,
though its general acceptance might have the excellent effect of making many a yearning unsatisfied
soul content with a second best mate.

For this is the untowardness of the doctrine of
affinities. There are souls that ever yearn and are
never satisfied ; or if they are satisfied, it is because

they are ever yearning, which is to their conceit a
sign of psychologic elevation.   Or, persuaded by the
books they read that no soul can pretend to refinement without yearning, then will they yearn.   But
in no such case can there be peace or wholesomeness, while there may be a great deal of the ridiculous.
For it is an essential part of the aforesaid doctrine,
persuasion, superstition, affectation, simulation, or
hypocrisy (as it variously is), that an " affinity " being
found, you have a divine right, if you be a man, to
take possession of it ; or, if a woman, to be absorbed
in it.   The actual consequence is some wickedness,
much unhappiness, more of a ludicrous kind of
feigning foolishness, and a good deal of substantial
inconvenience.   Assuming a general truth in the
theory, we need not worry about affinities born a
hundred years too soon or as many years too late ;
but it really is disturbing to observe that certainty
of recognition is not a gift allowed to everybody.
There is such a thing we may suppose.   But it
takes a questionable shape when pretended by
wedded husbands and neighbours' wives ; and (as
might be with a hound between a distant fox, an
adjacent violet bed, and an approaching pannier of
red-herring), it is evidently so bewildered a sense in
many of our fellow-creatures that they know not
when they have found what they seek.   Now, and
now, and now again they detect their very own
" affinity " in different persons ; sure in every case of
the divine "at last," and in every case rediscovering
the universal hollowness of things before long.
" Miserie, ah ! miserie ! "   Ay,. and vanitie, and
falsitie, and fripperie, and spuriositie, and some other

things with names that never appear in the books of polite lexicographers.

It was the intrusion of this rascal nonsense that brought affinity into disrepute very soon after its introduction. English being the language of a humorous people little inclined to mystic sentimentalisms, it did not long retain "affinity" as a word of serious meaning in relation to love. After a little while it became a joke ; a common joke ; a tiresome joke ; and then was heard no more : which, upon the whole, was the accomplishment of a good riddance..

To conclude, the solicitations and on-drawings of "affinity" are of two kinds ; and, if the one kind seems to be a calling of the divine to the divine in man and woman, the other is the call of the spirits of earth compounded in the clay of them. To go studiously through the various manifestations, emotions, and transports of love, is to discover that it is of two kingdoms apart ; and that the lower kingdom displays everywhere correlatives and travesties of the celestial passion—in its seizures, pleasures, influences, and effects alike—such as Milton's Lucifer might have devised in mocking competition for ascendency in the human creature.

AMOUR

One of the numerous equivalents of "love," and the one which, for obvious reasons, has been adopted by the French. For when rightly pronounced (as it is on the stage, for example), with

the bleat in the vowels prolonged in a dying fall,
the word defines and differentiates the passion as
cultivated in France with singular precision.   So
felicitously, indeed, does the sound of the word (let
us hear it: " Amōōur!") represent the distinctive
character of love in its French variety, that it
strongly supports the onomatopoetic or " bow-wow "
theory of the origin of language. No spoken language
suffices for the needs of love ; which therefore, like
maternal affection, has to eke out the vocabulary of
every known tongue with breathings of its own,
incapable of syllabled expression.   It is only natural,
then, that the spirit of these ejaculations should pass
into such words as *may* be commanded, modifying
them in various countries according to the character
of the thing expressed. Thus we have the Italian
" amore," the Spanish " amor," and the French
" amour "; each word revealing in the sound of it
the differing characteristics of the passion in different
races.

All words expressive of abstractions are associated
in our minds with something appreciable by the
senses ; and the true inwardness of " amour " is
understood when we remember that its invariable
association is with perfume, or (not seldom) with per-
fumery.   And when we say perfume it is not of the
breath of roses that we speak, but the exhalations of
musk or stephanotis.   It is further significant of the
difference between " amour " and " love " that " love,"
when unqualified by any kind of adjective, is instantly
accepted for what it is at its sweetest and best.
And not only so, but even when linked with a
qualifying word of baseness the ray about it is

undimmed : it is the adjective that takes the darker
hue.   On the other hand, no French poet or novelist
can fancy that he has put " amour " right with the
public till he has coupled it with an allusion to " la
tourterelle."   Imported into England, it has never
been naturalised here ; and though no doubt it has
its uses in this country, it is rarely seen and yet
more rarely heard.   There is, indeed, reason to
suspect that in the budding years of girlhood the
word is sometimes murmured where friend walks
with friend in groves of academe ; but these are but
bubbles on the lip of a brighter infancy.   Soon
there comes a time when these same sweet girls of
English growth would as soon nibble at olives as
say " amour."   Their elders shun it equally, on
fuller information ; and though it is useful, and
sometimes indispensable, for the meaner employments of language, it can no more be admitted to
domestication than the Chinese labourers in a British
settlement.

These remarks do not apply to " enamoured," or
apply in a very remote degree.   We have no compendious word of a like signification ; its adumbra-
tions are without repulsiveness ; and it attains to a
certain breadth of innocency through being applied
to music, power, and other delights.   Yet there is
meaning in the fact that with us " enamoured " is no
word of wooing between young man and maid.   It
is only possible in the case of widows.

AMOURETTE

This is **not a** dictionary **word in English,** which has nothing that can be called its equivalent ; and yet no love lexicon would **be** complete without **it.** In conversation **with** ourselves we **do indeed speak** of **our "little loves "** ; but **the expression is an** uncertain one, and cannot be acknowledged **by** the lexicographer. Though **of** doubtful parentage, " amourette " **is in all** its meanings **as** innocent **as a** Dresden shepherdess, and as dainty **and as** sweet to every regard. **It has** nothing to do with **flirtation :** a flirtation is quite a different **thing.** There **is a** good deal **of heart** in many an **entanglement—a good** deal even of broken heart ; but it **is not that either.** Amourettes that become entanglements **change their** character ; but to admit that they ever **do so become** is **only** a concession **to the** ninety-ninth student of this **dictionary,** who, unlike the remainder, must needs **be** humoured **as a person of imperfect** sensibilities. Purity, **tranquillity, and a** something that answers to disembodiment are **the** distinction of these **little loves. The** great passion declares itself in warmth and light **as of a summer's** day ; the most welcome **of our little loves, which are** those that come late, **rise upon us** like the evening star on **the calm** profundity **of** a summer night. **A radiance** that tranquillises in embracing ; distance without **longing ;** nearness without approach ; contentment **without** the spoken word—such are **the tokens of the** bright impassionate kindlings of affection **which** are less a delight than a good to whosoever experiences them.

They may be the least enduring or the most lasting
of all.   They may run their course and descend into
the limbo of happy memories in a stretch of time no
longer than a honeymoon, or they may continue in
undimmed serenity for years as many as all the days
of a honeymoon.   For the most part they glorify
our younger · time, when they come and go like a
May morning ; but not to be so forgotten.

This is known to hundreds and hundreds of wide-
girdled wives with boys and girls of their own about
them, and to as many of their corresponding spouses.
The one keep in the lavender-closet of their sweetest
and most secret thoughts, the other find lodged in
the bowls of their favourite tobacco-pipes, memories
of the youth or the maid who, without being quite
loved or quite loving, made for them the Eden of a
long-past amourette.   But amourettes as golden
befal men of whom a stranger would say "This
should be an uncle and a bachelor"; and if not
"amourette," it is difficult to know what to call
the fond intensity and full romance of love which
racks many a breast ere yet the first Eton jacket has
shed a button.   But that mysterious subject comes
under a heading of its own.

ASSIGNATION

A romance word, the concrete idea of which is a
cloak ; or, to be more specific, a Spanish cloak.   It
was from France, however, that the word was imported, for the more elegant and comprehensive
expression of " appointment " when they who were

to meet were lovers.   Its advantage was an additional air of secrecy, mystery, which is at once
the lover's refuge and delight.   Moreover, it carried
with it suggestions of the clandestine ; a certain
admixture of which was thought necessary (at that
period) to give " character " to love-affairs.   Although
its use was unchallenged by Propriety for many
decades, at no time was it deemed of cloistral
simplicity.   Within the recollection of our fathers
it still passed amongst persons of discreet taste ; but
it had already begun to lose character by that which
was supposed to confer it, and is now employed only
where taste and discretion are entirely absent.

ATTACHMENT

Attachment, when sound and honest, is a good
linsey-woolsey sort of feeling, hard wearing, and,
indeed, often more lasting than that which it does
duty for without pretending to be.   It is a kindness
that never rises into love ; though, just as the Undines
know their want of soul and yearn to share the gift,
it is sometimes dimly aware that it would be love if
it could.   On the other hand, love is capable of
falling far below the loyalties that an honest attachment abides by.   Like affection, it is all for service ;
but, unlike affection, is indifferent to service in sweet
and gracious ways.   Not puritanically, which is to
be close and harsh, not quakerishly, which suggests
the pretty coquettishness of wild-flowers peeping from
a bank, it yet cares nothing for gauds and garlands.
With the conscientiousness of Dutch housewives, it

loves all that corresponds to neatness, wholesomeness,
order ; but being destitute of imagination, it sees
neither duty nor delight in adornment,

> Taffeta phrases, silken terms precise,
> Figures pedantical,

it could not, would not use in the business of courtship ; preferring rather that all should be expressed

> In russet yeas and honest kersey noes.

To be just, to be true, to find no duty understood
too late, to be content with neither happiness nor
unhappiness unshared, such are the topmost virtues
of attachment ; and they are all of indoor range and
application. There is nothing inspiring about them,
no upliftings of heart and voice. Attachment speaks
in plain prose both from taste and incapacity ; and
is, indeed, of so unpoetical a temper that could it be
taught to speak its mind in verse it would probably
rhyme "lyrical" with "hysterical."

But this, of course, does not hold good of attachments formed by men and women who were lovers
once—all of a bygone day. They would know
better. When we speak of attachments we must
needs include these, for there are many such that
help to keep the world together in peace and content.
Still, they are descents from a higher estate ; whereas
there are thousands and thousands of our fellow-
creatures who were born incapable of nor can bestow
any stronger feeling than attachment. It is not in
them ; and what they lack cannot be supplied by
study. Intellect has nothing to do with it, nor
even genius. Love has no preference whatever

for persons of education and refinement, and would
as lief inspire a country lad as anybody else.   And so
it is that while the gentleman who puts on a velvet
jacket the better to read Herrick will never, never,
never rise above an Elzevir attachment at best, the
maid who sweeps his room has a nest of birds in her
breast that sing all day long as well as Herrick, and
better too.   Yet it is the humdrum and half-awakened
that are most subject to this poor gentleman's inability;
the drudging, the bourgeois born ; solicitors, lexicographers, small-coal merchants ; persons of anxious
acquisitorial instincts, and (generally speaking) such
as have large appetites for dinner.   But what matter,
since for these attachment is enough ?   Most of them
would not know what to do with more : the auroral
flashings and surprises of it would be a constant
worry to them till they were discontinued.   A
sincere attachment consorts with all that they are at
best, harmonising if not elevating ; and leaves nothing
to be desired when reciprocal.

Young lovers who have just come into a princely
passion may smile at the mediocrity of attachments,
but they are not to be contemned.   There are
thousands of homes in country parishes, thousands
more in factory towns, thousands more yet—(equally
lowly though much larger)—in Regent's Park,
Queen's Gate, Tyburnia, the Belgravian Squares,
and other more eligible situations, where unvaried
comfort is secured by a well-placed attachment.

ATTENTIONS

The general meaning of "attention" is to bend the mind upon anything,—to stretch the mind in a specific direction : from which it is evident that no word comes more naturally than "attentions" into the lover's dictionary. There it is a word of two meanings. In its first signification it is nearly equivalent to "addresses" : for attentions precede addresses and merge into them. When all goes well with a man to the point of embarkation upon marriage, he commonly passes through the following stages on dry ground : he is smitten—usually an affair of a moment ; he hazards attentions ; he proceeds to more ostensible addresses ; he enters upon full and accepted courtship. It appears then, that in its first signification the word "attentions" carries with it all the meaning of "attend," to stretch the mind in a specific direction, while at the same time it is another word for overtures. But it is obvious that the initial design of overtures is to call upon oneself the attention of another, and to draw that other mind in a specific direction ; from which it further appears that the Latin original of "attentions" is turned to the utmost possible account.

The second signification of the word is more figurative, and divides into several branches. In all cases "attentions" carries a meaning of heedfulness, consideration, watchful care, ready anticipation of needs and wishes, the constant affordance of *petits soins* above all ; and the presence of a tender politeness in everything. Well may we understand, therefore, how precious attentions are to those on whom they are bestowed ; and reflection carried a little farther will show how much they lose who deny or cease to practise them, since they are an education in gentleness and grace. Rendered in public—but not with ostentation, which detracts from them altogether—they are prized as homage, such as gentlemen in days of old proclaimed in wearing their mistress's colours ; and when the recipient is a good creature, as she often is, the pride she feels in their bestowal is so far from arrogance that it sinks at once into a sweet humility. There are men who render attentions in every public place scrupulously enough,—partly from a conscientious deference to what is expected, partly in consideration of what is due to themselves, partly from fondness and acknowledgment of desert ; but that done, they go no farther. They show no lack of kindness, no discourtesy ; but the lady's colours are folded away in her lord's crush hat, and do not reappear till he requires it again. Even so she is content, for there are multitudes less fortunate ; and just as they choose their finest gowns to wear abroad, why should not women prefer attentions that adorn to such as are merely comfortable, and that can be done without when nobody is by ? Are not concealed privations more endurable than the poverty which every one may gape at ?

We see, then, that there are two sorts of attentions, the single and the double : one open to view, not unmeant for display, ritualistic rather, and sharing the nature of sacrifice in the Temple ; the other little different so far, but crowned with the addition of a

thousand solicitudes that have no formality.   Home
is the sphere of these *petits soins;* and they are
practised with a watchfulness that will never be seen
to watch—a prevenient care that shuns detection as
a first principle of conduct.   To contrive in the
dark and bring all about as if by accident, there lies
the charm of this sort of attentions ; and as the others
are never wanting where these are bestowed, she is
a happy woman who can boast of them.

And to think that any man may confer this happiness by the mere cultivation of habit !   With a little
good-nature to start with, that is all that is necessary.
For good nature grows with the habit of solicitude, the
habit with the good-nature, till all is confirmed and
flourishing.   Strange that this charming fact should
be so little known !

BASHFULNESS

THERE is bashfulness, and there **is** shyness.
Though they are alike they should **not** be confounded. The difference between them is that
shyness appears in both sexes, while after childhood
has passed (when we are not very distinctly either
one thing or the other), bashfulness belongs more
properly to womankind. This leads to a remark
which may as well be made here as elsewhere. Men
and women would understand each other better if
they avoided **a** very common error : the error of
assuming that there is no difference of sex in the
passions, emotions, and other interior qualities of
mankind. That difference does extend to the pas-
sions. Some are more alike than others, as greed,
for example, which **is** the same thing in both man
and woman ; but **of** most passions it may be said, as
is written in Genesis, "male and female created He
them."

From this it would be no unreasonable inference
that shyness and bashfulness are the same things,
variously modified in the one sex and the other.

But that does not seem to be the case. Most men
are neither shy nor bashful ; and though a few are
both bashful and shy, in that case they are either
very young or irreclaimably feminine. Women may
be shy as well as bashful, or shy only because they
are bashful, or shy without bashfulness. For shyness
is " reserve " in a condition of alarm. It is an
emotion called out by dread of approach, fear of
being drawn into familiarity; and therefore one
which both men and women feel, and even the fowls
of the air and the beasts of the field. And though shyness is more common amongst women than men, only
at a certain time of life is the difference considerable.
Shyness is little more apparent in middle-aged
women than in middle-aged men. In earlier days
the difference is greater, for this reason. There
must be shyness where there is bashfulness ; bashfulness is a womanish quality ; but women lose their
bashfulness as time goes on, and with it goes the
accompanying shyness. This fact helps to mark the
distinction between the two, which is this. Shyness
being the common feeling of " reserve " in a condition
of alarm, bashfulness is a similar consequence when
certain feelings proper to womankind are thrown into
a similar state. It may be modesty in alarm ; it
may result from that accessibility to surprise which
makes flight an instinctive impulse with women even
when escape is not intended ; or it may arise from
fear that feelings which should be concealed are too
visible : or that the feelings themselves are not
what they ought to be. Now all such emotions as
these are accompanied by a sense of shame. Therefore they abash, and the consequent confusion of

mind and aspect is bashfulness. A torment to those
who endure it, it makes a pleasant show to others,
and is well thought of. Therefore it is feigned
sometimes, along with the innocence it so prettily
betokens. But there may be innocence without
much betrayal of bashfulness ; and it might even pass
for a true saying that they who blush at little will
not blush for long.

BEAUTY

There was a philosopher — and a very fine
statue of him in a listening attitude may be
seen on the Thames Embankment at this hour—
who died of melancholy after making out that only
4,000,000,000,946 different combinations of musical
notes are possible. He loved music, and these
figures proved to him that a time would come when
there would be no more new tunes.

It is a large number — 4,000,000,000,000 —
and yet (supposing the calculation accurate) there
are just as many reasons for saying that beauty
and music are alike. They are alike in this very
particular of yielding an all but infinite variety
of charm. For where the change of a note will
make a difference, so also will the turn of a line
from brow or chin, the depth of a dimple and its
position, the heightening or the softening of a tint,
and many other trifles. Nor will the likeness
between music and physical beauty seem less if
we look round upon the world and ask of its various
men of taste—as the black man of taste, the yellow

and the brown man of taste—what music is and what
beauty. Where this is done, it will be found that
disagreement on the one point is generally accompanied by a corresponding measure of disagreement
on the other. The beauties of China and its music
are equal wonders of superstition to European
missionaries and sea-captains ; and while " Adelaida "
is but a sort of howling to the Chinaman, his exuberantly idiomatic tongue barely enables him to
express his loathing of British loveliness.

This difference of taste lies in different ideas of
harmony. Harmony is beauty ; beauty is harmony
in its many diversities ; but the Negro with his
tom-tom, the Chinaman with his singing as of
Madame Mouser in an agonised falsetto, have
their own ideas of the harmonious, which are not
those of the Western world. The little more of the
slanting of an eye, and how much it is at Pekin,
and how entirely a matter of disgusted indifference
in London and Paris. Figure ? A bolder sweep
of fulness beyond the very full, and the aesthetic
sensibilities of Young Abyssinia are strung to lyrical
pitch ; while in Europe (not excluding Holland)
commiseration would view the sight through tears.
So much do the races of the world differ where it
would seem no difference should be. Yet how
fortunate is the dispensation ! What a world it
would become if the white, the black, the yellow,
the male sex and the female sex, were engrossed
with one idea of beauty, no matter which ! What
languishings, what jealousies, what wars, what forays,
what domestic inquietudes, what beatings, burnings, poisonings there would be till the last Helen

had been absorbed into a population all whity-
brown! From these miseries we have been preserved by an order of things which, however unsatis-
factory from the scientific point of view, must be
regarded as Providential.

In every race the conception of harmony, though
hedged within certain bounds, admits of great
diversity ; wherefrom ensues the happy consequence
that, go where we may, every Jack has his Jill.
Another consequence is that the most perfect beauty,
though by all admired, is not by all desired. It is
true that great beauty must be greatly harmonious,
but not true that the greatest beauty must needs
strike upon the sensibilities of the greatest number.
A beauty less perfect may do that, and then find
itself rivalled by physical excellence of a lower
degree.

Were it otherwise, beauty would be answerable
for more general madnesses than three ; and yet (to
speak of women) only three have been recorded in
the long history of the world. There is the story of
Helen, of Cleopatra, and the Scottish Queen Mary,
of whose beauty some are enamoured to this day.
Heaven alone knows why, however ; for the only
existing portrait of the Egyptian princess, and the
ninety and nine of the Scottish princess, are less
delightful both in form and colour than any of those
that were viewed by a thousand housemaids in a
thousand looking-glasses this very morning. It would
be a pretty thing if half these young women could
play such havoc with the Antonys of hall and village
as made Cleopatra glorious. But no. The harmony
of beauty must be concordant with much that lies

E

behind the brows of him that looks upon it, or else it is nothing but a picture. Its loveliness may delight his eyes, but it moves him no more to love than would the vast 'circumference of Abyssinian grace. "If she be not fair to me, what care I how fair she be?" That is the humour of him, and going from the presence of the divinity in a whistling mood, he encounters a third-rate pair of eyes and mouth to match which draw his very soul to them; satisfying him in a moment that if they are not simply beautiful it is because of their tangle of meanings, and because they express all the beauty of the world in confused epitome.

But where he finds this transcendent charm others see nought but a common prettiness; in some other piece of common prettiness these, each in turn, discover the same transcendent charm; and all the while few bethink themselves that here is an infinite subdivision of the wonder that while whole nations and races of men adore the slanting squinting eye, to others it is odious. According to their innate conceptions of beauty, men differ first in gross and then in detail; and, thus, by one of those ingenious contrivances for which Nature is famous, disagreement averts contention and bloodshed.

Of all things in the world, beauty is the greatest pride and envy of women. Birth they think more of than men, yet were it possible to discover an ugly princess an un-Serene Highness would be found who would gladly be the lovely daughter of the merest privy councillor. The great author of "Adam Bede," who had no beauty but the contrary, rated it

above genius, saying that she would gladly resign
her title to fame if only she could be beautiful.   Now,
her gifts being what they were (so great that she
could frankly lament the charms denied to her),
it would appear that there must be more suffering in
the world than comes to light.   And it is evident that
this suffering flourishes not so much in Patagonia,
or amongst the Fans and other African tribes, as
amongst women of the higher races; for there are
fewer deviations from the standard of beauty where
life is simple than where it is involved in the tearing
complexities of civilisation.   If all were known, then,
it might be found that while men deplore the in-
equalities of wealth in civilised states, women grieve
at the more unequal distribution of beauty: a likelihood which, in common kindness, should never be forgotten.   On the other hand, women should remember,
and remember young, that if beauty is harmony,
harmony is beauty.   It is so in everything ; and should
they ask for an illustration of the fact where they
are concerned, let them think of the loveliness of
many a plain face when a smile plays over it.
Further, they may reflect that the beauty which
comes by that way has the surer hold and is more
lasting.   Great beauty of face and form is a fine
estate which no one would refuse.   A nun would
take it, though it were never to be seen except by
the other nuns and their ancient Lady Superior.
Yet it is an estate that is held from hour to hour
upon the sufferance of accident.   Its tenure is a
vanishing tenure ; it soon runs down from wealth to
a bare competency, thence descends through pitiful
breaks and rallies, and so to spectre-haunted ruin

long before life ends.   Great the height, terrible the lingering fall.   A more modest fortune is surely one that wisdom would prefer, and that a lover should choose for his mistress if he could.

Indeed, he has usually an instinct that way, though more in kindness to himself than to her.   Just as he would be loved for himself alone, so he would have her immoderately beautiful for no one else.   Were he less selfish he would look beyond her triumphing days to the days of decline, and would think of the time when "Ah me! going off!" would be said in her bosom with more than a sigh—with a pang. Better the lowlier estate of loveliness in no extreme of beauty.   Loveliness may go with the highest beauty, no doubt, and then it is perfect; but more often it does not.   And—(praise therefore to all the gods!)—loveliness may be somewhat commanded.   Any girl starting in life may choose to have a share of it.   If she be of comely feature; shapely too, mayhap, with a spark of veritable sunlight or starlight under her brows, of sweet and honest mind,—all that is needed to make her lovely is the habitude of kindness.   And the habitude of kindness is a matter of choice, and loveliness is more than beauty.

"BEAUTÉ DU DIABLE"

In French, we are given to understand, "la beauté du diable" is a light expression, signifying the beauty of youth.   In English there is no corresponding term, which is strange; for we undoubtedly have the thing, and sufficient need to speak of it. But whatever the French idea of the "beauté du diable," it has no association in England with the beauty of youth. The French signification becomes quite comprehensible, however, when we gaze upon the pictures of girlish innocence painted by Monsieur Greuze, who helps us to understand it by a diabolic artlessness all his own. Or should any one say that the beauty of youth "plays the deuce" he would be understood ; but only in a limited sense, for it is capable of directly opposite effects on the observer.

There is a true beauty of the devil, and no doubt it may appear in youth. For it is not the other beauty depraved or changed, but one that is original and distinct. As long as it is in the bud no sign of its true character appears ; when it breaks from the bud it may be mistaken for a better thing ; but when it enters on its prime, " la beauté du diable " can be mistaken no longer.

With certain mergings and blendings, beauty is of three varieties. There is a stately beauty, which may be either fair or dark ; the angelic fair ; the dreamy or the sparkling brown. There is another type, "the Village Rose" it might be called, as delightful as any ; but, with all the charm of beauty, it lacks the distinction which confers the name. The beauty of the devil is also in three varieties, but each is more strongly marked. There is the darkly brilliant, the sumptuous fair, and the angelic fair. These three sorts of beauty derived from the Pit correspond with the world, the flesh, and the devil. What they are in aspect they are in spirit. There

is little deceit or concealment about the first two.
They fly the flag ; the air about them is musical
with "vogue la galère !"   But as to the third, the
third is all deceit ; the superlative of subtlety in
treachery.   All have their victims, like every kind
of spider ; but the first variety is the least deadly of
the three, next the second, most the last.   All are
endowed with extraordinary fascination ; which is
not so much accidental to the "beauty of the
devil" as its essence.   And it is fascination of such a
character, that it repels almost as often as it attracts ;
and there its distinctiveness comes out.   Different
in kind, it surpasses in magnetic strength the fascination of the higher beauty ; which, though it may
not always attract, never repels.   The diabolic fascination still holds when the diviner one would perish.
It lasts when it is known to be of the serpent—the
mask of heartlessness, the lure of baseness.   A
few committed faults, and beauty not of the devil
loses its charm for him who is aggrieved.   Outrage, outrage with mockery even, and (as likely
as not) the "beauté du diable" will fix its fascinations deeper, though the outrage will of course be
mourned.

To love where the beauty of goodness is "is a
liberal education" ; to be enthralled by the "beauté
du diable" is degradation certain and complete.
And yet no man, however dull, is unaware of the
difference between this and that kind of beauty, or
doubts that the difference is absolute, or that whether
the one have or have not any relationship with
divine things the other pertains to the infernal.
Only to look on it and watch the part it plays is to

revive the question whether, after all, those godly men are not right who say that the devil is allowed the run of the world, with freedom to compete for its sovereignty. Again, we are reminded of what has been said before, that love is of two kingdoms apart, and that the sweetnesses of the one are closely travestied in the basenesses of the other. They are followed as if in the derision of confident superiority ; as plainly appears when of all the several types of the "beauté du diable," that which deceives the most, robs the most, lures most certainly to degradation and torment, is the one that apes angelic beauty. With its lily looks and Marguerite mien, no coiner ever matched that imposture ; which, since it is rarely detected till it has passed through the rubs of the world a while, finds an easy way to hearts which those other varieties—the bold, frank, joyous beauties of the devil—could never subdue. Some honest attraction may underlie *them*, none under this ; which (not by effort, but quite naturally) wears its utmost loveliness of candour when its lies are basest.

Enough of the beauty of the devil, except to note one sign which appears in all its varieties : a dry glitter in the eyes when *genuine* emotions—genuine emotions which should be soft—stir in the bosom below. That women can tell of a corresponding "beauté du diable" amongst men seems very likely ; but on that point little is known.

BEREAVEMENT

Bereavement is of several kinds, each of which is the worst when we are called upon to suffer it. This is generally true, but especially true in love-affairs, for the reason that love has no *little* losses. Unlike as they may be, its bereavements are so heavy that lovers who view them in all the security that mortals can enjoy would hardly know which to choose were choice forced upon them. Death? That is the first terror that starts up, for death may come at any moment. Youth will not insure against it, beauty tempts it, and fidelity is everything but an elixir to keep the loved one in life. The world dissolves for her who wakes with the thought in her mind that her dear and faithful Jack, now on the seas or engaged in pacifying hill-tribes in a jungle-country, may be dead before she can dream of him again. To go down and read in the newspaper that she has indeed been so bereaved, would be, she thinks, completion in one stroke of the worst loss and misery that fate can have in store for her. But when she finds instead a letter from the dear and faithful Jack himself, ocean-full of life and jollity, and glowing here and there with the ardour of sunshine amongst the Shans, she wonders whether it would be a greater grief to know him dead or find his love transferred. First picturing one bereavement and then the other, which is she to choose? She sees him in an honourable grave, his last thoughts of his Lucy ; and, comparing that scene with a fancy sketch of Jack gone from her into the arms of some Cuban beauty or more deadly manœuverer of "the Hills," she hardly doubts which bereavement would be most terrible. On the one hand there is death to happiness, but not to love and the pride of love returned ; on the other there is death to both love and pride as well as happiness. But whichever bereavement happened it would be thought the worst, though there might be some change of mind about it in after-years.

But sudden and desperate bereavements are not the only ones that love is subject to ; and some that linger on the way are hardly less painful and lasting. There is a bereavement of bloom, of youth, of beauty which is sorely felt, though its distresses are never acknowledged. Perhaps that is why Nature adds to the other wedding-gifts one that is best of all, ordaining that marriage shall begin with a new equipment of beauty for the bride. Had she a grace yesterday ?—now she shall have another and a different one. Showed she the dawn of a brilliant womanhood ?—now it shall shine out, to her trans-figuration.

But, alas and alackaday ! this same kindly Nature is one of those who prescribe that to whomsoever much is given more shall be added. For it is to women who marry happily that the best of this endowment falls. They have little share in it who make a luckless choice, or who find themselves less prized than their hearts' desire. And it may happen to any woman that as soon as she has won the affections of her dearest and best, every charm that he praised will begin to fail. In a year she may be quite bereft of them—first to her dismay, and then to her bitter sorrow. They who are very beautiful are mostly very insolent ; and some may be disposed to laugh when they hear of the poor lady's distresses before her looking-glass, and her heartache at the thought that indifference must soon be her portion. And this fate, which all fond women dread in such a case, many find. With the ravage of their beauty a slow bereavement of love begins, though what they are fated to lose may be dearer to them than ever. And what makes the matter more pathetic is that the signs of waning affection are watched for as if they were all in the natural course of things ; and since there can be no complaining, however great the grief, the practice is to harden one's heart as expeditiously as may be. There are husbands who take the injury to themselves. They look on the misfortune as theirs ; and the sense of it as such is heightened by a feeling that it was not in the bargain when they married. Nor need they take much pains to conceal that view of the case, for it is one that seems perfectly natural to women themselves. Yet their own sense of bereavement is the same ; and it can bring moments as bitter as any other loss as long as fondness remains. This every good man knows, and the knowledge weighs with him.

BETROTHAL

See art. " Affiance," under which head the decline of this worthy word is touched upon. Of native ancestry, an honest word and full of meaning, it has fallen almost entirely out of use among persons of taste. It is still seen in the public journals, where it is of indispensable service in recording the marriage or the engagements of high personages ; and it also appears in novels of that excellent but expiring kind where depth and purity of sentiment are more considered than the avoidance of solecisms. To boys and girls too—though not much to boys—it is acceptable as a romance-word, signifying knightly truth and tenderness. When they say "betrothal" they straightway think of showers of roses, sylvan bowers, and that sweet seclusion from the world with the one beloved which is the deepest joy. But romance expires early amongst young people nowadays, and there is small charm in "betrothal" for sweethearts who have arrived at the full maturity of two-and-twenty. No well-conditioned matron speaks of betrothal now. No young mother, dreaming on the future of her new-come treasure, says even to herself, "when my babe is betrothed." Had the word been better liked it would have remained in use, true though it be that there is an end of the old ceremonious troth-plight in England. Yet it continued long after Reformation times—a ceremony under sanction of the Church, contracted with oath, kiss, and ring, with feasting and minstrelsy, and held to be so firm a tie of espousal that on the one side it was "husband" and the other "wife," if so the contracting parties had a mind to call each other. What says Olivia in "Twelfth Night" on an occasion of less ceremony—

> Now go with me and with this holy man
> Into the chauntry by : there, before him,
> And underneath that consecrated roof,

> Plight me the full assurance of your faith,
> That my most jealous and too doubtful soul
> May live at peace :

And what says the holy man of this same ceremony?—

> A contract of eternal bond of love,
> Confirmed by mutual joinder of your hands,
> Attested by the holy close of lips,
> Strengthened by interchangement of your rings ;
> And all the ceremony of this compact
> Sealed in my function.

This was betrothal; and though the custom declined, the word remained in lingering use till about the middle of the century, when it went out together with the degraded remnant of another old custom : the choosing of valentines. Perhaps it fell into dislike with the reaction against Byronism, or haply with a more familiar acquaintance with German love-making as described in German love-tales.

BLANDISHMENT

Admitted here as an example of words that should not be included in any lover's own dictionary. For though blandishment may be nothing more than a guileless kind of soothing, such as mothers use with wilful sons, it is the one word that gives a name to honey-sweet caresses, smoothed and sylla-bub'd and blended to deceive. Though administered in words and looks, blandishment is a kind of confectionery intended for a kind of stomach. For the mind is not all head and heart, as might be gathered from most writers on the subject. Honestly carrying out its correspondences with the body, the mind is as much stomach as heart or head ; and its appetites may be as confidently appealed to as its wisdom or its sentiment. This men know by observation, women by instinct ; and hence the flatteries of the one and the blandishments of the other.

The more innocent kind of blandishments may have some sincerity, as, for example, a sincere desire to please ; but there is rarely any more love in them than frankness in flattery. Themselves deceits, they are often assumed as a covering for deceit ; of which a rude illustration was afforded by Lucinda, when, idly sailing with her lover on the lake, she drew his face to her bosom while she blew kisses to his friend upon the shore. More commonly, perhaps, blandishments are administered to soothe suspicion or wean from doubt ; but sometimes they are the expression of intermittent remorse, where as yet no shadow of distrust has arisen for removal. It seems likely that some idea of "making up" for secret treachery may mix with these remorseful blandishments ; but however that may be, their distinguishing character is excess. They are frequently so overdone (defensive or evasive blandishments rarely have that fault) as to arouse suspicion, so that the poor man whispers to himself, "What does this mean?" By and by he may find his question answered by the quick and unprepared embrace, the sudden kiss with closed eyes and brow thrown back, which say as clear as words, "For some one else in my thoughts ; not for you."

Judging from the ease with which it is employed by young and inexperienced persons, blandishment must be a natural **honey-like** secretion, answering to that which **collects** in the lubricatory glands **of** certain forest creatures.   But **it is only** natural **to** dishonest minds.

BLISS

This is another of those **words** which, rising from **the ranks,** soar above common **uses.**   Of Saxon descent, **it** originally stood **for what** is now called " blitheness "—**a word** for any jolly lad or merry lass. **But it no** longer applies **to** the ordinary kinds of happiness.   **Were** power, honour, or wealth itself to claim it, **they** would appear ridiculous in a moment. **Bliss is no** word for **them,** but is appropriated to the happiness which **is divine** or that which is half divine. **The** joys of heaven may be called bliss, **but only** such earthly **joy as** lovers **know or young mothers** happily wed.

Here, then, two things pleasantly appear.   Firstly, we see in the undesigned employment **of a word** (for " bliss " was not *deliberately* **set apart** for its present **uses**) **a universal** recognition of **" the** kindred points **of heaven** and home " ; and next **we** see a similar recognition stamped on the belief that the greatest happiness **of all** is that which any cottar may possess. An old woman trudging to chapel, clogs in one hand, umbrella in the other—she may **have** it ; for saintly spirits sometimes **go in that** humble guise. Or **any** fisher **lad** with a bonny wife—they may **have so much of it, in equal shares, as** to fancy **there can be none for anybody else.**   And what **is it ?**   **The** happiness **that could not be** claimed by honour, **power,** wealth, without making **them appear** ridiculous : **bliss.**

BLUSHING

Mr. Darwin is of opinion that " blushing **is the** most peculiar and human of all **expressions ; " and it** is disappointing therefore **to find, on** reading **farther in** his essay on the subject, that he does **not** acknowledge any relationship between blushing **and** love. His conclusion is that **it is in no** sense an affair of the heart at all. The **ruddy suffusion that we call a** blush is too sudden **and too partial to be traced to the** heart's action ; **and is** probably ac- counted for by " the intimate sympathy which **exists** between the capillary circulation **of the surface of** the head, **and of the** brain." **Blushing is caused by two or** three **kinds of mental disturbance.** " **The** mental **states** which induce blushing **consist of shy- ness,** shame, **and** modesty ; the essential element in all being *self-attention*." That is to say, even shame, shyness, **modesty would not** have **been** attended by blushing **but for these** feelings over- taking us in the presence of others. This they **do,** however, very often ; and observation being drawn upon **us** accordingly, our own attention is turned to our personal appearance. The consequence is that " the capillaries fill with blood **over about as** much of us as is visible, **and so we blush."** " **Blush-** ing—whether due to shyness, **to shame for** a real crime, **to** shame for **a** breach of the **laws of** etiquette, to modesty from humility, to modesty from an

indelicacy—depends in all cases on the same principle ; this principle being a sensitive regard for the
opinion, more particularly for the depreciation, of
others ; primarily, in relation to our personal appearance—especially of our faces—and secondarily,
through the force of association and habit, in relation
to the opinion of others on our conduct."

While delivering this opinion, Mr. Darwin is not
unaware that young people in love with each other
blush beyond the average ; but he explains it by
the observation that "young men and women are
highly sensitive to the opinion of each other with
reference to their personal appearance." This all
young people are, and of course young lovers more
than any ; hence their frequent blushing.

There can be no doubt that Mr. Darwin is right
as to all that he includes in his theory. Yet it is
possible to question whether he would not have
admitted more had he been able to push his exact
methods of inquiry into certain sacred ground.
But there was no possibility of his doing so. The
free investigation which nothing forbids when
employed upon one set of persons in hospital, and
another in an idiot asylum, is inapplicable to a
third set of persons in love. Could these be con-
vened for inquiry (and Hyde Park would scarcely
hold them), we should hear from nearly all that
there is a blush peculiar to their condition. That,
of course, would not be enough to prove Mr.
Darwin's theory incomplete ; but the assertion
would be of great weight if the only evidence that
can be adduced is this sort of evidence : the testimony of individual feeling and consciousness. And

that it is so is pretty clear. What can an observing third party know of the cause of lovers' blushing? He sees them blush as they approach each other. If they are aware of his presence, or if they suspect that they may be noticed (which is always the case when they are under observation), the blush may certainly accord with the Darwinian theory; that is to say, it may be and probably is a shyness or modesty-blush occasioned by the feeling that an inquisitorial eye is upon them. But lovers blush when nobody is looking: and what is the cause then? Observation is absent and cannot answer. Nobody can tell but the blushers themselves, and they can speak to nothing but their own individual interior sensations. Those sensations are, in fact, all there is to go upon; and the question is, what are they, and what do they indicate?

It is to be remarked that the sensation is the same when we "turn red" from any of the causes to which Mr. Darwin limits blushing; and this sensation is shame. At one time we know we blush from shyness; at another we know that outraged modesty is the cause; at another, that it springs from distress at some breach of social etiquette. But neither the difference in these cases nor our knowledge of the difference varies the sensation; which is never distinguishable from shame. But lovers blush when they are aware of no such provocations, and when the feeling they do experience is as far from shame as pride is, or joy, or triumph, or anything else that is the opposite of shame. No sensitive lover ever imagined aught to the contrary; or can believe that there is not a blush of love which one's own " personal

F

appearance " has nothing to do with nor anything in conduct either.

Had Mr. Darwin known these things more intimately he would have felt less secure in the belief (on which his Theory of Blushing rests) that it is unnatural to blush in private. He doubted whether it ever happened ; but many a maid could have told him that she had found it the most natural thing in the world. At a thought, at the utterance of a name, at the sound of the crumpling of a piece of paper under a pillow, there comes a sudden flush which is different from the tardier reddening of passion. More might be said. We might ask if Darwin, had he taken love-blushes into account, would have been so sure that the roseate effusion is limited to face and neck. In severe cases the flush of love is certainly felt all over ; and it is rash to deny the visibility of what is shrouded from sight and absolutely denied to scientific observation.

But this article has grown to disproportionate length. Of course so famous an opportunity of warning Science against its fury for dissecting sentiment and skinning the Beautiful could not be neglected : but retaliation can be carried no farther at present. It only remains to be said that although no one ever *gazes* at a blushing face (except for scientific purposes) it is beautiful to glimpse at : and that blushing is so excellent a sign that Lady Mary Wortley Montagu is perfectly credible when she says that in her time it was valued by the Turks themselves. Circassian women who could blush commanded a higher price than those who were incapable of blushing.

BRIDAL

A word which, from its likeness to "bridle," has engendered a variety of confused misconceptions in the popular mind; especially amongst town-folk. The error has been assisted by the general idea of a bride as one who gives herself up to the control and guidance of another; and also, perhaps, by the fact that he who undertakes her direction is called a bridegroom. There is, however, no connection between "bridal" and "bridle," either as signifying restraint, guidance, governance, or as meaning that portion of gear or harness which, when fitted to the head of a horse, puts the noble creature under control. "Bridal" was originally "bride-ale," which is Old English for "marriage-feast"; but centuries ago the word passed from that gross form into the pretty contraction and disguise in which we have it now. Long before Shakespeare's time it must have changed its meaning to the ear; otherwise, "saintly Mr. George Herbert" could not have written of Sunday—

> Sweet day, so cool, so calm, so bright,
> The bridal of the earth and sky :

which is just what marriage itself should be.

"Bridal" is a word of charm, with a music in it that calls out troops of associations, all of youth, innocence, morning joy. It has differentiations from "wedding" which should keep it in use, spite of the sentiment of which this old worn world begins to be ashamed, as a City Father might be of wearing flowers at his ears. "Wedding" is more of a Martha-word, "bridal" more of a Mary-word. Both beautiful, one speaks of glad faith and willing bonds, the other of the joy that twines the bonds with roses. "Bridal" is the word when blooming young folk marry, "wedding" when youth has learned to walk sedately. "Wedding" carries with it the meaning of a day of equal happiness; "bridal" crowns the bride and leads her forth as Queen of the day.

BRIDE

Most men have seen a bride, and all married men have had one of their own, or perhaps two. Yet no man who desires to speak understandingly ever says "bride" without a feeling like that which overcomes him when he is doubtful of a pronunciation. For what is a bride? There are moments when the question may be answered confidently enough. As a young couple advance to the altar, or as they return from it, or when they sit at the wedding feast, any man may say without hesitation, "That is the bride." But even then he will be conscious of certain dimnesses of meaning, the same that steals over us when we speak of sylphs, nereids, nymphs, and other creatures of imagination; for to conceive of a condition or state of being which has no distinct origin either in time or circumstance, no ascertainable beginning and no distinguishable end, is confusing work. In this view of them, brides, who are often called "visions," might almost be thought illusions; and according to the little bird who knows so much, this is just what most brides think of themselves when they cease to be brides. They look back, and " it is a dream."

Bridehood might be supposed to begin when the wedding-day is named ; but there is no appearance of its beginning then unless the day named be only a week off, which brings new conditions into the case. Or the appointment of bridesmaids would .seem to mark a date ; for how shall there be captains before there is a commander ? Yet this will not always serve either ; the proof of which is that bridesmaids are often appointed, with every ratification of pledge, embrace, and kiss, long before any young man has been found to play an essential if secondary part in the affair. On nearer inquiry, it would seem that there was more in Mr. Carlyle's Clothes Philosophy than he knew, being such a very poor lover himself. So far, no one has plumbed the symbolism of attire, or tracked to its mysterious depths the psychologic influence of scarfs, robes, veils, garters, garlands, and other ceremonial caparison ; and it is far from im- probable that, with all the solemnity and poetry that encompass it, bridehood begins with the Ordering of the Clothes. At dawn in the shop of the shoemaker, it grows to perfect day in the haberdashery depart- ment, and mounts to zenith when the wedding-dress comes home.

This must not be supposed a mocking theory. It is as serious as innocent. All observed facts sustain it with one consent ; and to resign it is to be thrown violently back upon the question, What then, is a bride ? There are mysteries in the matter, certainly ; and some that Man has never approached.

After ages of observation, he sees in as much ignorance as ever that when a young " engaged " woman comes to her full estate of bride she undergoes a change. What it is he knows not. To him it is invisible, incognisable ; but he perceives that it is very clear indeed to her female friends and relations, and that it is a change which makes a profound impression on them. Some inkling of its nature should be gathered, it might be thought, from this impression itself, or from the signs and tokens rendered by it ; but no— the impression has its own mysteries and explains nothing. Evidently, however, the bride-transfigura-tion which no man-creature beholds is of a spiritual, a moral, an emotional character ; and perhaps as near a guess as any is that it partakes of elevation to the peerage, the creation of a queen-bee, and a garlanded sacrifice on her way to the altar. It is but a guess, however ; and except in the latter part, it leaves unexplained the mystic enclosures which her female friends cast about the bride—circling and enshrining her as if in an impalpable sanctuary. This they contrive to do by their mere presence, and so effectually that no man, however unconcerned he may be with what is going on, can be insensible of mysterious exclusions. But there is one for whom they are particularly intended : the youth who at a somewhat later period will be called the bridegroom. Feel them as he may, however, he is only at liberty to understand one thing from these mysteries : which is that there is a sacrifice afoot, another Andromeda on her way to the monster's maw. It is against him more than all that the bride is enclosed as in a sacred grove ; and a circle of flaming swords could hardly warn him more clearly than do so many pairs of deprecating eyes that his place is without, in the desert of his own inferior nature.

Had we here a survival from old-world myths and ceremonies it would be explained at once ; but though some such survival there may be, the secret lies deep in the differences between woman and man. Who has explained the little maid's adoration of dolls and the little man's contempt of them ? And in the whole round world, where can be found a young fellow who, whether he were to be afterwards married or not, would take a month's delight in being a bridegroom, set in a worshipping court of gentlemen friends ? There is not one. But for the marriage itself, no man would have aught to do with bridegrooming ; he would flee from it with the utmost speed of avoidance. With women it is different ; so different that were it possible to be a bride from the ordering of the clothes to the throwing of the slipper—the bridegroom to be a miniature portrait up to the moment of his appearance in church, and destined to evaporate at the first crack of the postilion's whip—a coveted delight would be provided for hosts of girls. Evidently, it is a distinct condition or estate, this of bridehood ; just as the rapture of doll-devotion is distinct from maternity. Separate, though not of course dissociate from marriage, it is a garden about the hymeneal temple ; and what it is to wander there is only known to brides and brides' companions. But neither can they tell. Could they do so, we should probably hear of a certain wild religiosity of senti-

ment, pagan but not unseemly, dating from a time
before the whisper went abroad, "Great Pan is
dead."

For persons of both sexes there is one equality,
which is death.   For the gentler sex there are two
more ; bridehood and motherhood.   Good democrats
who rejoice in the one equality should protect the
others ; and especially they should look to it who,
being eager for the advancement of woman, would
have marriage neither bond nor sacrament, and
motherhood a state-affair.

BRIDEGROOM

Through the wrongful introduction of an *r* into
this word, it takes false meanings as it falls into the
ear.   The original word was not "bridegroom," but
"bridegoom," *guma* being Anglo-Saxon for *man :* so
that "brideman" is the right word.   Yet "bridegroom"
does very well, and, indeed, conveys the true meaning
to us nowadays.   The associations with "servant"
are entirely appropriate, and must have grown about
the word *bryd-guma* from very early times.

Irksome and uninteresting as bridegrooms are to
themselves, they are useful to the student of sociology.
During the short period of their existence,[1] they
strongly illustrate the courtesy-submission of men
to women in the Western world, and the recognition
of what may be called Rights of Sentiment in the
gentler sex.   In most parts of the East the bride is

---

[1] It may be calculated that a lover becomes a bridegroom about the
time the wedding-dress comes home, and so remains till the payment of
the first hotel-bill, should he take his bride abroad.

somebody, but the bridegroom is everybody. It is for him that the feast is made, and the flowers strewn, and the music blown. With us it has been different ages beyond ages. The old Scandinavian tales inform us that the women of the North, with Vikings for sweethearts, had well-acknowledged and well-exercised rights of sentiment. There is abundant evidence, however, that in days of old bridegrooms bore themselves with a large and gallant conspicuosity which they no longer affect or desire. When much in love it rejoices them that they are about to wed, but they find no pleasure in being bridegrooms : when they are not much in love they seem to endure it better. There is no magic for them in the ordering of clothes, but a nuisance ; accompanied in many cases by a dim prognostic melancholy, whispering of a time when there will be a forced economy of hats and no further care for the set of a shoe or the cut of a coat-sleeve. We have spoken of the half-religious, half-reproachful seclusion of the bride in the last days of her maiden-hood ; this they feel as if they had done something to be ashamed of. The more sensitive will confess that they go about in that state of mind which falls to us when we wake of a morning and know not what oppresses us till the remembrance of a fault or a misery starts up. Were the bridegroom even as the bride, a circle of attendant swains would move about him, exalting his spirits and wafting him to the height of the occasion. But that he would not have if he could, nor could he if he would. The men of his acquaintance hold aloof from him. They kindly shun him whenever it can be done without ostentation, and carefully present a side-face to his condition : for which he thanks them.

Fortunately, it is but a brief phase of existence. The actual, unconcealable bridegroom-period is much shorter than the bride-time: which is lucky, considering how differently it is spent.   He knows now the depth of his sincerity when, talking with her at the beginning of their bliss, they each declared a strong preference for quiet little country weddings.   He hardly knew how well he meant it then ; she, in her simplicity, only thought she meant it.   Yet if he be a handsome bridegroom and a tall, he will muster his vanities, call up his pride, and, when the time comes, start bravely out and go through the day gallantly. Never, perhaps, is manly beauty so much of a stand-by ; but unfortunately it is not common.   Some of the best of men are neither absolutely tall nor positively handsome.   Others, who might be called plain, range from 5 feet 7 inches to 5 feet 3 inches, and have neither the distinction of a military bearing nor the assurance which a noble beard confers.   It is ill for them in the church and at the wedding-feast ; for, turn where they may, they see their imperfections thrown off from the mirror in every eye, and know themselves but little joy to the bridesmaids.

That is as matters stand ; and they are not improving.   Were it possible to ascertain the amount of anguish endured on this account per annum, it would be found an increasing quantity.   Not that Englishmen have declined in strength, stature, goodliness, but that Englishwomen (long known to every discriminating and impartial foreigner as the most beautiful in the world) are rising to such heights of loveliness that it is a wonder. And ah! what a mistake are these superb growths, however kind the intention. Nature, never weary of compensations and adjustments, finds out that in her brightest kingdom bachelors hold back too much. So many comely girls willing to be brides—so many young men with no mind to be bridegrooms. Then, through the operation of some obscure law, the order goes forth, " Let these comely girls be more comely still. Beauty they have, but give them more ; and since the little that can be added may be over-looked, make them at the same time magnificently tall. Shape them like goddesses, but goddesses like Flora." It is done, but with what success ? Nature evidently fancied that even the young men of a dying Nineteenth Century would run into raptures of matrimony when surrounded by these blooming daughters of Anak, these broad-bosomed Amazons with expansive minds. But there was an error in the calculation, though a pardonable one. The Great All-Mother cannot be expected to take account of mere ceremonial, and knew not what terrors she was adding to the *rôle* of bridegroom.

BRIDESMAID

Bridesmaids are a blend of contradictions. They are of dual character, of which the one part is discordant with the other ; though the two are mysteriously made to agree. Ostensibly, brides-maids are of the Court : maids of honour attendant on the coronation of a bride. It is equally clear,

however, that they are of the temple : priestesses of
sacrifice.   Apparently, the idea of being bridesmaid
precedes the idea of being bride, and embodies as
much romance as that idea with less of serious
undertaking and responsibility.   Yet there is gravity
in the romance, as we may judge from the fact that
the friendship of young girls is stamped with its most
sacred seal when they engage to be bridesmaids
to each other.   Sometimes the pledge is carried
out : in which case the friendship assumes a religious character for ever after.

The institution of bridesmaid is probably coeval
with marriage itself ; with marriage in its more
gracious forms at any rate.   The central intention
of it was, no doubt, standing by the bride to the
last : which is the character it still retains.   But
sometimes the bridesmaids at a wedding are too
many (eight is no uncommon number) ; and then,
like strings of pearls as large as hazel-nuts, they lose
the significance intended and assort with common
things.   One bridesmaid has sufficed ; two are better ;
three should never be appointed : it is an angular
group and all at odds.   By rights, they should be
just as many as the supporters of a canopy.   And
then four signifies a square, and a square typifies
security : as the four towers of a keep, the four walls
of home.   Or, when there are four bridesmaids, you
may fancy them messengers from the four quarters
of the world, or angels conveying the much-prayed-
for blessing of " Matthew, Mark, Luke, and John."
Many figures and resemblances are in favour of the
number four ; but, however philosophic and well-
meaning, he was wrong who suggested on educa-

tional grounds **that** bridesmaids **should** represent
Spring, Summer, **Autumn, Winter** ; **or, as** you might
take it, childhood, girlhood, womanhood, and **venerable** age.   More paganism would be better than
such destructively moral allegories.   **To have** their
right meaning, bridesmaids should be all young girls
in the flower and promise of womanhood.   Even as
pageantry and appurtenance they **are then most**
seemly.   Clustered **near the bride, they** are as much
in place as the star that stands at evening in the
hollow of the moon.

BRIDESMAN

No doubt there **was a** time **when the brides-**
man was **an active** and important personage at **the**
wedding-ceremony.   By degrees, however, he **has**
declined from his **old** estate, and is now, like the
two buttons at the back of his smart frock coat,
hardly more than a survival from ancient uses.   Yet
the presence of the " best man " **at a** wedding is
essential to the right proportion and just harmony
of things.   It would not be seemly were the bridegroom to appear unsquired and alone.   With the
bride and her maids should go **the** bridegroom and
his man.   And though his natural instinct in these
times is **for** retirement, a well-selected bridesman
may play a very useful and graceful **part** ; **as,** indeed,
he usually does when conscious **of the** requisite
qualifications.

The difficulty **is** in choosing **him.**   For none
but a devoted friend should **be** asked **to** undertake

the matter; and while the number of such friends is generally small, the qualities demanded by the occasion are not a few. Unless the "best man" be young he will not set off the bridesmaids handsomely; on the other hand, his youth may excite remark should he be many years younger than the bridegroom. He should be naturally gay, and capable of sustained buoyancy in depressing conditions; for though weddings are no longer festive, somebody should pervade them with a smiling face to recall the fact that the occasion is really a joyous one. He should be a goodly man, but when his comeliness much exceeds the bridegroom's he scatters around him discordant ideas and disorderly suggestions. And here, too, the bride herself is concerned: for, explain it as you may by a fleeting sensitiveness to public opinion, no bride was ever quite happy at the altar when the squire of her chosen one was taller, handsomer, more gallant than he. Evidently, therefore, few bridegrooms can have at command a best friend who assembles in himself the desired qualifications; which suggests that a provident and sage young man would look about him in his earlier years for a friend who would pair with him advantageously in a bridal procession. Were this a common practice, many more weddings would go off harmoniously, and much human misery would be spared.

CALF-LOVE

A CONTEMPTUOUS name for a mysterious but most fortunate visitation. Usually occurring to young men at a period of life which corresponds with the first week in Spring, it is as surprising to itself as we may fancy the earliest snowdrop. It is as innocent too, though not nearly so cool and as soon to perish. But the simile can be bettered. Were a rose to push up from the new-sprung grass, burn from white to red in the glances of a bright but un-impassioned sun, and then, dying down, leave jewels in the earth where it bred, there we should find a likeness more complete.

It would be a mistake to call the love so derisively named premature—as much a mistake as to call a night illumed by "northern lights" premature day. It would not be what it is were it not a distinctly separate kind of affection ; and it is sometimes pre-luded by a greater mystery yet—that love, so like the grand passion as the minstrels conceived it for Arthur's nobler knights, which seizes upon the mere child.   But it is not the fortune of every little man or every little maid to go through that dream-passion; while most adolescents of the ruder sex, from the lad who drives a plough-team to the boy-poet rambling in his college fields, are more or less acquainted with the emotions of which calf-love is the name. It is doubtful whether young lasses are *ever* visited by a corresponding ferment of sensibility : that is to say, exactly corresponding.   No man can say more on this point than that he has never seen reason to think they are ; which, however, is a negative observation, and quite without value.   The generations of man go to their graves, one after another, in ignorance of much that lies in the breasts they repose upon. But even when we turn to the only authoritative witness on the subject, the love-tales published by women, no sufficient evidence appears.   We do, indeed, find in those compositions many a hint of " vague yearnings," vacant romance-dreams, or dreams that would be vacant in the very heart and centre of them but for the creation therein of an ideal adorable. But here we see all the difference between the abstract and the concrete—between the dreams of Columbus on the boundless main unknown and the changed order of his visions with land in sight.   The boy-poet wandering by the river's brim, the lad who plods with the plough-team, they must needs have encountered some actual Divine Object before they begin to dream at all.   Not till then is the one caught up into his rapture—not till then does the other forget to whistle as he goes, gee-woh-ing without knowing and the very whip of him pendent in willowy meditation.   And besides, while " love," "affection," "attachment," are terms of general application, and just as appropriate to one sex as the other, "calf-love" is manifestly not. We know by a common perception of the nature of things that it *cannot* apply in the case of young women ; and since there is no corresponding term in existence that does apply to them, the inference must be that the need of such a term has never been discovered. The budding girl has her dreams and her idealisms, but there is nothing corresponding to calf-love in her experience. She passes from the dream in the heart of the rose to its full-blown perfection in reality.

But let not a mocking word, as "calf-love" is, lead us to the conclusion that here she has a superiority. It is not so. Since women live more for love than men do, their immediate transition from dream to reality seems natural enough, and no doubt is part of a well-ordered scheme of things. But yet it may be questioned whether women of nobler heart and brain would not be the better for a calf-love of their own ; though it cannot be pretended that they stand so much in need of that refining passion. It is even surmisable, indeed, that some women more or less renowned did share the sudden kindlings and illuminations of the love which is hight of calf, what though they had no occasion for its purifyings and withholdings. For there is all that in the boyish passion which, wrapt in folly as it often seems, every young gentleman's good angel delights in.

The truth is that the term "calf-love" was the invention of the same small wit that makes fun of old maids. Not but that appearances have favoured its adoption. The brooding, hang-dog look, the

G

mooning melancholy rather cherished than suppressed
which enfold the lad, his moody musings, his
withdrawal to heights of solitude where his nearest
relations are intruders, do lend themselves to ridicule.   But wise men know that calf-love is very
much more and very much better than a foolish
growth of disordered sentimentalities. They know
that for the right sort of lad, the boy with mind in
him, it is a sun-burst of illumination ; while as for
the common young man, though he may seem more
foolish still when overtaken by it, he will be none
the worse either in his wits or in his morals.   On
the contrary, his perceptions of what is highest,
fairest, sweetest in the world will be both broadened
and clarified.   He will feel where, before, nothing
touched his sensibilities to awaken them ; and, for
one particularly good thing, he will put the distance
from heaven to earth between himself and whatever
mermaids, sirens, and other alluring she-monsters
may fall in his way.   Therefore it was truly said
that were calf-love a marketable commodity, every
wise father and mother would go to market for six
months of it and present it to their sons on their
eighteenth birthday, if not previously supplied.
There is magic in it : mystery beyond understanding.
Fired by this same calf-love—as he may be in a
moment, and truly in the twinkling of an eye—he
who was yesterday all prose looks out upon the world
with a poet's eyes, and is lifted into ranges of vision
and regions of feeling which poets fancy their peculiar
heritage. Some fair young stranger's face comes
into view, and at once a dozen invisible little keys
get to work in the young man's interior, throwing

open as many avenues of perception and sensibility. Till to-day they have been closed ; now they are thronged with a fresh birth of thoughts, dreams, emotions, aspirations, while at the gate of each avenue where they swarm an angel stands on the watch for unclean and ignoble intruders.

Shall the moralist set no store by that? Shall even the lad's mother, hateful as are to her the signs of his ultimate reversion to Another Woman, set against it a *per contra* account of vapourish conceits, languishing airs, dying moods, secret rites over stolen gloves, preposterous worshipping of faded flowers acquired by strategy? What of such trifles as these? Or, to go farther, what if the Divine Object be unintelligible as such? It is of no consequence, and should excite no irritation. Thirty years old, forty years old, what does it matter? It is, indeed, a subject of great psychological interest, but it need not concern the family. The abiding good of calf-love is that, drawing him into a realm of enchantment, it awakens in the boy-lover's mind whatever capabilities of beauty and fruitfulness there are in it : then what matters it whence the witchery comes? It has no substantiality ; it leads to nothing, out of his tormented bosom ; and, indeed, the witchery does not proceed from the lady at all. It is his own work. The charm of the enchantress is conferred by him whom she enchants. Her magic is bestowed on her by the lad who wonders and trembles at the spell, and passes away with the more glorious illusions and environments it calls about him. Therefore let be! Calf-love may be only a fever, a ferment of the blood, but it is all good and no harm. For as long as it lasts, at any rate, it fills the boy's mind with a portion of the light of genius; and he must be a dull dog to begin with if some rays of it do not linger in him to the last days of his life. More than that, it is an illumination which, for short, we will call moral; leaving it to be further explained by whosoever can account for its spontaneous generation at the sight of one who may not have a spark of fancy or morality to communicate.

CAPTIVATION

Captivation is itself extremely captivating. Its possessor is a pleasure to behold, in her sparkling variety; and it is no such oppressive endowment as we may suppose magnificent beauty and majestic mind to be. It exactly fits and contents the moderate ambition which asks for nothing in excess. Enough to be very pretty, very witty, very winning; and, after all, it is more human to captivate than to subdue.

Captivation is of complex character, being made up of a multitude of bright little gifts set off by as many graceful little arts. But to be complete it must partake of the greatest of all gifts and the one that is least indebted to art: the gift of "charm." Indeed, there can be no captivation without some admixture of that inexplicable quality. Within a pleasing exterior you may be a museum of graceful arts, and a whole polytechnic of shining accomplishments to boot, and yet miss the distinction of captivation. For that an infusion of charm is wanted ; and since charm is not a thing that can be acquired, all depends on the amount of it that you were born with. Thus it is that there are so many different degrees in captivation. It naturally varies with the extremely variable quantity and quality of its constituent parts. At its best, it is one half charm at least ; and for the remainder, a blend of gentle but efficient manners, brilliant arts, sparkling graces, and the kind of cleverness which is valued in the horse. Good-nature is another necessary ingredient ; but though it is essential that it should be obvious it need not be embarrassingly deep.

Pleasing as it is in the general, captivation may be turned to fatal account. For in this compound quality charm answers to genius, the rest to talent or skill ; and the whole is commonly attended by the same restless desire to be doing, the same appetite for "making one's proofs," which is so insatiable in actors, poets, pigeon-shooters, and other persons endowed with the artistic temperament. Art for art's sake, and, above all, for our own enjoyment of its exercise, is more than an æsthetic dogma. It is a natural instinct, and one that born mistresses of captivation can no more subdue than the painter of symphonies and nocturnes. They, too, wish to test their gifts from time to time, to revel in their exercise, and to enjoy the view of a completed work. The consequence to the captivated is not always serious, for few artists of any kind succeed to the utmost at every attempt. But in the pursuit of these triumphs much suffering is inflicted, much torment endured. Vivisection could do no more sometimes; indeed, the object aimed at is the production of extreme agony. That, however, is no uncommon result of "art for art's sake"; and we are to remember that no siren ever believed that the pain she caused outdid the pleasure she bestowed.

The essentials of captivation are found in both sexes, but women themselves rarely speak of "captivating" men. The word is vulgarly inappropriate, just as gleaming jewels are when men display them for their own adornment. "Fascinating" is a word more often used; but perhaps the true masculine of "captivation" is "conquest." One argument for that suggestion is that from the bottom of their hearts, with every fibre of their bodies, to the last recess of their directing thoughts, women prefer being conquered to being captivated. On the other hand, they are much happier as captivators than as conquerors.

Captivation may be found in full flower in a girl two years beyond her teens, but in most cases it matures much later. The corresponding quality in the other sex never appears in very young men, where it would be out of place; indeed, its most effulgent and victorious period seems to begin just before the turn of middle life. But it does not compare with the female original. It is less spontaneous; it wants root; it is inferior in the play of advance and retraction; the active and energent principle in it — art — is coarser, and lacks the flexibility imparted by constant and ungrudged practice.

Captivation is extremely pleasant for all within

its scope but not within its grasp. To those who possess it largely it is delightful ; and not less delightful because it is not all gift, as beauty is, but some-part management. It has its penalties, however. Captivating persons are seldom capable of the tenderness and glow which it is their triumph to inspire in others, and a time comes when they are feeble to hold where they fain would cling. There is little love in them, and what love there is for them passes. This should be some comfort to those whose sweethearts they win away.

CHARM

Charm has been described as " something which exerts an irresistible power to please and attract." It is a right definition, and perfectly acceptable if "exerts " is not understood as implying effort. The word must be taken in the gentlest sense of " putting forth " ; as a bough puts forth its buds, or pearls their radiance.

The etymology of the word " charm " is beautifully harmonious with the thing signified. Springing from *carmen*, a song, it thus proceeds : a song, incantation ; incantation, enchantment ; enchantment, charm ! All is there ; and the more to satisfaction because " charms " had the meaning of " songs " long after Shakspeare's day, when there was a double force in the lines beginning " Music hath charms," which is lost nowadays without being missed.

Music and enchantment : the word charm was born of these, and what parentage could more fitly or fully account for the thing itself—this "something which exerts an irresistible power to please and attract"? That it is enchantment we know who come within its influence, vainly wondering what its source may be and what its secret. And it is equally mysterious to those who possess it. Genius is also a mysterious possession. But genius can be employed at will; its possessors are conscious within themselves of its action; and there is no such consciousness in those who are gifted with charm. Though they must be aware of its power, they cannot command their magic, nor view it as others do, nor feel the play of its influence; their part is to abide within it, like the Man in the Moon in the light thereof. But though enchantment is of many kinds—of earth, of sea, of sky, of air, of things seen and unseen—it happens that none is so like the witchery of charm as the witchery of music. Harmony is the life of both; and both speak a language for which we have no words to a sense within our senses, a mind within our minds.

There is hardly an hour in our lives when we do not know that we could be much less agreeable if we liked; and yet agreeable folk are as anxious as the disagreeable to believe that they are what they are because they cannot help it. In this we may see how general is the recognition of charm, and how sincere the homage it obtains. We would rather be supposed to partake of enchantments entirely beyond our control than capable of cultivating a virtue. The explanation is that while virtues may be acquired, or at any rate fostered, or at least imitated, charm is beyond all that: a gift of the gods more excellent

than human effort can attain to. So indeed it is,
and as such may be trusted.

At the word "trusted," many grieving hearts, both
married and single, send up a shivering little cry of
" no." They are understood, but the grief and the
exclamation proceed in every case from error. The
mistake that accounts for both is the mistake of
confounding charm with charming manners. They
are not the same things. It is true that in perfect
beings they go together. But charm often under-
lies manners which are only just good enough to be
called good ; while as for manners, they are but
manners and may or may not deceive. Girton,
Newnham, and the other ladies' colleges will never
be complete till a chair is established for the teaching
of this distinction, amongst other matters essential to
a right equipment for the struggle for love which so
many brave young creatures are ever about to plunge
into. There may be treachery in fascination, the
professor would teach, for that is sometimes a black
magic and sometimes a white ; but there is no deceit
in charm. That mystery, he would say, might even
be described as an effluence of the spirit of candour ;
the candour of generous and gentle minds. To
account for the way in which it seems to hang like
an aura about those who possess it, it might be
pictured as candour unwilling to be kept in store for
special occasions and particular uses. Escaping from
its natural confines, it dwells openly on brow and lip
and speaks in every word and gesture. A minor
point for observation is that inasmuch as charm
touches the senses, appealing to them as bloom and
beauty do, it is through voice and movement more

than anything else. Why through voice may be readily understood, for there are voices that play upon the sensibilities of sex with magic force. Why through movement is less plain, but the secret is probably the same ;—harmonies are evolved indefinable even to the emotions that must obey them.

Mind there must be where there is charm ; but amongst its many tokens of a divine origin must be counted the fact that brilliancy of intellect is rarely its companion. The light that naturally belongs to it is a steady, sweet, and cheerful wisdom, which lasts and helps it to last. This brings us to another difference between charm and fascination : charm endures, fascination decays. After a while fascination dies out in a gently-disappearing way, as if content to go ; or, not content to go, glares in ghastly-smiling travesty when there is no more help from the beauty of this flesh. The better thing adorns the tenement it lives in from first to last ; and sometimes changing a little but never growing old, often gives to age a loveliness of aspect hardly promised in youth.

Yet with all this, and though many talk of marrying money, or beauty, or birth, nobody talks of marrying charm. Is that, mayhap, because the generality have not learned to distinguish it from fascination ? And to those who have learned, is it, perchance, something like very great beauty, the acquisition of which in wedlock might possibly make life too serious ? If so, it is indeed time that an understanding of these things should be imparted to young men and maidens in the last year of their studies. For (especially where love inclines), charm is the surest warrant of good-companionship, high, sweet, serene, and lasting. It was of a woman endowed with charm that Steele said, " To love her is a liberal education."

CHILD-LOVE

This is one of the wonders of the world. A flower rooted and blooming in the air could hardly be more strange than the love which many a little man of ten years old shyly cherishes for some little maid no more grown up than he. And had we to choose a flower to emblem it, fancy would err in taking the violet, the primrose, or any such pale and unimpassioned piece of Nature's handwork. Rather the briar-rose ; sweetbriar ; *Rosa rubiginosa:* with its full share of thorns, perfume breathing from every tiny leaf, and its breaking buds so lovely in their deep red rosy innocence that nothing in Flora's kingdom can match with them.

Child-love is not a mere affectionate friendship,— no romantic attachment like that which bound Celia and Rosalind to each other, or such as couples the brace of lads who go apart on all possible occasions to read together, stroll together, fish together, dwell together in a maze of aspirations and confidences like those that united Irving and Carlyle in their boyhood. It would be reasonable to think it a sublimation of something that is not love though akin to it ; but in truth it is as much the true passion of love as the briar-rose is a rose. It is the true passion in all that poets tell of its intensity, its absorption, its fancy-kindling romance. No symptom with sweetness in it is wanting, none that is pain in sweetness, and none that is pure pain. As the full-mustachio'd lover dreams o' nights, so does the little lad with his heart a burning bush of *Rosa rubiginosa.* As the one tosses on his bed, making verses, so does the other and quite as good. There are times when both are aware of such carollings and chorusings in the world within them that nothing can compare with it except groves of wild angels, singing on a heavenly May-day where sounds are always felt and never heard. Or if there are days for the six-foot sufferer when the world is a desert—all greenness taken from the earth, all the virtue of light gone out of it, no food so sweet as bitterness, no couch so grateful as a pallet of straw in the darkest corner of a rat-abandoned barn—why so there are for the little one ; whose miseries are seven years ahead of his mustachios without being any the more tender with him. There are the same restless dreamings : the same slinkings into solitude and enjoyment of it ; the same doting upon stars, flowers, and the lovelier *little* things ; the same delight in leafy nooks ; the same preference for twilight ; and, to make all complete, there is the same sheepish sense of shame in the boy of twelve as in the young man of twenty.

Jealousy ? If that be, as women say who have known the world, the only test of love that can be relied upon with reasonable security, here is no lack of it either. At eighteen years the love-experiences of youth are mostly bitter, which is the reason why so many young men find that to be sensitive to-day is to be saturnine to-morrow. But at twelve these experiences are worse, a third part at least being sheer

torment.   For in the first place, at that age concealment is left to do its fatal work ; and in the second
place, nine times out of ten there is no capability of
response in the object of your affections.   Should
she be older by a couple of years she is above them,
and ah ! what desperation it is then !   Should she
be younger, or of an equal age, she knows not when
nor how she stabs you in company with other little
boys ; parting oranges with Another when you are
by, or nestling to him over a picture-book *for hours*
though she knows that to-morrow you will be far
away at school.   It is easy enough to smile at the
agony of such moments, but St. Lawrence on his
gridiron knew none more real or more poignant.

However, it is but a fleeting passion.   With all
its genuine fervours and distresses all is over in a few
months.   Only the mystery of it remains, and this
cannot be got at very easily.   Beyond the fact that
they do no harm, but good rather, nothing is known
of these little love-affairs though much may be
suspected : as that they are a tardy growth of sentiment—a development of the later centuries ; and
that with all the poetry, all the exaltation of the
true passion and none of the grossness which science
and cynicism bid us suspect, they flower in the
northern nations alone.

CLANDESTINE

An ill-fated adjective, which, though of blameless
origin and majestically syllabled, is never associated
with any but mean designs and ignoble purposes.

Of these there are plenty of all sorts ; yet its range of application has been narrowed till it is almost entirely confined to the stolen interviews and secret lawlessness of lovers. Its only comfort is that worse might have happened to any adjective ; for the offences which " clandestine " is coupled with are not all as black as they are painted, and some would be found as white as angels' wings could they be seen out of the dark in which the offenders choose to shroud them.

The clandestine may be shameful, of course ; but only as cloaking deceits, treacheries, faith defrauded, promise broken, or whatever else is shameful whether concealed or unconcealed. But lovers know, and Mrs. Grundy herself should remember, that there are feelings of shame where there is no shame ; and it often happens that only to spare themselves a little innocent confusion do the poor young things steal under shelter of the clandestine. Isn't it in the very nature of love to be secret ? Even to itself it would be so at its beginnings. Only by littles does it creep out for acknowledgment in the breast it was born in, as if ashamed to be seen by the other passions. Neither man nor woman feels an imperative need of seeking the woods to think upon a hatred or a jealousy, but how many are compelled to hurry to some deep retreat when they would dwell upon their love ! And even when the lover knows himself secure amidst sequestering shades, his sweeter thoughts do not come forth to light as readily as others would. The feelings that he would array for contemplation evade him. It seems as if there are woods and shades in his own mind where they hide

from settled view, and where he has to seek them
out. So secret can love and lovers be even to themselves, and so innocently clandestine. The little
notes that travel by covert ways, the little meetings
secretly planned and enjoyed, these are open to
remark, no doubt ; but what if they are contrived
from shyness and not for slyness ? And when the
case of an enamoured pair is such that even in a
wilderness they would hardly dare to say aloud, " I
love her," " I love him," what wonder is it that they
should go about to screen the embracing of eyes and
hands and hearts from all knowledge and surmise?
And without such embracings they would go mad
or die. It appears, then, that the word "clandestine'
should be employed with a more humane discrimination, or else should share the privilege of " secrecy "
and be allowed two meanings, one innocent and one
not. The word " secret " has attained to a greater
respectability through mere association with diplo-
macy, the police, and the least of the learned pro-
fessions ; an association which surely is no more to
be regarded than a similar connection with youthful
innocence.

Yet Heaven forbid that a moral dictionary like
this should cast 'a doubt upon the existence of
ignoble secrecy in love-affairs. There is such a
thing. There are sly concealments, goings and
comings that are felt to be more shame than joy
even while they are hazarded : let them be branded
for what they are known to be in the hearts of the
offenders—unworthily clandestine. Time was when
there were girls who loved the clandestine for its very
naughtiness, finding some kind of romance in it.

That time is past. Did any such persons remain, they should be admonished too, and yet not as criminals absolute. There are deeper transgressors with whom we have nothing to do; and these being reproved, the wise will have little more use for the word clandestine, remembering that love can hardly breathe but "under the rose." Where was it born or where cradled but "under the rose"? Could it hear, could it speak, "but under the rose"? The whole realm of its delight is there; or if it must pine, it pines "under the rose."

COMPLIMENT

It may be argued that compliment is no part of the language of love; but the contention will not hold unless, amongst many sorts of compliment, those are selected for objection which are formally or trivially polite. And let no man be so deceived as to fancy that even the least of these is unwelcome if only it be seasonable and betray pleasure in pleasing. Like the little birds in a nest, love is always agape; and no sweet word is too small for acceptance dropt into a woman's bosom from the lips she is most inclined to.

Compliments are what they are to those who receive them. In this they resemble gifts; and no one should err in making compliments who remembers that in fact they *are* gifts. For remembering this, he will bear in mind that they should be chosen with the same regard for the proprieties as when gifts that cost money are intended; and of course with the same preliminary questioning as to whether a right to make any such offerings has been conferred on him. Carefully observed, this is a safe rule of guidance.

To be sure, there are many who say that they detest compliments altogether, and will not have them. In these cases, however, it may be that only the hateful sorts are hated : such as the gross, the presumptuous, the insincere, the smirking, the sniffing, the larcenous-insincere, and the other-than-expected. If, on the contrary, there are folk who gorge all manner of compliment, they are but so many examples of greediness :—the fault is in their untempered taste and voracity. Some there are too, who, while they are at no pains to reject insinuated praise, never pay compliments themselves, and think their abstention a Roman quality. It is not that, but a Gothic medley of the churlish, the grudging, and ungracious. Not always, however. It may come of nothing worse than a desperate want of aptitude for saying handsome things handsomely.

But compliment in general is no concern of ours, except as there seems to be little merit in withholding what may be prettily and honestly bestowed, and is never ill taken when well sped. This it must always be from a lover's lips. And then there is something ceremonious about compliment ; and in the whole round of love-affairs there is no more stupid mistake than the banishment of ceremony. In many a case, the one and only thing wanting to perfection in the intercourse of married lovers is an occasional waft of ceremonious affection from husband

to wife.   The delight it is to a woman when the lord
of her heart says courtly things to her from the
distance of homage he never knows for she will
never tell.   But it should be understood that nothing
that can be bought in Bond Street is more prized.
They are jewels, but jewels that adorn her *for herself*
—the interior, ideal self, which rejoices and is proud
to be decorated too.   Every such gift is stored away,
and when she brings them all to memory it is like
the opening of a casket.

But does she really set store by such wordy
trifles, putting them by for remembrance?   For the
ten thousand and twenty-ninth time, Strange is the
human heart!   It is the adoring exclamation, the
passionate endearments she listened to in the onset
of their love that she has little memory for, and the
reason is plain.   She paid no more attention to
them at the time than she might to the particular
and individual noises of a storm at sea.   They
thrilled her, those passionate outcries, but yet they
were felt as some-part generalities—the customary
clamour of trumpet and shawm, of harp and pipe
and psaltery, heralding her into the paradise where
many had entered before.   But the pretty courtly
compliment of a more sober time is no generality.
It is minted for her, with her own image on it ; and
no hand had anything to do with the coining of it
but the one it came from.

It would seem a pity, then, to exclude these toys
of speech as too trivial or too precise for well-settled
lovers to use.   After twenty years, a simple, pretty,
hearty compliment (deserved) comes as fresh and as
grateful as the first nosegay.   Be it remembered!

CONFIDANT, CONFIDANTE

A statistical inquiry into the conditions, relations, experiences, and accessories of love-making would yield many particulars of value to psychology. Were such an investigation opened, one point of it would be to ascertain how many persons of the male sex, being in love, have confidants of their passion, as compared with the number of female persons in the same case. The figures should also show at what age the obligation to seek a confidant seems most uncontrollable—tables being prepared to exhibit the variation of that feeling in either sex at stated periods between sixteen years old and sixty.

As one result of this inquiry, it would probably be found that men who have confidants are relatively few, and that nearly all come within the age-period of eighteen to twenty-three. On the other hand, it is conjectured on reasonable grounds of observation that the whole female population above the age of sixteen has had one or more confidantes. A further difference would probably appear ; namely, that confidantes are not only indispensable accessories to young women in love (being, in fact, the third leg of a stool for indispensability), but are also a luxury apart. Sometimes, indeed, confidantes are created for their own sake, on the basis of an anticipatory or provisional *affaire de cœur*. But that is rarely the case with young men—never unless they are partly young women ; and it is to be observed that while the indispensability of confidantes to the fairer sex seems only natural, similar indulgences by young men appear *un*-natural. Looking back along the history of men and women to its beginnings, the psychologist knows precisely why ; but this is not a psychological dictionary, and we proceed to add that it is nothing out of nature when young men make confidants of a deep, a raging, an *unhappy* passion. And it is the unhappy passion that men are most ready to confide, the happier ones women. Except in the case of young poets—of whom, however, there are a great many at the age of nineteen—it is for the easing of pain and not for sympathy that the unloved lad bellows on the bosom of his friend. He would just as lief complain to the rocks and woods and streams, like the love-lorn shepherds of old, had he half the shepherd's belief in listening ears unseen.

But if he seeks no sympathy, neither could he find it if he would : such is the nature of mankind. Possibly he would prefer that his dearest friend and comrade should feel for him rather than not. On the other hand, his friend would like to feel for him, and tries to do so ; but however generous the effort, it is seldom attended with success. The explanation of the failure is not want of goodwill but some strange lack of comprehension. For though a man may know the passion of love in himself full well, his conception of it when it rends another man is of something foreign, crude, vapourish, elemental, curious—amusingly curious. It is not *quite* as if he were looking at one of the animals in Mr. Riviere's picture of " Circe and the Swine," but not unlike. A strange perversity this, and yet so common as to be almost universal ; and the consciousness of its existence, which all men feel, must needs limit the

number of lovers with confidants of their own
mannish sex. But women—it is different with them.
They have unbounded sympathy with each other
in love-affairs, a feeling heart for every woe, an embracing imagination for every joy ; and no moralist
can doubt that these instinctive characteristics have
as much to do with their running together with their
love-secrets as any impulse less divine.

The mingling of kindred souls is one of the
dearest pleasures of youth ; and, fortunately, it is so
ordered that kindred souls are more plentiful at this
time of life than at any other. And one of the very
sweetest of these pleasures is communion over the
sweetest of secrets ; wherefore there would be some
unkindness, as well as no success, in preaching
caution in that matter. Nor is there much call to
preach. Men need little warning for one reason,
women for another. They do confide, do embrace
each other's confidences ; and they are not unfaithful.
It is a common assertion that women are given to
prattling with unbenign intent. But considering
what numbers of confidantes there must be in the
world, and considering the delicacy and exuberance
of that which was imparted to them, the harmony of
society is impressive evidence against that assertion.
Inasmuch as they do prattle, it would seem to be
in a sort of Freemasonry, quite amongst themselves ;
but the word " inasmuch " here would be better
" inaslittle." A line is drawn. The subject is
sacred.

CONQUEST

When we speak of conquest, mutual attraction is of course excluded. Conquest is aggressive here as elsewhere ; but it differs from that which soldiers enjoy in being all glory and no gain. Indeed, there would be little glory either if what is acquired was ever coveted or valued in the least. But there are two kinds of conquest : the involuntary, and that which is designed or intentional. Considering that involuntary conquest signifies surrender to beauty, charm, fascination, at the mere sight of them, it would appear to be that which is most highly valued. Yet whether from loftiness of mind induced by conscious irresistibility, or whether because victories won without effort are lightly esteemed, unintentional conquests are least prized of any. But there is another reason, and one that brings out the true inwardness of conquest, which is sport. All sport is at bottom love of conquest ; but while men go forth to shoot bears, rabbits, tigers, and all manner of difficult animals, the conquest of man is the only sport of woman. If now we conceive of a sportsman in some strange country, where the animals run after him to gaze at his gun and die immediately they catch sight of it, we may learn from his indifference to the sport why woman's involuntary conquests are little prized.[1]

---

[1] Rothkopff has observed that the prosecution of conquest is never so keen as in the shooting-season, and in country-houses where sport is the predominant passion with the host and the gentlemen his guests. And the German writer suggests the explanation (which, however, is of doubtful originality) that their ardour for the chase excites to boiling-point the corresponding instinct in the breasts of the ladies then staying in the establishment.

Conquest as a pursuit is certainly of the nature of sport, even the terminology of the two being for the most part identical : thus we hear in each case of "bringing down" and "killing." As practised by ladies, the sport is most like that of the fowler who takes his game in nets, either for immediate execution or after detention for a while in a pen or cage. It is not their nature to pursue, nor is it with them a necessity except in desperate cases. They go to work with a magic resembling that which is ascribed to the Pied Piper of Hamelin : a magic which exactly reverses the process of hunting or stalking. Airs attuned to his delighted ears, beckonings that enchant his senses, draw the victim to where the sportswoman sits and smiles and weaves her harmonies. He comes, and being arrived within point-blank distance, is shot dead with a stare. Or a cord is thrown about his neck ; and then he jumps after her like a led monkey as long as she can keep his teeth from the rope, or finds his grimaces entertaining either to herself or her company. This might be called wanton or cruel if it were not sport ; or, to put the fair truth another way, but for its being sport the cruelty would be impossible to such gentle creatures as we know do glory in it. There is no way of explaining conquest except by putting it on a level with rabbit-shooting, when the cruelty disappears. Nevertheless, it may be held that conquest for conquest's sake falls short of positive goodness, and it is certainly no evidence of a loving nature.

Conquest has its curiosities, of which one is that while absolute beauty is not a necessary equipment

for the weaker sex, there are many examples of the
other doing quite without it.   Handsome and gallant
men are as much given to conquest as handsome
and seductive women, and they make as much havoc
(or it may be more) in cruel and unsportsmanlike
ways.   But many succeed who have no appearance
of being either handsome or gallant.   Quilps have
been conquerors, and their wives half mad with
jealousy.   To turn again to the other sex, it is
observed that a difficult conquest will sometimes
pique the adventurer to so desperate a determination,
and drive her to such extremes of encouragement,
that she puts the rope round her own neck, and
even exposes herself to the entirely unanticipated
consequence of being shot by a stare.   This dreadful
possibility should be borne in mind.

CONSTANCY

There is a taste in virtues as in lesser things.
We would not willingly deny the possession of any ;
yet we may have our own preferences.   To one, this
virtue seems over-rated ; another doubts whether
that is not held in disproportionate esteem, or
whether mankind is not in a general conspiracy of
make-believe in favour of a third.   And it is not
as if the virtues we think most of are those which
we happen to possess.   There are cheats in love
with integrity, hypocrites who would fain be
sincere.

Inconstancy is commoner than theft—perhaps as
common as untruthfulness ; and yet, for a fancy

virtue, none is more doted on than constancy.
There is hardly a soul but knows how high and fine
a quality it is, nor are there many who would not be
constant above all things. A humble virtue, and
yet so compendious! No creation of theologies,
nothing divine, but a sound earth-born virtue with
the distinction of being the same in all climates,
constancy includes one-half of all that heaven can
smile upon in this world below. Beginning in
friendship and love (themselves delightful to behold),
it gives to both their highest beauty. It implies
loyalty; duty has part in it; generosity is wrapped
in it, and the charity and tenderness and magnanimity which Bishop South aims at when he says,
" Constancy is such a firmness and stability of friendship as overlooks and passes by lesser failures of
kindness and yet still retains the same habitual
goodwill." This is said of friendship; but when we
come to love, it is not only the lesser failures of
kindness that constancy will pass by, but utter
bankruptcies. Then patience is called upon; meek-
ness, endurance, endeavour to win and reclaim; and
often with all this there is a martyrdom of heart
which, considering how it lingers, will compare with
the bonfires at Smithfield. Sometimes, however, it
does reclaim; and the more often when it is not
so much a constancy of duty as of tenderness. No
one can tell how many wayward spirits are brought
back to honesty and kindness by the dumb entreaty
of unalterable love.

There is a constancy as of the Nut-brown Maid
in the ballad—*if* it be true that she would not have
been so very constant had she not been so extremely

brown. With this kind of constancy we have nothing to do.

And there is, of course, a rejoicing as well as a mourning constancy : two rejoicing kinds, indeed, and very different. The one is happy in its own complete assurance, though it has never been tried either from without—as by neglect or cruelty—or from within, as by temptation. The other is still more assured and more rejoicing because (though this may be a secret from everybody) it has come through the fires of temptation and *knows* that it is staunch. Its firmness is a settled thing. It is safe, steadfast, and therefore must be happy as long as the love that has so well been tried is heartily returned. This is a more common case than would appear from the story-books.

Lastly, there is a variant that may be called constancy to constancy. It is most often seen in those faithful lovers who, their dear ones being dead, roll a stone before the place they held in their hearts, allowing entrance to no other love. But it may also be seen where the bereavement is not of death but treachery or desertion. It is a proud feeling then, and not quite heart-warm ; yet there is greatness in it too. Not only is there a clinging to constancy for its own sake, but the sanctity of love itself is vindicated. The baseness of others is not allowed to degrade its ideal. And thus the two fine flags of love and constancy are kept flying together over foundered trust.

COQUETRY

Coquettes, who are far more pleasing to the sex they do not belong to than their own, have much pleasure in themselves, and no name is to them so pretty as the one they go by. The reason is, perhaps, that " coquette " breathes to their ears with the meaning of " cockade "—a truly ineffable word, boundless in its association with the dashing, the gallant, the victorious in flying ribbons. But " coquette " was understood of old to mean " a prat-ling or proud gossip," and it is the feminine of *coquet*, a little cock ; which is not a comparison for any young lady to be proud of.

Coquetry has more often engaged the attention of students than anything else, perhaps, within the scope of this work. For it is not only a pleasing study and eminently curious, but one that seems to open an easier path than most into the recesses of female character. In that respect it is like a smiling glade on the edge of a forest, inviting to enter in and wander and behold. But the charmed inquirer has not advanced far before the glade itself turns out to be a well-pleached maze, resounding with confused voices ; while beyond lies the everlasting mystery of darkness, shot with beams from heaven and gleams from the Pit, which are so hard to reconcile. The student is exercised, and perhaps amused ; but he learns nothing, though he may be confirmed here and there in an old belief, as that the charm of coquetry is flattery. It is more than that, of course, for though flattery is the means, torment is the end ; yet it is by the one that the victims of coquetry are drawn into the other. And if torment is the aim, sport is the motive ; that is to say, the pleasure of exercising superior qualifications both natural and acquired, which is the soul of all sport.

The methods of the coquette are invariably the same, and their peculiarity may account for the idea that she shows us a way behind the veil that shrouds woman ·from man. The pretty little fluttering approaches of the coquette are not at all what she depends upon, and are nothing but calls to attention. They might, indeed, do her work off-hand ; but though a conquest so obtained may be satisfactory enough to some, it is too tame for the coquette. Herself a wild thing in the midst of all her equipage of refinement, she knows by instinct of a pleasure the exact converse of the angler's when he wades and leaps after the fish at the end of his line. Her flutterings of approach are but starts and preliminaries to allurement by flight. Not the advance —the flight is the thing. The rapture of being pursued, the exciting possibilities of stumbling, the delight in the pursuer's eagerness, the sweet malicious joy of baffling him from point to point and of throwing him out altogether at last—these are the pleasures of the coquette ; and it must be acknowledged that they are entirely sportsmanlike. Judged from that point of view, they are unexceptionable quite. (For supposed levity and cruelty, see art. " Conquest.")

As might be inferred from the nature of the amusement, coquetry is almost all in the hands of brisk, lively, vigorous young women ; and they appear to be most addicted to it and the most adept who are of a brown complexion, bright-eyed, red-lipped, with two rows of that particular kind of teeth which seem to have an own gift of smiling. There are fair coquettes too—of the brilliant and sunny kind of fairness ; but it is thought that they are fewer than the brown, and more liable to languish in the way when hotly pursued. Both, however, are declining in numbers. Coquettes are less frequently met with than in former times, for which there are two reasons, if not more. Coquetry is in its very essence a *womanly* pursuit, and womanly pursuits of every sort are losing vogue. Added to this, the male sex has become so numerous of late, and takes such advantage of its numbers, that coquettes have but poor sport nowadays. Many have given it up altogether and few are coming forward.

COURTSHIP

By general consent, the time of courtship is reckoned from the day when, the question being put, the lover is accepted. But in most cases the court-ship is over by then, if courtship means wooing. The lover is still the lady's courtier in the broad brave sense of the word, and is so more openly than ever ; but he was her courtier before in that accepta-tion, and much more her courtier in the sense of one who seeks and solicits. His suit embraced, there is an end of the soliciting. The devotional air of attend-ance, the timidity of approach, the eye-asking, the ingratiating inflections of voice, the silences that make a void for every question but one—these and all other addresses of courtship have passed away with the uncertainty that attended them. He no longer courts the lady's love, he has it; and all his business now is to rejoice in it, bask in it, heightening and brightening her affection by the effulgence of his own.

As they may still lose each other, something of the courtier's circumspection remains, no doubt; and if, by the last kindness of Fortune, they go upon an equal footing of affection, it is pretty to see how soon she will take her share of this watchfulness against offending. Still, there is no courtship; and though it may happen several times before the wedding day that he will have to go back to it for an hour or so to smooth a difficulty (or she put on a courting sweetness with the same design), that is no more than will occur after marriage; and on many occasions, mayhap.

What it is that makes this little stretch of time so memorable is not courtship but companionship; *their* companionship; the companionship that now begins, with its greater freedom of admission to each other, and with all the fresh wonders and beauties they find in the communion of two happy souls born for each other and come together. To be sure, the courting-time is sometimes memorable for another reason: the discovery of incompatibilities, blemishes, unfitnesses too small to carry a label but not too slight to grow. These, however, may be put aside till we come to the letter E and the word " Engagement." Under " Courtship " it is natural to include none but happy lovers. The companionship, then,

is what makes this time so fair ; for it is almost as
new a " life and conversation " as Eve's and Adam's
when they walked together after their first surprise.
If, indeed, there were no other men and women in
the world but these two newly-engaged persons,
their companionship would be an exact repetition of
Adam's and Eve's at its beginning. And as it is,
their whole imagination and desire are bent on
feigning that there are no other men and women in
the world.

It may be doubted whether these pleasures are as
fully known to great folks as to humble ones. They
smack of sentimentalism, of unrefined naturalism :
the vulgarities of common sweethearting. Moreover,
the forms, customs, and habits of association amongst
the higher sort of ladies and gentlemen allow but
little opportunity for such companionship, which is
to their loss, whatever they may think. But it is
only in town that the restriction is severe. If any
time of the courtship-period is spent in the country,
the most fashionable lovers—lured by opportunity
and the Natural Man—give way to common sweethearting and find it good. Love-making is always
best in the country. Cities are unfit, but not so
country towns. If we could but believe it, life is
nowhere so good as on the edge of a pleasant
country town ; and it is there where courtship-time is
filled most full of its own delights. The going out
together to the open fields has an appropriate charm,
and so has the coming home together where the
houses cluster and the hearth-fires burn. But
whether in town or country, in grass-bordered lane
or dingy street, the joy is being together ; and they

would describe that joy as a feeling of inclusion in
the same golden cloud that shrouds each of them
from all the rest of the world when they are apart.
Of talk there is little need.   It is the silent passages
of the conversation that are most profitable and most
enjoyed.   This is felt to be so much the case that
they manage to carry on the silence even while they
talk.   There are moments when, to the consciousness of one or the other, it becomes a little too
eloquent; its heart-beats are too audible; or perhaps
a mere feeling that it is time to say something over-
takes them.   Then their mouths open and words
fly out.   Brisk words they are too; but, lord!
what prattle it is that bandies past their ears, with
no intention but to cover the real conversation, the
silence that is to be heard distinctly all the time.

Although it is so good to be together, lovers
should be specially exhorted to remember at this
period that wisdom prescribes a liberal deal of
absence too.   Should there be jealousies (which
heaven forbid, but there often are) the absences
may be few and brief; but where there is as much
confidence as affection it is on all grounds a mistake
to be niggardly of absence.   In that happy condition
of affairs its torments have a piquancy which no
lover should deny himself the pleasure of.   When
he does so he brings upon himself another loss—
the delight of meeting again which those torments
prepare; and how keen a pleasure that must be is
known to every one who has chanced to witness it
unobserved.   Three beautiful sights may be seen
amongst the children of men: an infant waking
from warm sleep, its mother watching its awakening,

and lovers meeting when they have long been parted. And whether it be of sweethearts or of married folk, all that has been said against unceasing companionship is true. The worst is no libel; and a careful man should remember that whereas indifference is the malady which his own sex falls into from this mistake, the other sex is apt to be carried farther and become contemptuous. No doubt this is a danger which lies mainly beyond the days of courtship; but, with bad management, it may partly come into them.

There are some lovers, too, who will not only be for ever at their mistresses' side, but for ever offering the incense of their adoration. This excess may be pleasing to a few, but even with them it is not a lasting delight. "Why," complained one of these overlaboured ladies in a letter to a friend, "why, because he gives me a rose, must he thrust it to my nostrils twenty times an hour?" Every accepted lover who suspects himself of a too continuous and expressive ardency should repeat that question to himself ("Because I give her a rose," etc.), and should remember to do so every morning up to the third day before the wedding.

COYNESS

Coyness meant nothing more than stillness once —stillness and quietness. The maiden who had no prankishness, but loved best to sit soberly and speak little, was a coy maiden. Nowadays coyness stands for reluctancy or hesitation, but a reluctance that

I

need not be taken gravely. It may be sincere or half sincere, playful artifice or of serious meaning, an expression of modesty, a disguise for conscious warmth, provocation to ardour, shrinking from ardour, calculation in a state of disturbance, or coldness at a stand. Coyness may be either of these things or a medley of several, though not in a confirmed or inveterate spirit. It is understood that there is always a certain levity in coyness ; and therefore, and although it has a very pretty appearance whether it be natural or a good imitation, no one likes to be called coy. There is too much uncertainty about the appellation even when applied to damsels in their teens, and it goes very near the hazard of insult when risked upon ladies past twenty. This marks the character of the word and the thing, as commonly understood.

According to the best observers there is much less coyness of all descriptions now than there was in the earlier years of Her Majesty's reign ; a change which is partly explained by a fashionable rudeness in the social intercourse of young men and women, and partly by a general apprehension that, whether affected or unaffected, coyness bears the all-dreaded stamp of provincialism.

DALLIANCE

A LITERARY word, almost invariably preceded in prose and followed in verse by "sweet." This, which has now become a merely habitual qualification, was at first adopted of necessity. For what "dalliance" meant when originally taken up by romancers and poets was "foolish trifling." Foolishness was of the essence of the word ; and there is, indeed, a tough, insensitive, no-nonsense sort of maiden who calls dalliance "fooling" to this day. It appears, therefore, that the old poets and dramatists were obliged to write "sweet dalliance" or "dalliance sweet" whenever they intruded upon what lovers themselves leave unmentioned and unnamed. For it belongs to the silences of all religions and all sacred things ; and this our poets should have understood, since they found no good own word for it at the very late period in the history of love when they began to twang the lyre. And it seems indeed strange that, while they were about it, they could not hit upon a word without a meaning of foolishness. But there appears to be some fatality here. "Fondle"—from "fond," a word of like signification—is rooted in a meaning of folly; fondness being, in fact, an old and eloquent expression for foolishness softening into its worst. But then "fond" and "fondle" have so many innocent and tender associations (as when one says, "Her babe was fondled to her breast," or another, "I am remarkably fond of sucking-pig") that they appear without a blush in the lover's vocabulary. "Fondle" he can say unashamed. "Dalliance" reddens him angrily; as when, in some unguarded hour, he reads the word aloud from the much too busy, much too excited, poets of the period.

DETRIMENTALS

It cannot be doubted that detrimentals exist throughout every settled community; though in the rural districts they are sparse, and there is no complaint of them in what a great London dignitary used to call "the strata." Indeed, they are hardly known by name out of Society, where they abound.

The word "detrimental" describes these persons with unacerb felicity. It includes all the varieties of those disturbers who, being handsome and poor, or handsome, rich, and notoriously *roués*, or poor, clever, and characterless, dangle about half-fascinated girls whom they do not intend to marry, or would not be permitted to espouse; with the result that really eligible *partis* keep at a distance and no business is done. Usually endowed with great personal advantages, commonly possessed of a lively social reputation, and invariably devoted to making themselves agreeable, these persons are the pests of social life. A peril to unsophisticated girls, a terror to chaperons, a torment to mothers by night and day, they would be put under regulation in any thoroughly beneficent system of society. In England the great County Councils busy themselves with matters of much less importance to the happiness of citizenesses, who are more than half the population ; and if a Sub-Council of Matrons were established to deal with social scandals, disorders, and excesses, one of its first decrees should be that no ascertained detrimental shall appear in any public place between the hours of 2 o'clock P.M. and 4 o'clock A.M. unbadged. The badge might bear the letter D surrounded by willow-branches.

It would be necessary to have a care, however, in constituting such a council, and in laying down the principles on which the status of detrimentals should be determined. For it is one of the excesses of Society to think too much of poverty in this relation, and one of its disorders to think too little of character. There are matrons, for example, who make a jingling general rule of " Regimentals, detrimentals " ; and nearly all are disposed to bear too hardly on gallant young officers with more gaiety, temper, and manners than present funds or perceptible future. Portias from Girton or Newnham should be admitted to plead for these.

It is a curious circumstance that we never hear of detrimentals of the fairer sex. Yet there is a

well-recognised order of women which comes under
that designation most distinctly ; the main or perhaps
the only practical difference between them and their
male congeners being that the latter are rarely
married men, and that the former are always
married women. The ravage which this sort of
detrimentals, or deprivers and dissuaders, is answerable for, the loss and the grief they inflict upon
successive generations of pretty *débutantes*, become
greater every year, the harm they do exceeding
all that can be laid to the charge of the other detrimentals, many of whom are their own manufacture.
Nor is there much reason to hope that these ladies
could be badged to advantage ; otherwise it might be
suggested that up to the age of thirty they should
be compelled to wear a large parti-coloured rosette
on the left breast, signifying " Young Married
Woman," and after that age a small one of the
same, signifying " Old Married Woman."

DISDAIN

Behold the picture of Disdain. It is taken from Mr.
Darwin's book on the " Expression of the Emotions,"
and is no fancy sketch drawn by an imaginative male
artist, but the effigies of disdain caught by photo-
graphy from a woman's face as she looked away from
a despised lover. A lovely face as Heaven meant
it, and with no actual distortion here of its beautiful
lines. A certain drooping of the eyelids under a
placid brow, a slight retraction of the nostrils, the
corners of the little mouth drawn down by just as

much as may be perceived, and out comes the spirit of Disdain to make *that* of a beautiful woman ! As we gaze upon it we remember that the full title of Mr. Darwin's book is, " On the Expression of the Emotions in Man and Animals."

Young ladies who dream in pleased anticipation of the time when they, too, will move amongst despised lovers in all the glory of disdain, may now see what they will look like in the act of " killing off." If they are very handsome, and close their eyelids beautifully, and draw up their noses with a ladylike reserve, and lift their upper lips in such elegant restraint that the canines on either side of the mouth become visible, they will resemble the picture above printed.   But they may not be so handsome as the lady in the picture, which will take something off. Or their features may lend themselves less readily to delicate handling ; and if so, they will stamp such an expression of countenance on his memory as no woman could wish that any lover, however much despised, should carry about in him to his grave.   It may be useful therefore to schools and families if we repeat the picture of Mr. Darwin's young lady with her beauty slightly reduced, and the expression of each feature heightened by one degree.

How uncelestial is this !   And to think that any nice girl could put on such an expression, even for a moment, and think it lofty !   The remedy for that delusion is to practise the look of scorn before a mirror night and morning for a week—a cure which is strongly recommended.   One trial will probably suffice, but it is better to give personal respect the full dose for six consecutive evenings at least ; except in cases where the patient is subject to bad dreams, when the physic may be taken from the morning glass alone. The precaution of turning the key in the door before the mirror is approached will not, of course, be omitted.

Only on one occasion has this cure been known to fail. This was the case of E. B., a young lady of majestic build and a Juno-like cast of feature, very high and commanding, though at this time she was

(From Darwin's " Expression of the Emotions in Animals.")

not more than thirteen weeks out of the hands of her governess. After three or four trials before her dressing-glass, with the photograph of poor pimpled little Mr. R-ck-tts in her hand to assist the experiment (Mr. R. was something in the Custom House), the young lady declared that she found nothing disagreeable in her expression of contemptuous disdain ; and she still remained of that opinion when she added to her looks the touch of loathing which she was told *would* come out in many cases, and

which her feeling for Mr. R. taught her was only
natural.   It now became necessary to introduce Miss
B. to a part of the cure which is usually omitted as
superfluous, and as likely to wound the patient's
amour propre over-much.   It is this.   As she approaches the looking-glass she repeats aloud the
following words : " Physiological students inform us
that this feeling of contemptuous scorn is one of
those that bring into the human face points of

expression which directly link it with animal faces ;
bidding us suspect a common origin."   Defiant of
the theory, but nevertheless with this new light in her
mind, Miss B. made another trial ; and when now
she caught the play of certain muscles at the base of
her beautiful nose, and when for a brief half-moment
she saw one corner of her mouth open in a loop to
show the least bit of a gleaming tooth, she could but
acknowledge a resemblance to the butcher's dog, and
had her glass changed for another in an adjoining
dressing-room.

The purpose of this relation is to put young women out of conceit with disdain as something complimentary to themselves, as they are much inclined to think it in the first full spring of youth. It certainly is not complimentary to themselves as an affectation, and doubtfully so when it is sincere, and called out to punish an outrage to sexual pride. *Of course* that same pride is most natural. It is bred in the bone. It goes back to heaven-only-knows-what distance in the history of womankind, or how far down amidst the root of things. But if there be anything good and beautiful in the human breast which looks bad and ugly when expressed in the human countenance, it should be kept within the sphere which it adorns. It is not only humane to *be* nice, it is humane to *look* nice ; which indeed is being nice when any poor little presumptuous Mr. R-ck-tts has to be put down. And why—for that, after all, is the grand argument—why should any pretty young woman fancy it a triumph to look like the pictures in this article? The only explanation is ignorance, pure ignorance ; which, however, all know how to correct after reading these pages.

If anything remains to be said, it is this, perhaps. Men never display the disdain, the scorn that we are thinking of ; or, if they do, are thought brutish and unmanly. Is it possible to imagine a man meeting any woman with the look on his face that we see in our picture No. 1, let alone our picture No. 2 ? Of course men are men and women are women ; and, though it is quite safe to say that to give expression to this kind of contempt would be unmanly, it is not so safe to say that in a woman it is unwomanly. But what of the other epithet, brutish? And how far may it apply in both cases? And would it not be better for all hands to follow the masculine example of reserve, considering the lesson of the looking-glass?

DISENCHANTMENT

Disenchantment is the lot of all fine and sensitive minds, though not to make them all unhappy. Many of us know sooner or later that the enchantment was no spell cast upon our senses from without, to delude us, but a magic in our own breasts heaping beauty upon every fair thing which our eyes rested on. And why should we groan on that account? It is no misfortune to share "the light that never was on sea or land," the gleam that goes forth from ourselves, in the act of looking, to glorify everything in the world that we take delight in. True that it does not last for ever. A time comes when the glory fades and there is no more magic in us. Youth passes, and leaves us with "the light of common day"; but field and sky are none the worse because we have seen them under that other light. It is a lovely world still, though the glamour is gone that was cast over it when we were poets, and could clothe it in a poet's dreams.

When there is a like disenchantment in love who should complain? It is a most unreasonable thing; and yet many a young couple have no more grace and no more gratitude in this particular than the goose of Nunswood Common. This was a goose which in olden days warned a neighbouring saint against the approach of a terrible temptation. After admonishing the unhappy lady from the oak in which he took refuge, the holy man granted his benefactor the one wish of his heart; and in sight and hearing of the whole village, the gray goose soared and circled and sang with the larks a whole summer long. Then the spell came to an end; and then might have begun the enjoyment of delicious memories in a sober world of good green grass. But no. Mourning the past as no reality but a mocking dream, the wretched bird could not again endure to pad the common with his kind, became dejected, solitary, cynical, hypochondriacal, studied the composition of apple sauce, and the rest of the tale is too dreadful to relate.

Almost as much of a goose is Cymon, who, falling in love with the pretty Poppetta, made her more beautiful than any creature ever was, decked her from his own fancy with graces that enraptured and charms that surprised him anew every day, lived for a whole year in the heaven he created about her, married her in a heaven higher yet, and in six weeks was so unjust and ungrateful as to make a mortal grievance of her disenchanting him! As if she had anything to answer for! All this while she was only pretty Poppetta, nearly as much frightened as pleased at being made a goddess of, no more capable of weaving enchantments about any man than her kitten of knitting gloves, but yet a very nice girl and extremely fond of Cymon. The witchery was all his own; and though he charged his disenchantment upon her—(as if she ought to have told him from

the first that she slept with her mouth open!)—the
fault was merely his own incapacity for dreaming
on. This he should have known; and instead of
turning cynic on the pretence of wrecked illusions,
he should have blessed his stars for that long year
of rhapsody, smacked the comely shoulders of Poppetta in recognition of her merits as she stood, and
prepared himself forthwith to live with her the
hearty, lowly, honest life of good folk matrimonially
engaged. Not to do so, what disenchantment for
Poppetta!

For there are disenchantments real and dour
enough, and it is hard to say whether men or women
have the most of them or the worst. Perhaps if we
knew all, we should learn that women suffer disenchantment less often than men but more severely.
Less often, because women have a born gift of understanding men, individually and collectively, to which
there is no counterpart in the other sex. It is
Nature's recompense, perhaps, for the smaller share
of genius distributed amongst them; but a likelier
explanation is that their superior intuition is the
growth of countless ages of interested study, and
knowing more of men than men ever know of women,
they are less often deceived; and when they are
supposed to be blind, and act, and speak, and even
for nine-tenths of the waking day order their thoughts
as if they were, they usually are not. They have
stowaway perceptions which they habitually choose
to disregard; feeling that from the nature of things
they are better disregarded, and that the chief use of
their knowledge is as a stock provision against any
disenchanting surprise. Their superior intuition pre-

pares them for faults and imperfections, even grave ones; and most of these they are born with a readiness to make light of whenever the faults are balanced by a certain little group of sound masculine qualities. Not merely here and there, but in the breast of every right woman in the world these qualities are worshipped. They are the gods of an ancient, universal, undying paganism—a paganism as lively and sincere as any that ever existed; and no worship can be more truly called worshipping than that which is given to them. Where these manly virtues flourish they atone for everything. No matter how rude he may look who is known to abound in them, they beautify him. Notoriously absent in a Hercules-Apollo of a man, he is valued at sixpence. But they may be simulated; their absence does not always come out in the ordinary intercourse of young persons engaged; and many a Jill has gone proudly to church with her gallant Jack to find him in due time a coward, a sneak, an honest man in the cheating degree, a bully to herself alone, and hardly more decent than a dog. Disenchantment? There is no such disenchantment as this; and yet for very shame poor Jill must carry it off as if she knew not her own abasement, bearing its tortures year in and year out, even before *him*, as though unaware that any wife is more honoured in her husband than herself.

Ignorant of that half of the world which moves in petticoats, and comparatively unskilled in the arts of fascination, it is probable that men are oftener deceived as well as self-deceived; and therefore more open to the misery of disenchantment. But then

they rarely suffer as much under the operation ; and
though often galled, they are better able to bear
a disappointment which they soon take for no more
than an affair of domestic unpleasantness, like smoky
chimneys.   But there are wide degrees of disenchantment for men too ; and though the sterner sex has
never yet risen to the height of worshipping any
of the virtues proper to womankind, its disenchantments in love and marriage are the same that
women experience.   In both cases they come of the
concealment of mortifying faults under taking graces ;
and while on the one side these faults are all summed
up in unmanliness, what generally breaks the spell
in the other is some sharp betrayal of unwomanliness.
This is a fault which takes many shapes, of which a
too generous and startling abandonment of reserve
is one.   Women, fondly prized for the delicate sweetness of their nature, will make nothing, sometimes, of
throwing all that aside three weeks after marriage—
stripping themselves in broad daylight, as it were,
with one appalling word.

DOLLS

As applied to young women, " Doll " is a term of
abuse ; but foreign students of our language should
observe that the word is seldom employed in this
sense by men, and that it is not often applied by
young women to one who is at all older than themselves.

It is feared that weakness must be at the bottom

of the indulgence shown to "doll-girls" by men, true
as it may be of that sex that they are often the most
generous who are indulgent, and the sourest who are
most severe.   That, while they are in their teens,
girls of the same age rarely call each other dolls
appears to admit of only one explanation.   They
are not satisfied in their own minds that it is a
genuine term of reproach.   Doubting whether it
may not be interpretable as an utterance of envy,
they hesitate to disclaim the pretension of being in
some conditional and charming sense not undoll-like
themselves.   They see that the word is never applied
to plain girls, and seem to think that it is used with
most acerbity by young women past a certain age
who are less beautiful than intellectual.   And these
are evident grounds for preferring to be amongst
the accused rather than the accusers.

Very few girls, however, wish to be thought dolls
and nothing else.   Even those who *are* nothing else
have moments of conviction that to be pretty, to be
bright, to be brainless and useless, puts them at a
disadvantage everywhere except at picnics, at water-
parties, and at church.   And if they have any sense
of a future, and any intimations of what goes on in
the breasts of other women, they cannot but guess
what terrors they are to mothers with young-men
sons.   These poor ladies have a sad time of it
generally when their boys begin to look about them
for some other woman with whom to fly away, but
their misery is never worse than when the choice of
their own first-born lights upon a "doll."   This is
always the mother's dread.   When she pictures herself bereaved of her boy, she makes the best of it by

fancying him wedded in the next street to a healthy, good-looking, quiet, well-bred, sensible young woman; in low tones of colour; of graceful but deliberate carriage; cheerful, yet not gay; educated, but no novel-reader; a devoted wife, but by no means sugar-sweet or of a weaning disposition; one who knows the value of a pound; one who, while she plays her part sweetly and obligingly amongst her husband's friends, does so with the reserve induced by ever-present thoughts of the nursery; a manager, and indued with that fine convinced taste in dress which never allows the flutter of a tag six inches from the person. If called upon, the matron could hopefully resign her first-born to such an one as this, and per-haps with little feeling of offence and humiliation to herself. But she knows the rarity of such young persons; and though they do exist, she knows the aptitude of youth to rush blindly past their merits, fascinated by the shallow attractions of some doll.

And what is a doll? The alarmed mother sees the creature in every peach-bloom maid with angel eyes—any pretty, light, laughing little girl who may be presented to her in fluttering muslin and ribbons. Let all such take warning, then, and show in occasional flashes how sage and sedate they can really be. For mothers' hearts are prejudiced wonderfully when some young son is at stake, and they will not always remember how often it is that only their youth and the springtime give wings to butterfly girls, and that most of them have sense enough in their little heads to turn into staunch and careful wives three months after marriage.

Yet there are young ladies who are veritable

K

dolls, and can never be anything else until —— when? Every lad who reads this page should ask himself the awful question. Till when? Till the prettiness fades which dies early in dolls, and the child - like flightiness and the piquancy become ridiculous, as they do when the thirties begin and the prettiness declines. Then they are no longer dolls ; but *what are they*? We know how charming they may have been in their first condition. We know that however contemptuous we may have been in our boyhood of their waxen flaxen proto-types, some of us do delight at five-and-twenty in having a dear little lovely, lively, doting, ridiculous, sweetly-dressed doll of our own in living flesh and blood. Nor is there anything against it in human nature. What we experience is only the doll-passion postponed for some years, and made natural to us by altered conditions and the supply of a different article. The dolls that our infant sisters adored were equally without sense, equally soulless, and *known* to be nothing substantially but so much bran enclosed in a skin of white-kid-glove leather. Yet those dolls were a genuine passion ; and when we consider what a difference there is in these others— that they are as live as live can be, are all aglow from head to foot, and can laugh with eyes and mouth, and blush and pout and kiss and love and say the sweetest things out of their own heads— what is to be said against their being a genuine and well-satisfying passion too, though known to be dolls all the while? Nothing.

We talk of young men. But many a man of ripe wisdom would give much to have a Dora

Spenlow of his own to-day, were it not for the thought that he could neither wish her to die early nor to live long. There's the rub ; and now we come to the difference between childhood and the doll-doll and young-manhood and the doll-wife. Be his heart what it may and his imagination therewith, he cannot imitate the rapt fidelity of his little sister to her doll long after it had lost every lineament and integument that once proclaimed it such. For her, her darling and her beauty still existed in all its first loveliness when it was no longer a doll at all, but marred material and a thing of chiffons. And exactly what she saw at the head of her doll's tea-table he will see in due time at the head of his dinner-table, but without the glamour of her vision.

A complete dissertation on dolls — (and now only that kind is meant which is bought in bazaars and adored in the nursery)—would include all that is deepest and all that is thought mysterious in the nature of woman. It is everybody's remark that the instinct of motherhood is wonderfully seen in the love of the smallest little girl for a doll. And in that mystery there are sub-mysteries, such as the universal preference for girl-dolls over boy-dolls. Now this is contrary to the run of nature in the main direction ; and what does it suggest but that the prophecy of maternal love is accompanied thus early by intimations of an instinctive passion for dress, of which the preference for dolls with golden locks is a further illustration ? A much wider speculative field opens from the fact that while the idealism in a man-child's mind goes out in adventure and is scattered and cast upon many things, in a girl-child's mind it concentrates on this one thing with the most willing and most constant devotion. (And thus is idolatry explained and justified by Innocence itself; which, however, is but a by-remark thrown to theologians.) It is not so wonderful then, in writing a little book like this, to find that the imaginings and idealisings that surround the Doll are repeated in varying forms over and over again in the woman's life; and that we are constantly reminded of them in thinking of her various affections, and especially of such vagaries as seem strange to men.

DOUBTS

The worst of living in a sunny clime is the insects: the mosquito that hums around the curtains of your bed, the earwig and the spider and the scorpion, and a dozen other pestiferous and poisonous things. Love is a most sunny clime—warm, delicate, delicious to abide in; but there, too, the mosquito hums, and the earwig creeps, and the scorpion hides under your pillow, and the spider drops upon it from above while you sleep; and these insects (which have no particular names, but are all called Doubts) are oft-times so tormenting that the sufferer wishes himself well out of that beautiful country, and back in the breezy Plains of Indifference whence he came.

From constitutional differences, some sojourners in the Vale of Delight are much more open to attack from doubts than others are; but few escape whose blood takes the natural temperature of the place, rising to its full warmth. The best defence seems to be extraordinary good looks. It is said of beauty that it is but skin-deep, and of the membrane which confers loveliness that it is thickest when most beautiful. This statement is certainly borne out by observation of the varying liability of one person and another to the torment of doubts when they are in love. To such attacks the most beautiful are the most thick-skinned. With an exception here and there, the gloriously handsome man sleeps sound enough o' nights for all that doubt can disturb him, however much in love he may be ; or should some creeping thing have found entry, and he toss about a bit, he is not long disturbed. He bethinks himself of one adventure and another, and a waving of invisible arms, and the sighing of three, four, five inconsolable damsels, distinctly audible in the gloom of his chamber, soon lull him to rest again. And so with equally fortunate young women. Now and then they may be fevered for a little while by some stinging or some fretting doubt, but their youth and their beauty are in most cases as much a defence to them as his stout integument to the river-horse.

It is, indeed, no far-fetched opinion that the gift of beauty is the denial of sensibility ; which, however, is but a doubtful comfort to plain people. It is the sensitive and not very beautiful, or the sensitive because not very beautiful, who suffer most when they are in love from the torments of doubt. There is a saying that, by providential dispensation, all plain women believe themselves otherwise, and that few ugly men think themselves so. It would be a merrier world were that true. But the second clause of the saying needs narrowing. It should run, "The uglier a man is the less he thinks himself so"; while as to the first, that it should be commonly accepted only proves how successfully half mankind conceals her little miseries. It is probably true that, whatever their allotted portion of good looks, women believe themselves ten per cent, fifteen per cent, twenty per cent prettier than they are, and no kindly soul would have it otherwise with them. But to suppose them unaware of gradations of comeliness in face and figure, or insensible of their own position in the scale of beauty (there or thereabout), is a mistake that should impose upon no one ; and if all the dressing-glasses in the kingdom could render up the sad or the wildly-searching looks thrown into them after a ball, or a picnic, or a dinner-party, the error would be exploded at once. It is not always to admire, but often to compare themselves that women gaze into mirrors ; and oh! the doubts, doubts, doubts with which the poor ladies run to their glasses sometimes, and the heavy hearts they take to bed with them afterwards,—many a time quite without cause ! They say to themselves in the darkness : "And thy life shall hang in doubt before thee, and thou shalt fear day and night," and, after all, be as happy as ever before Sunday comes. But, cause or no cause, torments like these are as well known to the gentle creatures as to tempestuous and exclamatory man ; though they make it a particular care to have no Roberta Herricks or Georgiana Witherses to put their sorrows into verse.

There is only one sweet and pleasing doubt for passionate lovers, and it comes only once. Usually it occurs with the first waking moment on a certain

morning, and takes the shape of incredulity that
the word and the kiss of last night were really,
really said and done. " It is a dream ! " A meteoric
flash in the brain, a star-shower of recollections, and
the one delicious doubt comes to a delightful end.

DREAMS

⁚ By his dreams you may know the lover ; or
rather you would know the lover if you knew his
dreams. His age, his experience, his temperament,
his characteristics of head and heart would either be
brought to a very near guess or to actual ascertainment could you see what his dreamings are when he
is quite given up to them.

The ideal lover, for example, is he who is young,
ardent, imaginative, and in his first grand passion ;
and to make all complete, he should feel himself
safe in the affections of the sweetest, dearest, goodest,
prettiest girl for miles and miles about. Such a
lover has no dreams, although he lives for half of
every waking day in an intensity of dreaming. What
fills his mind is a universe of dream-stuff, not dreams.
To resemble it with anything in nature we must
look to that space in the heavens where palpitates
the Milky Way. His joy, his fancies, his hopes, his
recollections of yesterday, his anticipations of to-
morrow, the look of her this way and that way, the
voice of her now and now and now again, these and
a thousand picture-thoughts pass and change so
swiftly within him that they could not settle into a
dream of two minutes' duration. Delight in all is

so restless that it can fix **upon nothing, but shuts its eyes in** a moment **upon one** excessive **joy** to open **them** on whichever next comes thrusting forward. It is an illustration **of this** state of mind that as long as it lasts the lover may try what he may without **bringing before his** sight **a** complete vision of **the lady's face.** It may appear of itself unasked, **and be fully seen** for an instant ; but only **to be** chased **away the** next by **the very** eagerness **that** would **hold it for** contemplation. **But** let him now **try to paint the** air with her **picture** himself, and **the same eagerness runs before his** imagination so violently——settling now upon the beaming eyes, which **alone it** sees, and then **upon** the **lovely** mouth, the eyes vanishing——that **no** complete **portrait is ever visible.**

The lover **who has never** experienced **or who** doubts this is not in the first category. He is not young, or he **is not** ardent, or **he is** unimaginative, and therefore he can never make a lover of the first rate. In all likelihood he has none of these advantages ; which means that he must be classed as a fifth-rate lover.

It bears upon what has **gone** before that youngsters deeply **and** truly in love rarely dream of the adored **one in** sleep, however great their longing to do so when **they** lie down to **rest. It** is in after-life that such dreams fill up the night, **and** never so often as when the loved one has been long lost, or is long since dead, and the memory of **her has settled into** tranquillity. **By the** same token, when such a lover's day-dreamings are capable of taking shape and order—when he is able to weave them in his mind

to taste, and as a story-teller plots his romances—
he may be sure that he is no longer in the zenith of
the passion; though he need not on that account
doubt the sincerity or the strength of it. Duller
young men never rise so high; and the proof of
their dulness is that such love-dreams as visit them
in their leisure hours could be as readily described
as a scene in an operetta. Nevertheless they may
be very good young men, and their dreams prettily
touched with the romance of affection. And much
the same thing may be said of lovers well advanced
from youth who have already passed through an
affair or two. But with others more hackneyed, or
of a lower order of mind (more selfish, or more animal
perchance), what takes the place of love-dreaming is
a mere rehearsal of pleasures and advantages, very
like the dreams of the rising man when he lays out
the ten thousand a year he means to possess, or the
visions of the greedy man invited to dine with the
Merchant Taylors' Company. 'The descent ranges
from poesy itself down through pure romantic prose
to the dull and brutal novelette at one franc fifty.

Of a woman's dreamings when she is lost in
love it is more hazardous to speak; but it would
appear that though they are often as rapturously
idyllic as any they are usually more dramatic. That
is to say, they are more orderly, more composed,
more like the reveries called day-dreams. But then
her dreams are more continuous and lasting. They
are, in fact, continued from other dreamings before
she was in love, and when she was like the young
birds on the farther side of ocean who have visions
of the heavenly land they are drawn to in migration-

time and cannot rest for them.   And for aught we
know—(the doll-phenomena seem to tell us that it
is so)—she has a similar dreaming consciousness of
another heavenly land beyond the first ; a land
where every little parsley-bed is more beautiful than
a garden of Damascus.

ECSTASY

SINCE love is all extravagance, it is quite in order that the language of love should be exaggerated; yet there is a respect due to words which even lovers should observe. "Ecstasy," for example, cannot be chosen to express delight without a certain degree of irreverence; for it belongs to a state of mind which more nearly approaches the celestial than any other that we know of. Ecstasy may come of extreme delight, but it is something more; and no one should speak of it who is not conscious of being for considerable periods of time out of his mind.

That however is, to use a confusing expression, useful only because it is popular. "Out of his mind" is a phrase which seems to have been formed upon the analogy of "out of money"; the meaning being that what mind or what money there once was is gone. Therefore it is no correct account of ecstasy; which is more truly described when a man is said to be "beside himself." That, indeed, is a very good phrase for the purpose, and nearly perfect ; for the most common sensation in ecstasy is as if our minds were out of us and surrounding us. It is no longer as if they were contained within our bodies, but as if our bodies moved within them ; so that the picture of a man in ecstasy would be drawn in a halo of light were the painter a psychologist and a mystic. [Compare the old pictures of saints and others who were ecstatics, by painters who were perhaps psychologists.]

As to that, however, what do the dictionaries say ? They show that the Greek original of "ecstasy" was formed to express a temporary displacement of the soul from the body, into which some spirit of the demonic order was supposed to enter ; and when we turn to the best of English Dictionaries (the Imperial, so called) we find the first definition of Ecstasy to be this : "A state in which the mind is carried away from the body ; a trance ; a state in which the functions of the senses are suspended by the contemplation of some extra-ordinary or supernatural object." This definition is evidently intended to apply to the ecstasy of religious devotion. Those who explain the only other state of mind that should be called ecstatic come under another head, and are thus set forth : "Excessive joy ; rapture ; a degree of delight that arrests the whole mind ; excessive elevation and absorption of mind ; extreme delight ; as, a pleasing ecstasy ; the ecstasy of love."

The ecstasy of love, however, embraces nearly the whole of these definitions ; though it is necessary to warn unfortunates who have never known

the tender passion against some dubious expressions here.   Excessive joy, excessive elevation and
absorption of mind, may be accepted as truly
descriptive of ecstasy on one condition ; namely,
that the word " excessive " be taken in its original
sense of " going beyond " (going beyond the ordinary), and not in the common acceptation of " over-
much " : there is no too much in the case.   " Trance "
is a true word enough ; and when the lexicographer
speaks of a " state in which the functions of the
senses are suspended by the contemplation of some
extraordinary or supernatural object," he precisely
describes a lover's ecstasy without intending it.   But
he and his brethren seem to have been misled a
little by a bias to the original word as " displacement " ; and hence we hear of " a state in which
the mind is carried away from the body."   Religious
ecstatics have been willing to believe this true of
themselves in their transports ; but though it is hard
to say what raptures there may not be in the trance-
condition of holy men, there is an equal difficulty
in imagining that they ever felt their souls being
" carried away from their bodies."   The ecstasy of
love is a lower one, to be sure ; but here certainly there
is neither arrest of mind nor the sensible carrying
of it away from the body.   The feeling is one of
elation, of expansion, of outrush and overflow of
mind ; so that it seems to envelop the body as in
a living mist instead of being contained in it.   This
sensation is accompanied by a feeling of intense
stillness in the *corporeal* part of us ; which, when
it moves (as in the crossing of a room or a garden),
seems to move in a vacuum.   The familiar expres-

sion, "It was as if I walked on air," is significant
of this sensation ; and any one with eyes may see
that when man or maid "skims the plain" in an
ecstasy of love, there is a quick, sharp, high lifting
of the feet that tells the tale.

But as to the delirium itself, it is no more to be
described than seen. We can say that it is like
being lifted above the world in a cloud of happy
fancies, thoughts, and dreams, all attuned to a sort
of disembodied music that whispers on unceasingly ;
but, short of being a poet (which, however, everybody is at such times), no one can say more,
perhaps, unless he speak of the distance, the separation from all human creatures but one, which is
another strongly-felt sensation. But for the benefit
of persons of small experience and limited imagination, it may be said of the attendant music (which
they will understand has no more sound than the
indrawing and outgoing of our daily breath) that it
is of the Wagnerian school, flowing on with absolutely no recurrent melodies ; while as to the feeling
of distance or separation from all mankind save one
alone, some idea of it may be obtained by thinking
of the successive veils of gauze which are let down
at the theatre when evening comes on behind the
footlights. It is like being within the veils.

These delights—which are more than delights,
being at the same time inspiring, ennobling, clari-
fying—are no peculiar privilege. The peasant-girl
tossing hay in the fields is quite as likely to be lost
in them as the parson's daughter who writes verses
of high accomplishment ; the prentice shoemaker
banging at his lapstone may be meanwhile lost in an

ecstasy as fine as ever was ; and when we hear the
clink of the mason's trowel, it may be that the
sound of it is to his own ears quite as far off as to
ours—seeming to him a distant accompaniment to
the Wagnerian strains going on inside. Imagination
is willing to believe that much the same thing is true
of the poorest sempstress in the poorest little garret,
and only begins to dubitate when it ascends to
merchant princes and the higher aristocracy.

ELOPEMENT

Though elopement has still for very young ladies
the same fascination that buccaneering has for boys,
it is a fast-declining fancy. From time immemorial
till about 1825 A.D., elopement flourished as a wild,
romantic, and delightful because not quite wicked ideal
in the female breast ; an ideal, be it understood, with
a long, long history in the heart of womankind, and
associated to this day with the trembling pleasure of
being pursued. It is probable, therefore, that it will
never quite die out as a dream ; but whether from
the general fading of romance or the universal disuse
of post-chaises, elopement is no longer what it was.
The invention of steam is no doubt at the bottom of
this remarkable change. Destructive to romantic
feelings in many ways, the substitution of the rail for
the road has taken all the fearsomeness and poetry
from flight. The stealing out at early dawn, the
leap into the lurking chaise (the boat in the creek
and a moonlight night were only for a few at the
best of times), and then the pattering of hoofs to the

panting of hearts—that was one thing ; or even the swift ascent to the roof of the fast coach "Defiance" at the very moment of starting. But a cab to the railway-station and a scuttle to a railway-carriage— that is quite another thing, and one that no dreaming can englamour. The very naughtiness of elopement changes its complexion, taking a wretched resemblance to the " bolting " of a runaway cheat. Besides, elopement was always more of a business than a pleasure to gentlemen, and now they are supplied with an undeniable alternative in the registry-office ; resort to which is as gloomy as going to jail and less romantic than being buried.

ENCOURAGEMENT

A word of blame ; sometimes when the thing signified is withheld, oftener when it is bestowed too liberally, or heartlessly, or in mistaken kindness. Even when encouragement is blamefully withheld it is often done from *fear* of blame, which is the only solace of many a maid who, when her timid lover has vanished from the prospect of her life, sits down to mourn that she did not encourage him a little more. The memory of a dozen occasions rises up against her, when some answering kindness—though it were no more than a sidling nearer to him by five inches with a downward look, instead of moving off to a similar distance with an upward look—might have made all the difference in the world. But, with the intuition which it is never safe to disregard, she feared suspicions of " forwardness " ; and true it

is that if some lovers are afflicted with a timidity
which soon sinks to despair, there is another kind of
timidity that is quick to take alarm. It lies perdue,
but none the less lively, in lovers who advance
gallantly enough ; but finding a prompt and vigorous
encouragement, they begin to step backward at once
like my Lord Chamberlain.

Heartless and heedless encouragement both sexes
are guilty of. It is not flirtation, nor the sport called
coquetry, nor jilting in any shape ; but a colder kind
of trifling, pleasant as the six bright days in Spring
that smile upon the orchards, bringing forth their
bloom in happy ignorance of frosts to come. The
third variety of encouragement proceeds from nothing
but kindness, though it ends just as badly. Pity
is the name of this particular sort of kindness, and
being akin to love and naturally resembling it, a
very little goes far to mislead. It will not be
readily believed that men give way to its expression,
since they are not expected to perceive, and still less
to pity, anything like a burning uninvited passion
in any woman under twenty-seven. It will happen,
however, that they do ; and though harder hearts
and harder heads point out to them the better way,
which is to take no notice when requital must be
denied, they are not always capable of repressing
a show of tenderness, which only prepares a deeper
heartache in due course. But from their greater
gentleness, and from the psychologic circumstance
that pity is by far the strongest moral emotion in
all good women, they are the greatest culprits here ;
their punishment being that they are rated as heartless when their fault should bear a softer name.

L

There is another kind of encouragement, however, which deserves nothing less than servitude under the worst tyrannies of marriage for six months after the wedding day. This is when a calculating lady willingly listens, with flashes of heavenly smile, to the poor gentleman whom she has no idea of marrying if a certain somebody else can be brought to marry her. But though the poor gentleman may be deep in love, she is far out of it, and her place is rather in the Commercial Dictionary.

ENGAGEMENT

For matter pertinent to engagements see arts. "Acceptance," "Affiance," "Entanglement," where the penalties of gentility in this relation are touched upon. In the glorious topmost circles of society, however, these penalties are rarely incurred. It is one of the many advantages of being born into one of the hundred best families that you may engage to marry under circumstances nearly as favourable as those which tinkers, tailors, and candlestick-makers enjoy. The grand disadvantage which others labour under is that men and women are very often pledged in marriage—with no way of liberation for the gentleman, and but a narrow path for the lady—when all the knowledge they have of each other has been picked up at a dozen dinner-tables, or amidst the refined artificialities of as many balls, crushes, and garden-parties. From this danger the lower classes are preserved by the fine freedom of their sweethearting customs, and the Olympians by a broad

and open intercourse of mutually-related families,
every one of which has a good gossiping knowledge
of every other. Mark a circle of one mile radius
from the White Horse Cellar in Piccadilly, and it
will be found that at least half the employment of
its inhabitants is to acquire, enlarge, and impart a
nice acquaintance with the more distinguished
Emilys, Harriets, Williams, and Algernons within
its bound. Therefore, and considering the freedom
of personal intercourse, the disregard of concealing
either one's own defects or those of other people,
which are customary in those regions, there is
little risk of making engagements in ignorance of
character.

And so with the happy lower orders. They take
each other as sweethearts, and sweethearts they are,
and a-sweethearting they do go; but all upon what
may be called a half-pledge or provisional promise
system, which proceeds upon tacit understandings.
But this insufficiency of contract imposes no restraint
on present intercourse, which is generally very improper without the least impropriety. When my
lady's housemaid accepts the attentions of her
beautiful butcher, so smart and rosy, and so little
like business on Sunday afternoons, she does so with
the utmost frankness and to the total exclusion of
every other pretender. And yet he is but admitted
to probationary favour, notwithstanding the familiarity he is allowed; and then his company-freedoms
make probation more severe, being as well calculated
to bring out his worst qualities as those that are
most becoming. Nor is the advantage hers alone.
It is quite understood that the young man shares it,

and may lawfully take second thoughts half-way
through the sweethearting.

And this is high matter, going beyond mere
discoveries of conduct and character. For amongst
many mysteries there is this mystery : that while a
languid love will sometimes rise to settled ardour at
the least embrace, there is no assurance but that an
ardent love will sink to zero at the first touch of
endearments that yet were longed for. Whenever
this unhappy consequence appears, it is a better
reason for parting than any such trifle as loss of
fortune, for example ; and yet—on account of the
freedoms aforesaid—it comes in the way of pretty
housemaids and gentle young journeymen butchers
far more often than to persons of superior distinction.
A master butcher with three shops, and moving in
a private circle of corresponding elevation, has not
half the chance of the foreman of his least lucrative
establishment ; and as we go higher it gradually
dwindles till it disappears in the respectability and
vastitude of the upper middle classes. In this
particular they are by far the least fortunate ; the
only real security for them being to choose their
sweethearts in known households, where there has
been some old boy-and-girl intimacy.

And they, and indeed lovers in general, will do
well to follow the advice of all experienced ancientry,
and avoid long engagements. They are bad for
many reasons, but chiefly because they are companionship without the endearing familiarities, the
give-and-take confidences, the interchange of little
cares and generosities, the mutual understanding and
allowance, which make the habitude of marriage easy

and pleasant. Short engagements (which yet should not be very short, for they have their own delights) ripen both minds for that longer and closer companionship which, well matched, is itself unmatchable. Long engagements tire, and that is not the worst. Stars so remote that no glass reveals them stamp their presence on the photographer's sheet when it is placed before them for a long time undisturbed ; and in like manner, lovers should know, little faults are stamped on each other's minds enduringly for want of the dutiful kisses which in marriage would have rubbed the impression out.

ENTANGLEMENT

Entanglements, like debts, are oftener known than acknowledged ; and like debts should be shunned. Some, indeed, are so light and innocent that there would be no sin in wishing for them ; as when a young lass is caught into an admiration which lifts her above herself, and one day is almost love and the next is not nearly, and is neither to be encouraged nor very bearably abandoned. This is only an entanglement in the sense of being lost for an hour in the mazes of a romantic piece of wood, hardly out of earshot of the homeward road. Other entanglements known to women are always more plaguing than pleasing, and yet are difficult to break through : of such are the fascinations that are always felt to be doubtfully divine.

Men have their light entanglements too ; but in many a case they should be called strangling rather than entangling. Some of the worst of these are lawfully come by, and are only blamable inasmuch as a blindfold plunge into pledge and promise may be regarded as constructive indifference to suicide. It is a good rule, and one that should be steadily upheld in all Christian countries, that the man must stand by his promise to the maid, unless upon discovery of grave offences or sinister concealments ; while the maid may waft farewell to the man from any foundation of disappointment or distaste. It is not enough for disentanglement that she should like another more, but it is enough that she should like her lover less and in falling degrees. Thus the disadvantage that women suffer in never being able to "propose" is not altogether unredressed ; on the other hand, so it comes about that within six weeks of making himself the happiest fellow in the world many a man finds himself meshed in entanglements corresponding to those of a blue-bottle in a spider-web. To be sure, he has no fear of being eaten, but that is part of his sorrow. If only, with all her lovely looks, she were an actual vampire, an attack on him under the left breast of his waistcoat might be looked for as a full justification for shaking himself free. But he is not so fortunate. It happens as often as not that her appetite for eating him is provoked by love alone, and is merely figurative. It is no excuse for breaking an engagement that you fear to be devoured with kisses, and yet what an aggravation of distress that is when you are coming to believe that she whose sole design upon your waistcoat is to lay a loving head upon it is something of a slut, something of a scold, something of a liar.

The blood freezes at the thought ; and yet it is
one that will lie like a core of ice in the breasts of
hundreds of wakeful poor men to-night.

For where is the remedy ?   In honour, a good
reason must be given for breaking an engagement ;
and imagine the sufferer making up his mind to go
to the lady's father with an address like this :—

"Sir, six weeks ago I was so completely overcome by my affection for your daughter, in whom I
saw the reality or the promise of every perfection,
that I asked her to marry me, as you are aware.   To
my delight, and to my greater delight because I had
an inkling of what her answer would be from some
innocent betrayals of feeling, her reply was 'Yes.'
You remember, sir, that I immediately addressed myself to you for the sanction I rather doubted of, and
that you then sent me off to tell Susan that if she
was quite sure your consent would not break her
heart she might have it."   ["I do, George," we may
fancy the sire observing, with a cloud on the horizon
of his countenance ; "and perhaps without being too
indelicate I may imagine that each occasion was
celebrated by you two young people in the customary
manner."]   "You remember, sir," young Hopeless
goes on, "that up to that time I had very few
opportunities of real intimacy with your daughter.
I have been more fortunate since, and the wretched
conclusion I come to is that marriage between us
would probably be miserable.   No, sir ; I have no
reason to believe that Susan thinks so too.   I speak
solely for myself ; hoping that you may not consider
it unreasonable in me, though engaged, to take my
own happiness into account a little.   No doubt,

sir, you have a right to ask what Susan has done to
throw me into this despondency, and your invitation
to be frank is most kind.   In the first place, I doubt
Susan's temper ; in the next, her neatness appears
questionable ; and then I have witnessed in her not
merely an inclination to downright lying—which in
a girl of eighteen might be regarded as a faulty
impulse of youth—but some remarkably ingenious
and painstaking evasions of veracity.   Therefore I
hope I may withdraw without the addition of reproach
to a terrible disappointment."

Is such an address conceivable ?   Is it possible
to speak of such discoveries ?   And suppose that the
young man, if asked for further particulars instead of
being chased from the room, could only say that he
did not like the tone in which she called her little
brother " beast," how far would it cover a lack of
heinousness in the lady's offences to argue that no
mutation in nature is more surprising than the change
of nice girls with scarce visible faults into women in
whom those same faults luxuriate appallingly ?   Yet
it would be a just argument and of urgent consideration ; for five years of marriage may see the change
complete.

To be so entangled is misery to-day with a
prospect of greater misery ever after ; and yet to
endure the one and face the other without a word is
understood to be the natural obligation of a gentleman, once engaged.

EROS

The Greek name for the God of Love, who was much better known in England as Cupid till about the end of the seventh decade of the present century. "Cupid" then fell out of favour with the literary genius of the age ; which, being of a warmer temperament than preceding geniuses, or desirous of seeming so, and conceiving that "Eros" stood for a bolder, wilder, more faun-like and abandoned sort of passion, determined that the god should have no other name either in prose or verse. So far, however—that is to say, up to the date of the present publication—the change has been coldly received by a public already prejudiced against certain derivatives of "Eros." (See art. "Erotic.")

EROTIC

A word which is not found in Johnson. A new word in English, with nothing about it agreeable to native use or native taste, and one which has the peculiarity of distorting every pretty mouth that utters it. The violence of its effect in this particular is so well known that the word is never allowed to pass any woman's lips ; unless, indeed, she be a poet or romance-writer of the new school, and then only when she is composing Night Verses in the dark, or when she is reading her compositions in a corner to a boy-poet younger than herself. In our time there are many such poets—or "singers" as they prefer to call themselves, on the ground that groaning and the "woodnotes wild" of unallowed desire are the truest voice of song : and it is believed that nearly the whole of these poets have come into existence not merely *since* the introduction of the word "erotic," but on account of it, and through a determined habit of steeping their young souls in the pickle of its meanings.   Nurses in charge of rickety children use Mr. Tiddicomb's sea-salt for a similar effect, the aim being to make the little ones hardier. The design of the poetical young man is to become or to be thought of a hardihood altogether frightful ; but every authentic comparison of results is in favour of Tiddicomb's preparation.   If to be robust is to be manly, our young eroticals have the least possible success ; for no creature in the world can be more unmanly than your delicate-moaning, exquisite-squeaking, or high-resounding catawauler in erotic verse.

Ladies who suspect that these singers are not men at all may abandon every doubt on the subject. They are nothing of the sort ; and women are hereby exhorted to believe them entirely unacknowledged as men by men.   A gentle churchman now deceased used to say that every distinctly-marked specimen of the kind presented to his imagination the figure of a worm in the attitude of Signor Nicolini.   This was a palpably extravagant fancy ; because worms have neither arms nor legs, and (except in China) poets do not go about in limb-concealing attire.   Yet our erotic poets neither are men nor desire to be thought so.   Their own highest flattery of themselves is that they are half women.   They assure each other of this

distinction constantly in private intercourse. This is
what they hint at so complacently before the larger
audience of the public when they talk of their
"singing gowns"; and the most delicious compliment they ever hear is when you tell them that you
recognise in the noises they make the note of the
Eternal Feminine.

Erotic composition used to be called "amorous,"
and it would be a welcome change were it called so
again. Or "erosive" might be used as a synonym
with perfect propriety. "Exotic" it has a clear
association with; and any gentle student of this
dictionary who may be obliged to read aloud the
literature of the day is authorised to substitute
the one word for the other whenever she comes
upon it.

FAITHFULNESS

FAITHFULNESS even in love—where a certain lati-
tude is always allowed by the world-worn and the
sage—is ranked amongst the higher virtues ; and
fickleness is certainly a vice. Yet it often happens
that the faithfulness that lovers boast is only another
name for good luck. So much depends on the
choice they are pledged to. No doubt it is more
than good fortune, it is a merit to be able to choose
well ; for an ill mind, blind and ungoverned, is little
likely to do that. But his true match and counterpart does not come in every man's way, nor are
women more fortunate in that respect ; and we
know that the glamours and deceits which the best
of creatures are subject to make up half the lovers'
tragedies. It is the highest fortune when like falls
to like. It is the happiest fortuity when two good
fellows born for each other come within hail of eye
and voice with no one to say them nay ; and if,
being one of these much-favoured ones, you have
made your lucky choice, what is to be done but to

hold to it ?   Shall the **merchant** be praised for being
faithful to **his gold, or any** man **to the heart and** soul
of him ?

Faithfulness begins where there **is** misfortune, or
disappointment, **or** temptation, or provocation to
doubt.   **The least** meritorious fidelity **is** that which
is most **often heard of,** faithfulness **in** misfortune.
Yet misfortune is sometimes **a** sharper test than it is
commonly allowed **to be ; not** because the privations
of poverty are too hard to endure, but because
poverty's foul hand is apt to sweep away all the
beauty and grace, all that **was** so winningly bright
and bold and debonair in better days.   The ruined
man is often ruined in much more than his fortune ;
and we are to remember that many **people in** this
world, both male and female, never **were and never
could** be loved except for their extraneous charms
and adventitious graces.   And that is why that
" **When** Poverty **comes in at** the **door, Love** flies out
of the window," says the Englishman ; " Wenn die
Armuth **zur** Thür eingeht, **so** fliegt **die** Liebe zum
Fenster hinaus," says the German ; " Sans pain, sans
vin, amour n'est rien," **says the** Frenchman—usually
so sweet to l'Amour ; as indeed the German is, in
the abstract.   All that these sayings mean is that
there **is a love** which cannot **outlast** what gave birth
to it and nourished it ; in which there is hardly
enough surprise **to** make an epigram.

Faithfulness under temptation also counts **for a
very** small virtue unless temptation in one direction
is strengthened **by** disappointment in another ; but
here **a** halt must **be** called for the delivery of a
warning word.   Be it known **to all** young persons,

and especially to those who are conscious of a lightsome mind, that there are no more dangerous words in the lover's vocabulary than these two: "disappointment" and "temptation." Both are in many a case words of excuse for the merest faithlessness; and by simple repetition of them in tones of self-pity, it is possible to be converted from ordinary lightness to the basest self-indulgence and most cruel treachery. Yet there are disappointments far from imaginary and much above the trifling; and when in the midst of these temptation appears, faithfulness may claim a merit in turning a stony side to the tempter. But it comes nearer to a virtue when it remains unshaken by doubt; and when we say doubt, no trivial suspicion of trivial faults is meant, but the gravest doubt of wrongs, and perhaps of humiliation as well as wrong. To be steadily faithful then needs a true heart and stout affections —not always well rewarded. It is often seen, indeed, that faithfulness is but a wanton sacrifice, though the faithful soul can never be persuaded of that; and perhaps there is no call to mourn over a suffering virtue which never fails to find its own happiness in its worst distress.

FAMILIARITY

A line of introduction may be necessary for this word, which was not expected to appear, perhaps, in a lover's dictionary. The reader may be reminded, then, that familiarity has some relationship with the mingling of souls, the blending of hearts and lives, which are the theme of so many love-letters and the occasion of so many dreams. It is but a gipsy relationship, no doubt ; but then the appearance of " familiarity " here is precisely on that account.

Companionship, close, intimate, and above all exclusive—that is the object of the love-longings which thread the air with invisible bridges by day and night, but most when the witching-time draws on and in the waking hour of the morning. Were they not invisible, these bridges would be seen to start from the window-sill of some sleeping-chamber to the casement of another all over the country, giving it the appearance of being covered with a gossamer-web or vast celestial strawberry-net, its meshes sparkling with the desires that speed over it from point to point in every direction. Fulfilled, these desires bring to the sons and daughters of men their greatest happiness—the companionship above mentioned. But as all the world knows too well, it is a happiness exposed to many dangers, of which some of the most subtle are least remarked upon. Even of the sufferers, thousands have never understood that familiarity itself may be fatal to companionship, and often is.

Of the good reader's grace, let him not suppose that any wretched little cynicism is intended here. Familiar knowledge of each other is not meant, but familiarity in personal intercourse. No good-natured couple about to marry need fear the one, but in pity of themselves they should dread the other, in whatever station of life they may have been born or propose to wed. Good breeding is a presumption of delicacy, but no insurance of it : be that remem-

bered.   The refinement that is conspicuous in polite
society, punctually answering to all requirements, is
no warranty against a brutal absence of reserve in
dressing-gown and slippers.   They are quite true,
those stories of most respectable men who, going
into savage South-Sea islands or the like, have in
six months thrown off the decency that clothed them
in civilised life, becoming perfectly native.   And so
there are gentlemen at home—and what is more, there
are ladies (impossible to doubt their right to the
appellation)—who take three steps, four steps, five
steps back into the state of nature as soon as they
find themselves within the solitudes and enclosures of
domesticity.   When two such persons are joined in
marriage, their freedoms of speech and conduct are
probably conducive to mutual happiness ; but where
it is one and one, either wife or husband is doomed
to a torment that might be compared with being devoured by worms.

Prudery? there is no prudery in the matter.
It is all a question of civility, of common courtesies.
Every wise man knows that there is a familiarity in
the companionship of men and women, happily wed,
which goes far beyond every other for intimacy, while
it is sweeter in the sense of wholesomeness than any.
But no such companionship can flourish where
another kind of familiarity—careless of little decen-
cies, prying where it should not see, speaking where
there should be silence, coarsely unveiling thoughts
and feelings that when naked should be ashamed—
saps respect and tortures self-respect.   The shock of
discovering a familiarity of this sort has been fatal to
all that is best in marriage for many a pair otherwise

well matched ; and young persons about to marry
should look to it.   It must not be supposed that the
fault lies always with the man ; not at all.

FASCINATION

See arts. " Captivation " and " Charm," in which
some differences that distinguish fascination from
both are mentioned.   Fascination is always delightful to whomsoever it may shine upon ; and the
delight it gives may be as innocent as dancing, or
as the bouquet in a bottle of rare Bordeaux.   But
though fascination is often enrapturing, few are
indiscreet enough to call it " divine."   The divine
is precisely what it lacks.   In all its manifestations
it is either of the world (with its sweeter pleasures as
well as its other ones) or of the flesh (the delights of
which are not all wicked, or what shall be said of
beauty, strength, and the movement of happy life in
them ?), or of the devil : and devilish indeed it can be.
At its simplest and best, fascination appeals to none
but upper-middle-class emotions.   Thence descending, it runs down through ordinary human to such
as are unspeakable ; the which it not unfrequently
drives on with such fury that they rise again
into a sort of romantic blackguardism and heroic
brutality.
    Such is the range of whatever the mystic influence
may be which we call fascination in man or woman.
To avoid unnecessary consternation, be it understood
that the nicest young persons may be fascinating :
there is no assertion to the contrary.   The claim to

M

niceness is entirely justified when the qualities that
make for happiness underlie the fascination ; which
is always possible.   While charm is an unfailing sign
of indwelling good, fascination may commend either
good or ill to the beholder.   "It may be a white
magic or a black."   Being an inferior kind of charm
(answering to it, indeed, as physical beauty answers
to spiritual), and being at the same time all super-
ficiality, it *can* be imitated by the Satanic forger of
whatever is heavenly in the relations of men and
women.   And it is imitated with immense success.
A sort of fascination walks the earth, in forms most
beautiful, which wisdom and sobriety themselves
cannot always resist, though all the diabolism of
earth and its creatures is declared in it.   It not only
is, but looks, the apotheosis of the flesh and the devil
therein ; and the very delight it gives is mingled
with a delirium consciously ignoble.   This delirium
may be described as sweeping through the senses in
whiffs or wreaths, as some strong odour will : and
they who know it and its effects say they doubt
not that there is an actual likeness to it in the
tremors of a bird fluttering on the ground before
the eyes of a snake.   If the bird would but close
its eyes for a little while it could fly away.   But over
and over again it is drawn to look ; at every fresh
glance, another whiff of some strange ecstasy ; with
destruction in a trance for the end of it.

FIANCÉE, FIANCÉ

In the absence of any good, full-meaning, sweet-sounding word in English for persons engaged to marry each other, this (which might have come from the confectioner's with other apparatus in aid of domestic insufficiency) is not unseldom adopted. But rather than use it plain folk will make a long round of circumlocution, or take up with the barbarism of his or her "intended." Englishmen will never have their rights till this strange gap is filled in a language which has so many perfect words for love and home and all therein. Word-making is the special business of poets, and to them we look. Of the nine hundred and ninety now in song, nine hundred and nine—their breasts ever pushed to the thorn—trill unceasingly of love's entanglements ; and yet the necessary substitute for "betrothed" has yet to be invented. They should form a committee of suggestion under the presidency of Dr. Murray. He would probably direct attention to the old word "plight" as the better foundation to work upon, since "troth" is so heartily out of favour ; and there is hardly a word in the whole dictionary of broader base or more sweeping comprehension. "Plight" not only signifies pledge, promise, but embraces a world of meanings so wide that nothing within the prospect of an engaged couple seems to be omitted. It means to fold, to entwine, to complicate—words that abound in sweet suggestion. Duty and habitude are implied in it, whereby the word is further enriched for the present purpose. Debt also comes in, though mainly in the sense of duteous obligation ; and then, to make all complete, it has background meanings of imbroglio, risk, fearsomeness, danger. It is clear, therefore, that "plight" is the word that poets should work upon. (See arts. "Affiance," "Betrothal," " Engagement.")

FICKLENESS

Celebrated from all times, in all nations, and in every language as the most distinguishing character- istic of the female sex. Believed to flourish most wantonly in the warmer climes, where the strongest remedies have been tried in vain, it survives amidst the ice-fields of the frozen North, though doubtless in diminished activity. This difference is commonly ascribed to the sternness of the climate ; but it is also explained by the sparseness of a singularly scattered population.

An ever-flowing fountain of distress for millions in every age, fickleness has not been without com- pensation to the human race as a whole. If in its results it has decimated families, it has nursed the martial spirit in mankind, refined the use of the sword whilst extending its practice, and added enormously to the more poetic, passionate, and imaginative litera- ture of the world. In particular it may be said that while it has been the occasion of a vast deal of bloodshed, it has stirred the mind of men to the production of metaphor in unmatched abundance ; and no exercise is more conducive to the education of the finer literary faculties.

Yet because, like the sting of the honey-bee, the fickleness of woman strikes at individuals, whom it fevers, and not at communities, which it has possibly benefited, it is imputed to her as a fault. Inasmuch as it exists, it certainly has all the appearance of a fault ; and whatever good purpose it was originally designed to serve—(and war, famine, and plague are equally believed by philosophers to have their place in the economy of things)—that purpose, we may take it, has been sufficiently fulfilled. The genuinely fickle are survivals from primordial times. Some women, no doubt, are no more answerable for their fickleness than the tempest for its floods. They cannot help it. They must answer, as the waters do, to all reflections ; wherefore it profits not to speak of them. But there are others who seem to think that fickleness is both a privilege and an adornment, and are fickle as much from choice as from disposition. These ladies should reflect that they are without the excuse of their more elementary sisters, nor can they claim to be included in the apology for storm, famine, and plague. If they were intended to be what they are it would be another thing ; but since they are able to choose it is clear that they were not so intended, but were appointed to take an advanced place in the scale of nature.

Some words of reserve may have been observed in the foregoing paragraph : to wit, "inasmuch as fickleness exists" in womankind. For it certainly seems to be a diminishing quality, just as homicide is dying out among men ; and, with all respect to the older poets be it said, the faithfulness of women is as good for a song as their mutability. It becomes men to say so as lovers and husbands; while as philosophers they might remember—(amongst other things more frequently brought to their minds)— that since men cultivate themselves into an extra- ordinary number of varieties, the fickleness of woman should be less of a surprise.

FLAME

Up to the end of the eighteenth century or there- about, this bright and ardent word figured hugely in love-songs, love-tales, love-letters, and similar com- positions. By that time, however, it had not only lost its original force, but had become a moaning and a weeping word ; and soon afterwards went out of fashion together with funeral urns, which (swarming in the architecture, furniture and silversmiths' work of the time) were never complete without a little bunch of flames a-top. " Flame " also suffered in general esteem from its association with shepherds' crooks, groves, darts, and other classical fantasticalities, for which the world took a loathing ; so that now " we never mention it—the once familiar word."

Yet better image for the fires of love could not be. If the young lover will examine his sensations he will acknowledge the perfect fitness of the comparison. A spark from Delia's eyes, or some electric touch from the lambencies that play about her lips, fired certain combustibles in his bosom exactly as lightning might fire a wood-stack, only that lightning destroys. Thereupon there was a confused leaping of flame-like emotions in his breast, amidst a shifting

reek of roseate hopes and murky doubts and sudden
black volumes of despair. That was at the first ;
but soon the conflagration becomes more settled and
confined ; just as happens when a new world is
forming out of the clash of elemental matter. Passion
now sinks into a core and centre of white fire, from
the unsteady surface of which cloudy vapours or light-
bearing ethers arise. Of these last some seem to
burn in all but continuous flame, others to leap up
and out as if impatiently returning to some source
divine. Should the lover have the soul of a poet, it
accompanies these heaven-ascending flames part of
the way, bringing back more knowledge than ever it
had before ; and even though he be lacking in soul
he is never so dull but that he is conscious of the
novel aspiration.

Such are the lover's sensations as nearly as they
can be compared with anything ; and years and years
after, when the flames are all burnt out, he can still
tell of the white core and centre of fire within him ;
and perhaps he may add that but for its existence
his life could not have been so much of a garden
as it had been made.

To him the scientist would reply that these fancies
about fires, flames, and the rest of it, mean no more
than that the patient's blood is in a feverish condition,
indicative of physiological disturbance ; and that
the rhapsodisings of the lover precisely correspond
with the ramblings of fever-patients in general.
These explanations are intended to take the conceit
out of love as a divine passion, and to lower
the pretensions of poets ; but there really is nothing
in them. Physiological disturbance, with more or

less of one kind of heat or another, is everything in this life. Working in the brain of Wellington, it won the battle of Waterloo ; in the brain of Newton, it unveiled the law of gravitation ; and the scientist should know that when physiological disturbance ceases in himself, he will neither discover, nor invent, nor expound any more. All depends upon the nature, the bent, the end of it ; which is to make of one man a fool, of another a beast, of another a genius, of another a saint—and a saint so madly wise, perhaps, as to be indifferent to martyrdom. Patriotism is fever. Pity—the more tender it is the more truly may it be described as physiological disturbance. Wherefore the lover may be as happy in his fantasies as Shakespeare in writing the "Midsummer Night's Dream," and live at an altitude almost as high ; and yet the physiologist is right in all but his willingness to confound everything in mire.

FLATTERY

According to Irish annalists, the ancient name for the greater chieftains of their country was "Flath" ; and considering that every tribesman lived in the presence of his Flath, and that nowhere in the world is flattery so accustomed, so adroit, so finished as in Ireland, it might be supposed that we have here the origin of the word. But we may not enjoy the pleasure of believing in a derivation so rational and satisfying. It seems that we took "flattery" from the French, who had it from the Scandinavians, with whom it signified "to stroke gently" or caressingly.

That is very much what it means still, with the mingling of an intention to deceive by false praise— to win by fawning adulation. It has been much employed, therefore, in love-affairs, and mostly by men-folk. For a man may be truly in love without being veritably honest ; and when that is the case he will not scruple to commend himself by what he still thinks venial, however gross he may make it ; taught as he is by clouds of ungentle witnesses that no man need fear to flatter in excess. Women resort to flattery too, but less often and with a difference. They find blandishment more effective, and it comes more natural to them. The pleasure of being flattered is that you are licensed from without to think well of yourself. Blandishment affords another delight ; in the thought that some fair creature is not quite controllably fond of you. And all that is known of the two sexes renders it credible that flattery is the greater joy to the one, blandishment to the other.

Not without design was it written above that flattery " has been " much employed in love-affairs ; for there is reason to believe it one of our many declining industries. Various explanations of the decadence may be given, and it is probable that all of them count. To flatter with credit a fine " manner " is needed ; and most men of the present age are conscious of having no manners of the requisite kind. They complain that just as their forefathers exhausted the capacity of the race for drinking port wine, so their prodigality of courtliness hardly left to their successors a single grace where- with to bless themselves. That is one account of the decline of flattery. Another is founded on the revelation by a long series of lady novelists, each more explanatory than the last, that what women really like is not to be flattered but bullied. They feel that any one of their *own* sex can treat them tenderly, and they hardly know that they are in the hands of a man unless roughly used. Valentine was endured, it appears, only so long as women were slaves to conventionality ; but in their heart of hearts Orson was always the man.

The youth of the time hastened to profit by this unexpected disclosure, and young women of the superior classes have nothing to fear from flattery now.

FLIRTATION

A pastime which, like card-playing, is innocuous only when nothing is staked that can be missed if lost, while it is most harmful when the stakes are abstracted from partnership capital. The game is usually played by the ruder sex for amusement alone, its chief pleasure being the titillation and excitement of vanity. By the other it is played for amusement too ; but also for practice in various kinds of fascination, and to satisfy curiosity as to the inner nature of men. From the female side, therefore, it may be argued that when conducted with discretion and conscience, flirtation has serious uses. Instead of being called a game, it might be likened to adventuring into a half-known country ; and not from mere idleness, nor from mere love of excitement, but with a

view to ultimate settlement in some part of it.
Nor is it necessary to assume that a conscious or
formal intention of settling exists in the lady's mind ;
for daughters are by nature migratory creatures, and
may be expected as they grow up to share the prevenient instinct of other birds of passage.

But capable as it may be of friendly explanation
in moderate cases, flirting has a bad name and has
earned it.   The charge that it is an education in
flippancy, equivoque, lightness of manners and hardness of heart, is not without foundation.   More
seriously offensive to others is the well-observed fact
that flirting is often employed interferingly, for
mischievous and destructive purposes alone.   Accomplished mistresses of the art will resort to it with set
and sole design to humble the charms of another
woman in her lover's eyes ; which is malignancy
enough, without the worse than piratical outrage of
drawing him off and then flinging him away.   But
that is not uncommon either.   There are ambitions in
this art as in others ; and few of its superior practi-
tioners can forego an occasional triumph of this kind :
the Double Firsts of flirtation.

As an art, however, flirtation has gravely declined.
It will never die out.   Its rudiments are probably
indestructible.   But in no class of society, from that
which pretends to the highest elegance and *savoir
faire* to the most rustic, is flirtation ever seen nowadays except in its ruder forms.   The *finesse* of a
politer time has been completely lost.   The fashion
of social intercourse between well-bred young men
and women is to be rough, unceremonious, familiar ;
and what no doubt is still flirtation has coarsened

into something which is not readily distinguishable from general bad manners.

FONDNESS

Fondness is a pretty word, and yet a deep word, and one that will not be spoken lightly and triflingly; but, hanging on the lips as if to ripen there, drops from them with the after-sound of a kiss. Perhaps it is all the sweeter because it conveys a meaning of forgiveness. Indeed, it is through the gate of that word that we find our way from the present meaning of "fondness," which is "lovingness," to its original and long-lasting signification, which was "folly." In times of old, to be fond was "to act as a fool" in a general way. Later, the fond man was one who could foolishly submit and dotingly forgive. Nowadays, a man may be called fond, and even (tautologically) dotingly fond, without at all understanding that he is made ridiculous by the epithet; neither is ridicule intended.

If any inference is to be drawn from this, it is that mankind, unlike its satirists, is slow to see folly in affection carried to extremes. Ticket excess of love as the extravagance of fools, and little by little the meaning goes out of the badge, which becomes a mark of goodness rather.

We perceive, however, that distinct traces of the old signification of "fondness" cling about the word when we say "a fond husband" and then "a fond wife." So brought together, these expressions reveal a difference, though a subtle one. In the first there

is a suggestion of the possibility of weakness ; a
whisper of a tendency to doting and unseemly sub-
mission.   On the other hand, " fondness " and "wife "
agree as fitly as the breath of the rose and the
rose.   From which another inference may be drawn,
perhaps.   We find here a universal unconscious acknowledgment that love and governance are for the
one sex, love and obedience for the other : verily,
even to this day.

Yet there is such a thing as excessive fondness
even amongst women ; a fondness of which the folly
might be disregarded were it not for the suffering it
brings in its train.   Not of course that it does so
always, far from it ; but still, suffering is not unseldom a consequence of excess.   Wherefore, when
any young damsel detects her heart in boasting that
it is very, *very* fond, let her raise her hands to her
forehead night and morning with the prayer, " That
I may remember fondness was and may be folly."
The formula cannot be relied upon absolutely, but it
has been found useful.

FRIEND

Although friendship and love are nearly always
combined in the affection of men for women and
women for men, they are different things.   That
has been said a thousand times ; but it is not so
commonly understood that there may be great love
with little friendship, just as there is a strong friendship which is incapable of becoming love.   But for
the first of these two things there would be fewer of

the worst of husbands ; and but for the second, not so many faithful and yet scarcely-pleasing wives.

The rule has been stated, but it is not without variations. Amongst men there are a few, amongst women a greater number, who hang for ever on the hither side of the border-line between friendship and love for some person of the opposite sex. And all the while the prospect on the farther side is not unpleasing to them. When such an one fancies herself over the edge, it is without any feeling of alarm. There is no start of repugnance at the thought of walking hand in hand amidst the paradisos of marital affection with the gentleman whom she ever thinks of as Mr. A. or Mr. B. But if there be no alarm, neither is there any desire ; if no tell-tale start of repugnance, yet none of the wished-for intimations of delight. Were her feelings to go back a little it would be better, she sometimes thinks. But no : tap she never so often at the barometer, the index will not budge from " Set Fair," nor decline by one degree into the prophetics of ardency. The test is this : she can think of wedding another not only with toleration but with a prospecting eye ; though the thought that he may do so draws a shadow after it. If thereupon she asks herself, " Are you, then, so fond of him ? " the instant answer is "*Very* fond!" But nothing is altered.

The probable explanation is that the poor lady is incompletely designed for marriage. Her call to that state is so distant and so dimly heard that though its harmonies are readily listened to they are never quite made out, and its appeal is never wholly understood. But whatever the explanation, there

she is ; and whatever the mystery of her being, she
herself is natural and unaffected. She has a clear
meaning in her own mind when she holds her lover off
with the assurance that there is nothing dearer to her
than his regard, and that she is and must remain for
him what she hopes he will ever be to her : a tender
and affectionate friend ! All men—perhaps all
women—are not gifted with perception enough to
comprehend the sincerity of that state of mind, or to
understand that there is neither confusion nor illusion
in it ; and therefore many hard and contemptuous
words are bestowed where none are deserved.

That women are capable of forming friendships
with each other like the friendship of man and man
cannot be doubted ; but it may be denied that the
capability is common. The romantic attachment
that binds young girls in couples is another thing
altogether. Friendship it must be called, but it has
its own origin, its own exotic character, and must be
regarded as a passion apart. Flowering in the first
period of youth, with youth it perishes and never
reappears. Nor is it often followed by friendship
of a more sober kind, but rather by shy estrangement
and avoidance. And it certainly seems that the
strongest, soundest, truest friendships of women are
reserved for men. This is partly accounted for by
the idealising of the sexes, the one by the other,
which is one of the first laws of human nature ; but
partly also—(the truth must be told in dictionaries)
by the greater faith of women in the sincerity, the
comparative un-complexity of men. It has been
doubted whether a friendship between man and
woman is ever without some admixture of the softer

passion ; and young women complain that they dare not seek or encourage such a friendship because of the risk that, sooner or later, it will yield a crop of undesired attentions. In that they are probably right. Yet there is a friendship between the sexes which has nothing to do with sexual affections ; though none so strong as that which love begins. It is never so true, so lasting, so serene a sentiment as when it is the outcome of a love that once was and is no more : except as a never-uttered memory.

GALLANT, GALLANTRY

IN its older and better sense, gallantry is one of the finest things in the world. To be gallant is to be nearly all that makes a man, as distinguished from a schoolmaster, a merchant, a lawyer, a politician, or other fragmentary portion of the social machine. The word is from *galer*, which was "to rejoice" in Old French, and no man may rejoice in himself if a gallant man may not. For to be gallant is to be gay, splendid, brave. He is high-spirited and daring—he is generous, magnanimous, and courtly, is the gallant man. "A gay, sprightly, airy, splendid man," says the soberest of lexicographers. Says another and more knightly authority, "A gallant man, whose thoughts fly at the highest game."

And yet gallantry is out of favour, or seems to be so. For centuries it was esteemed the epitome of all that becomes a man in his relations mundane; but now a gallant man is never heard of, nor has been these seventy years. Though it has so many

bright and various uses, "gallantry" is a word that
in our own time is cashiered from conversation ;
except when a stockade has been attacked in
Burmah, or a young lady has been saved from
drowning, or a policeman must needs be praised
for the audacious capture of a thief. "The gallant
soldier," "the gallant constable," keep the word in use
as a professional term descriptive of courage and
dash ; but as descriptive of chivalry in social life,
or as a faggot-word for gaiety, generosity, courtliness, splendour, bravery in its double sense, gallantry
is in general avoidance. The thing is not ; and,
to judge by appearance, there is not only a common
incapability of continuing or reproducing it but a
feeling against it. The times are showy enough,
and show belongs to gallantry ; there is luxury
enough, though of a sad lumpiness, and abundance
is a very good appanage to gallantry ; but luxury
and show will not make a gallant man. Gallantry
has no dependence upon riches, but may exist un-
impaired in all essentials about the poorest gentleman. For it is bravery of spirit, courtliness of intention, fineness of demeanour, a well-chastened,
well-governed, well-apportioned radiance of manners
that makes a gallant man, as he stands naked of
exterior advantage and adornment : while as to
that, it is enough if he be well dressed and is never
without a guinea to spend in a pretty way.

Can it be, then, that gallantry has *really* gone
out of favour ? Is it imaginable that the gallant
man has no longer a charm for women ? Is there
a woman in ten thousand whose heart does not
warm to such an one *nolens volens*, or whose ideals

never did include a gallant man? It cannot be. Fancy banishes the idea at sight; art scorns it, science repels it, poesy will have none of it, and every feather in the peacock's tail disproves it.

And yet when the women of the day write love-tales for their sisters, how often do they choose for hero the gallant man—" the gay, airy, sprightly, splendid man "—knightly, courtly, " whose thoughts fly at the highest game "? Why, never. Without neglecting sublime manufacturers and sardonic literary persons, their choice most often falls on large, sullen, lumbering brutes ; shaggy ; bellowing when moved to speech ; richly endowed with the peculiar courage of butting animals, but with little that " bravery " signifies. Contemptuous of women (who are but "little girls" to these prodigious creatures), they are so devoid of courtliness as to count it good breeding to be rude. So strange a reversion to barbarism can only be explained by despair of gallantry as quite extinct, and by the need of creating fresh ideals in order to reconcile girlish minds to the supersession of romance by dulness and incivility.

That, however, will never be done. Young women are making the best of their lot, even to the length of pretending to like the boorishness of the young men about them ; but gallantry is not out of favour, nor ever will be with the spindle sex till the farthest planet has been discovered and the last Jew has abandoned the faith of his fathers. It has only fallen out of fashion perforce, like the taste for diamonds in the Argentine Republic. Gallantry will have its day again ; though not among us,

perhaps, till it has been regrafted from new and
natural growths, as was done in the case of the
grape-vine, the potato, and other failing vegetables.
And fortunately, there are places in Europe where
gallantry may find virgin soil : in Prussia, for
example, and in the Calmuck territories of the
Czar.

Yet gallantry should be every young man's education the world over. Its virtuous and embellishing
essentials should be taught in all the schools, upon
a foundation of example at home wherever possible.
Till its renewal by that means, or till its re-introduc-
tion from abroad, we must look for a continuation
of this Age of Melancholy, with its utter deadness
to the gay, the sprightly, the airy, brave, courtly,
and radiant, which is the description of gallantry
and the gallant man.

Of the starved and shy practice of gallantry
which still obtains here and there in courtship, it
is unnecessary to speak. Performed funereally—as
seems but natural since the spirit of the thing is
gone—it is a mere ceremonious survival. There is
another kind of gallantry, to which no praise can be
given. At all times an excess, a disorder, a sort of
drunkenness, it never had much grace, though the
ancient practice was to heap it over with floral
affectations. Nowadays it does without grace altogether and dispenses with affectations of every sort.
Otherwise, it is the same kind of drunkenness, and
one that we have nothing to do with.

HABITUDE

THE name of a good genius which has brought happiness unperceived to many who never recognised their benefactor. It is no virtue, no angel from the skies, but a common hearth-born spirit as a cricket might be; and yet altars might be raised to it as Love's physician and resurrectionist of peace.

There is a secret which hosts of young lovers are left to find out for themselves, though at least one married couple in every street could impart it to them: it is that a mysterious chance awaits all who wed for love. Unlike those who do not, they feel sure of happiness. As the wedding-day approaches their spirits run toward each other with increasing ardour, in the certainty of blissful union; which, to their wonder, may fail them instantly and altogether.

It was so with Robin and Robinetta: a pretty young couple who had known one another for nearly a year before marriage, though their acquaintance was not six hours old before each had made known to each an affection which yet they were too shy to

avow, till a stimulus was found in the celebration of the young lady's twentieth birthday.
Thenceforth they lived in a rapture so far above
earth that (unless he happened to be very much
in love himself at the time) no poet could describe
it. Their one misery was that they could never
be together often enough out of eyeshot of the
world ; for both belonged to an order of small
gentry which, though not uncheerful, is strictly
governed by old-fashioned respectabilities. In the
hearts of them, the last week of their unwedded life
was like the rushing of two precipitous streams to
make one deep lake of rest. But it would be better
to say in plain prose, perhaps, that they married in
a transport of heaven-knows-what expectancies, to
find heaven-knows-what disillusions or what disappointments. All that they themselves could tell,
is that there was a difference in a day, and one
that widened every day thereafter. To both it
was like waking from an exquisite dream with the
certainty of never dreaming such dreams again ; and,
to bring matters to the worst, they could see in each
other's faces, hear in each other's voices, feel in the
touch of each other's hands, that the disappointment
was mutual. This, which should have made them
forbearing, and would have done so in any other
calamity, only sharpened a resentment which both
believed just, though neither could have told why.
Concealment of a feeling that was reflected from one
to the other so evenly became impossible ; and in
less than three months these poor young people fell
to bickering, and would have accused each other
vehemently had they known what the offence was :

which, however, was as much beyond them as the
mystery of their being.

The misery of the unhappy pair was none the
less for their inability to make out the why and
wherefore of it ; and no one can tell how much more
it would have grown to—perhaps to passionate out-
break and running away—but for some clinging
memories, a feeling that if one was wretched so was
the other, and, above all, a pride that held violence in
restraint. And so they lived on together in secret
hope that the deadness of indifference was not far off.
They lived on together, and that was enough. For
they were not unchristian folk ; they were humane,
these two, and had been bred in habits of civility.
After a time they began to tire of their impulsive
jarrings, though without coming any nearer to each
other. The fretfulness of baffled and resourceless
sympathy wore down, and then came a space of
barren tranquillity, and then a peace not altogether
rayless. Habitude had been born between them.
Companionship brought its unfailing round of little
duties and amenities. Small troubles, common to
both, sowed in the dark a new growth of small
tendernesses. Now an endearing weakness appeared
on the one side, and now a kindly patience on the
other ; and all these things did habitude foster and
increase till the love of Robin and Robinetta rose
again from the dead—changed into a smiling, sweet,
and comely affection. The proof that it is now
unalterable is that it is changing them. Already,
at thirty-two years of age, Robinetta's handwriting
resembles her husband's so much that they are
hardly distinguishable ; and it is evident from the

face and figure of each that they are conforming to
the downright physical likeness which is so often
seen in happy old married people.

Young lovers, and especially those who happen to
be ardent and romantic, are charged to remember
this little story, and to think well of habitude : which
is not familiarity, they should understand.

HARMONY

See " Affinity," where it appears that pining ones
in search of their "affinities" might be described in
plainer terms as looking out for some person of the
other sex capable of living in harmony with themselves.   That is at least as good a way of putting it,
and more obviously in accordance with the univers-
ality of things.   For all the laws of all the universes,
and of every part of every one of them, come under
the word "harmony."   In music we say that the
composer makes the harmony ; in the Creation it is
harmony that composes all things, from the solar
system to "this little hand."   Everything in nature
seeks completion, growth, health, continuance in
harmonious union.   It is the one universal desire,
which even some mindless things seem able to express ; as, for example, the one bell in the church
tower.   At every sound, a poet would say, the solitary bell calls for a response in harmony with its own
voice, seeming to listen for it, time after time, in painful expectation.   It is only seeming.   The call is in
our own fancy, where, however, it would not be but
for a feeling in the whole mind of us that the one

note can have no completeness and no satisfaction in itself till it is wedded in concord with another.

In Steele's *Tatler* there is an ingenious essay in which the several varieties of women at an assembly are likened to musical instruments. "The person who pleased me most was a Flute, an instrument that, without any great compass, hath something exquisitely sweet and soft in its sound ; it lulls and soothes the ear, and fills it with such a gentle kind of melody as keeps the mind awake without startling it, and raises a most agreeable passion between transport and indolence. . . . By the side of the Flute there sat a Flageolet ; for so I must call a certain young lady who, fancying herself a wit, despised the music of the Flute as low and insipid, and would be entertaining the company with tart ill-natured observations, pert fancies, and little turns, which she imagined to be full of life and spirit. . . . But the most sonorous part of our concert was a She-drum, or, as the vulgar call it, a Kettle-drum, who accompanied her discourse with motions of the body, tosses of the head, and brandishes of the fan. Her music was loud, bold, and masculine. Every thump she gave alarmed the company, and very often set somebody or other in it a-blushing." There was besides "a certain romantic instrument called a Dulcimer "; the Kit, remarkable for "a great many skittish notes, affected squeaks and studied inconsistencies "; the prudish Virginal, the hoyden Hornpipe, and others ; nor does the paper end without inclusion of "your Larums or Household-scolds, and your Castanets or impertinent Tittle-tattles." It is then proposed that, "considering how absolutely necessary it is that two instruments which are to play together for life should be exactly tuned and go in perfect concert with each other," matches shall be made in future between Drum and Kettle-drum, Lute and Flute, Harpsichord and Hautboy, and such-like assortments.

A pretty conceit, and good for guidance : though of little service to lovers at first sight. These good folk put themselves in a moment beyond direction, and either need it not—Lute and Flute coming together by attraction of natural harmonic forces—or heed it not : persuaded by some strange defect of ear that the Larums of their choice are miracles of sense and spirit, that their Castanets are the smartest of "agreeable rattles," and that it must be a soul-inspiring thing to live from day to day and every day within sound of the Bagpipes and the Drum. But all love is not love at first sight. There is a more deliberate passion that comes on by quick degrees, indeed, but yet with halting intervals : and each of these intervals supplies an opportunity of looking with comparative coolness into the harmonic constitution and promise of the beloved object. In so doing it is of course necessary to take account not only of the music but the music-room. The kettledrum is not favourably heard in a rustic cottage, and some of the sweetest instruments lose tone unless backed by the sounding-board of a well-stocked wardrobe, or when removed from the vicinity of a coach-house and stable.

A further consideration comes into play when the match has been made and the long duet of connubial life begins. It then behoves each to remember

that he or that she is not only the instrument but
the instrumentalist. Till a little while ago this was
always understood, together with the lessons and
the obligations implied in the understanding. But
now a new doctrine has been imported into the relations of men and women : according to which it is
an imperative duty to One's self to live One's own
life. This is as much as to say that even in a
duet it is all in the justice and beauty of things
to choose one's own tune (with liberty to the other
one to do the same, of course), and to perform it
without regard to any one's pleasure but one's own.
It is a stupid doctrine and a drunken ; with nothing in
it at the end but headache for certain, and heartache
if the wherewithal for the severer malady remain.
To live in one's self, to one's self for one's self, one
must live *by* one's self ; which is not the case supposed. The binary or dual life is the most perfect
of all for human creatures, for the reason that it is
in the nature of things a harmony ; and one that
becomes divinely complete when, the instruments
being rightly paired, the instrumentalists in the instruments attune every wish to concord. Not that
all discord is forbidden. In life as in music there
are discords that sweeten harmony.

HEART, THE

Physiologists not a few ridicule belief in the
heart as the seat of the affections. Some peoples,
they maliciously remind us, are equally sure that
love is an affair of the midriff ; an opinion which

the sensations of rejected lovers may, indeed, be held to countenance. It is in the midriff that these unfortunates seem to suffer most—with a billowy uneasiness, as it were. But how does that bear on the general question? If, as seems highly probable, this theory of the seat of love originated in a country where the females outnumbered the males, and were at the same time remarkable for their severity, it is quite accounted for by local circumstances. Other nations have never doubted that the seat of love is the liver; and so familiar is this idea amongst them that their word for liver has taken a romantic cast, and is freely admitted into their lyrical compositions. They sing, " My true love's liver is mine, and mine is his," for example. But here again we are not without explanation of the error. If the torments of rejection sensibly vibrate on the diaphragm or midriff, jealousy as surely tells upon the biliary organ. Every robust lover who has gone through a sudden bout of jealousy will acknowledge this; and it is a singular merit in that noble actor, Signor Salvini, that while he throws heart into his earlier scenes as Othello, a subtle substitution of liver begins from about the middle of the third act. Evidently, it is but natural that a violently-jealous people should place the seat of love where the higher races are more often disturbed by *entrées* and east winds.

For the rest, it is plain that chagrin is not love, neither are the pangs of jealousy; and it is *chagrin* that shakes the midriff, the fury of jealousy that assails the liver. But with both the fury and the humiliation there still remains some love; and were

it not that scientific men are incapable of the tender
passion (a suppressed fact which the delicacy of
their wives enables them to conceal), there would
be no need to tell physiologists where the remnant
of an abused or a scorned affection is felt. It is
felt in the heart, where it was consciously born.
The chagrin in the midriff, the fury in the liver if
you please ; but the love in the heart : where both
the rejected and the jealous lover find it only too
surely between one paroxysm of those other organs
and another.

Were there a little rose-coloured realm of matter
in the brain, as there is a much-revered patch of gray
matter, and if, moreover, this rosy patch lay near
the breeding-place of fancy, it might be supposed
that love had at least a consulting-room in the head.
But no such thing has been discovered ; and it is
too much to ask sage or lover to believe that love is
either born or nursed in the brain. Persuade an
alderman that he is hungry, not where he fancies,
but in the hindermost part of his skull, and, then,
perhaps, his daughters may be made to doubt that
their bosoms are love's domicile. But this is allowing too much. It would take a miracle to bring
the dominion of the heart into uncertainty. By the
witness of a thousand sensations, it is there that
love is born ; there is its cradle, school, house, and
citadel ; and no one who has ever been bereaved can
doubt that there it makes its grave.

HONEYMOON

Though lovers would seem to be all of the morning, morning is no time for them. It is a common observation that before twelve o'clock they are vague, void, wit-asleep, as if they had become nocturnal, like the bird who " in the belfry sits " or puss on the wall. By mid-day they are awake and natural, remaining undistinguished from their fellow-creatures for a space of time which varies according to the season of the year. It is longest in the winter months, shortest in summer ; when the languors of afternoon revive in them the only life they care to live. From that time till nightfall, and through the night, and to the waking hour inclusive, they remain in the rapture of enamoration ; which is said to be always deepest, sweetest, and most thoughtful-melancholy when there is a moon.

Indeed, there can be no doubt that it is so. The connection between moonlight and love is thoroughly well established. It was an early discovery of the ancients, without being much to their credit ; because from the dawn of Sensibility to the present hour it has been the several and individual discovery of every man and maid caught up by the tender passion, supposing them to have tidal souls of their own. " Tidal " souls, be it observed. The word has a cogent meaning here, and one which Shake-speare had in mind (though he could not bring it into his verse conveniently) when he wrote—

The lunatic, the lover, and the poet
Are of imagination all compact.

The poet, the lover, and the lunatic or moon-moved
one are put together as equally made up of imagination, but there is one great difference between them.
It is the wits of the lunatic, his intellects, that are
tidal; and when, under the influence of the disturbing planet, they are drawn from their base, he dilates
into madness. With the poet and the lover it is
the diviner part that lifts in moonlight to its native
skies—filling to pain with dreams, yearnings, inspirations which the lover has no word for at all, and the
poet but a small assortment; as he presently finds,
poor man!

This may be said without denying that genius is
to madness near allied, or that Shakespeare meant
to put the lover where he placed the poet (and
where, indeed, we know he has always resided), next
door to lunacy on the heavenly side. All that is
intended here is to note the fact that just as moonlight, streaming upon land or sea, lifts and expands
the poet's soul more than any other natural influence,
so it is with the lover who is lucky enough to have
a tidal soul too. Under the same mystic influence
he feels the same spiritual dilation, becoming more
of a lover and a bit of a poet into the bargain.

It does not appear, however, that these observations in the pathognomy of love have anything to do
with "honeymoon." Nothing can be more natural
than associating that passion in its hour of fulfilment
with the red round orb of a summer night; but the
original connection is doubted. To be sure, it was
an old custom of the northern nations to marry at
the full of the moon, or when that variable luminary
was waxing to the full; and it is to the purpose

that we hear of honey-drinks given to the bride and bridegroom at wedding-eve and wedding-morn, and sometimes for days after. But "honey-moon" is "honey-month," the sweet month after marriage. Not that it was always customary to make a month's holiday of it, stealing away for a moon's space into seclusion. It was honey-month to new-wed squire and dame though they stayed at home and saw company three days after marriage—to the farmer though he never lost sight of his fields for an hour of daylight ; just as it is to thousands of humble folk who take up the daily round of care before the parson who married them is well out of bed again.

But whether the custom be new or old, the "going away" is the crowning delight ; and the high princely ones who can never contrive it in any right manner (not that "going away" could have much meaning for them, however managed), and the workaday people who cannot contrive it at all, are to be pitied from the heart. For half the girls in the world, years of dreaming are accomplished in a glorious wedding : veils, wreaths, bridesmaids, bouquets, horses prancing, sunshine dancing, and coachmen all a posy. An innocent triumph, by no means to be depreciated ; but after that should come the honeymoon romance, in at least twenty chapters of nights and days. What does the scoffer know about it, or they whose souls are no more tidal than the waters to which Mrs. Bond's ducks repaired ? The Romeo and Juliet scenes are beautiful because they are true, and admirable because the fitting words are given to what millions of Romeos and Juliets have felt without being able to express, or daring

enough to think worthy of celebration. And the
Romeos and Juliets are in number and generation
without end. Taking all the various State depart-
ments together, without excluding the Customs
and the Post Office, there must be hundreds and
hundreds of Romeos in Her Majesty's service alone
at this moment ; while in thousands of homes, gentle
and simple, Juliets are coming up like so many
flowers. No kind heart can think it well that any
one of these should settle down without a honeymoon in some sweet sequestered place ; and luckily
for certain of the gentlemen in the Post Office and
the Customs, a fortnight in house and garden of some
old country inn may be as a couple of weeks in
paradise.

So good an end and a beginning is the "going
away," that it is a sorrow to know of the loss of it
by any nice young man and woman. Loss ?——it is
a pathetic loss ; and considering the multitude of
benevolent associations, from the Non-Conversion of
the Jews Society up to the Decayed Dictionary-
Makers' Pension Fund, it is a wonder that no one has
imitated the enlightened tenderness of the late Miss
R——. Dying unmarried herself at an advanced
age, and having no relative but a nephew comfort-
ably settled in the bacon trade, she directed that
her fortune of £60,000 should be employed in the
following manner : To be kept at interest ; and the
interest to be used in supplying half a honeymoon
in country idleness to so many poor young couples
whose united ages amounted to fifty-three years or
no more, and three-quarters of a honeymoon, or
three lunar weeks, to others whose youth yielded

together forty-seven years or less. The only conditions were that the parties should be worthy though
lowly, industrious though poor, of a distinctly
imaginative turn, and healthy and fond.

HUSBAND

How this word may sound in the female ear, or
what sensations vibrate in the female mind when
the word whispers through it, is unknown to men.
It may be suspected, however, that there is not so
very much magic in the word, and that " husband "
passes for more than it is worth in genuine emotional
meaning. There is expression in it, a good deal of
expression ; but whether it has gathered in course of
time and use as much significance as " wife," or even
as " hearth," is doubtful. The truth appears to be
that the word was hampered from the beginning with
unfortunate associations and assonances. Husband ;
house-bond ; bondsman ; servitude ; domestic servitude : there is a clustering of associated meanings
here which is unfavourable to romance and quite
below the range of loftiness. It is all very well to
say that husband as housebond, or stay, support, and
girdle of defence for house and home, is a really
noble appellation. No doubt it is when we think
of it. But it is a common experience of the human
mind that what we most deliberately think will not
always abide in our thought ; and do what we may,
the idea of housiness and housebondage will still cling
about the word " husband." Nor is it quite without
significance that " housewife " was allowed by general

consent on the female side to degenerate into " hussy."
It is further to be observed that " housewife " was
thought, by generations of women who might have
been expected to hold the name in highest reverence,
not too good for bestowal on a case for needles and
pins.   The philosophic must needs reflect on these
things.

There can be no question, however, that "husband"
ranks high in the vocabulary of love and home. All
that is suggested is that it would rank higher but
for its unfortunate connections.   As it is, its clearest
signification to young unmarried women is that it
reflects dignity on the woman married ; while to
the fortunates in that condition its greatest bulk
of meaning is expressive of home comforts and
sanctities, fenced in with a trustworthy affection.
And a fine bulk of meaning it is ; and by the tone in
which the word "husband" is generally uttered we may
see that it is not only a word of trust but of endearment ; and yet—and yet another seems to be needed
that shall have the tenderness of " wife."   For the
man who is hero and prophet and lover to the woman
he belongs to, " housebond " is too poor a word and
goes too near the ground ; while as to " wife," if
an angel came to sit at a man's hearth she could
wish in reason for no other name.   Or must we regard
it as an involuntary tribute to the female sex—which
is generally believed to supply the greater number
of heaven's own angels—that neither " father " nor
" husband " carries such a burden of sweet and noble
meanings as " wife " and " mother " ?

In a world which, upon the whole, is peaceful and
content domestically, there are many different kinds

of husbands and yet only two or three ideals at most. How, then, is the general peace to be explained? The secret of it probably is that well-conditioned people learn without repining that the romance of love must be taken as romance, however vivid it may be. Though it is seldom continued into wedlock, what of that, say the well-conditioned to themselves, since the companionship of marriage has its own happiness, apart from the romance that preluded it? To find the romance and the reality different states of being is nothing to mourn over, if the dreams of the one are followed in the other by a lasting endearing interchange of homely service and dutiful affection.

IDEALS

IT would probably tend to a better understanding between them if the sexes could come to a frank explanation of each other's ideals. Much is known, no doubt, and much reasonably surmised on both sides ; but yet a great deal remains obscure and unavowed even in this generation, when the gentler sex seems so well disposed to meet the other half-way in a candid disclosure of sentiments hitherto concealed or disguised. Women hold congresses nowadays ; and it is time, perhaps, to employ this machinery in threshing out a subject of far more importance to them than the suffrage. A few hundred delegates carefully chosen, a few sub-committees sitting in secret, a clear, bold, outspoken report from each committee, and Man would profit by an authoritative exposition of Woman's Ideals of Man. It is probable that there would be some surprises, it is likely that there would be some pain ; and there is a certainty that while a considerable portion of the male inhabitants of Britain would be cast down by the reports, a few would swell to an intolerable degree of arrogance.   But with an excellent system of police and habitual obedience to its officials, there should be little fear on that account ; and it cannot be doubted that the general result would be highly beneficial.

This would soon appear in many ways.   Both consciously and unconsciously, there would be a striving to attain to the ideals proclaimed at the congress : and that would be improving to the nation at large.   Bone and sinew would be encouraged, a fillip would be given to independence and daring, a gallant carriage and pleasant speech would become every man's ambition, and the pretensions of mere intellect would be brought within bounds.   Not that the tyranny of one sole ideal need be feared, as we should find from the reports.   For, naturally, the sub-committees of the Woman's Ideals Declaration Congress would be drawn from ladies of different periods of life, and of at least three classes.   The first would be taken from girls unmarried, its members ranging between sixteen and nineteen years old ; the second from the young married— twenty to twenty-five ; and the third from the ex- perienced married : which last committee would be advantageously composed of women of forty.   Thus we should have the romance-ideal which every generation of budding girls keeps fresh, and another and another more or less modified from the first ; and very profitable it should be to study and com- pare them.

We should probably learn, among other things, that while young girls commonly set up an ideal Prince Charming in their bosoms, that is not the

way with the lads.   No doubt that when they have
any share of sensitive imagination these youngsters
have their love-dreamings too ; but until their
affections settle on some pretty maid in actual flesh
and blood, they contentedly leave their ideals in a
nebulous state.   Till then, the fair, the distant, the
unattainable creatures about them are only like other
beautiful things in nature that stir their young minds
to dreamy response : such as sunsets, moonrise on
the waters, and so forth.   They create no particular
ideal, to weave romantic scenes and histories about
her, though it is believed that most young damsels
enchant their days by employments precisely similar.
It is not that they are in love with this or that
person, any more than the lad who goes wandering
off into his solitudes without exactly knowing why.
Their condition is to be absorbingly in love with
love ; as indeed they seem to be in much less
marriageable times—the times of the first doll.   In
the doll they are supplied with an eidolon, visible,
tangible, about which heaven and infancy alone know
what phantasies are cast, or what dramas invest it.
Later, no doll would serve : an ideal palpable to the
mind's eye has to be created, to live and reign in
the maiden's breast.

Doubtless, it is not all a work of fancy.   The
beautiful young men who sit in these shrines—now
in the garb of a soldier, now of an angelical ecclesi-
astic, now of an athlete in cricketing cap and spot-
less flannel trousers—are partly drawn from books,
partly from own-imagination, but partly also from
shy appropriations of the actual in the person of
some godlike apparition, dimly seen from time to

time through wavering glances. But though the appropriations from real life may be large, and in some points very precise and particular, the whole is still an ideal ; and it is nearly always a worthy one. There may be mistakes in modelling—misconceptions. Features across which Nature herself has written " Splendid Brute " may be worshipped as the very mask of knightliness, or a head marked " Handsome Fool " be taken as Apollo's own. But the worship is for strength, courage, gallantry, generosity—manly will and manly grace and manly tenderness ; and we should probably find on anatomising the female breast, at any age and however married, that the original ideal is still there. At forty, indeed, there is less insistence on beauty, or perhaps an altered conception of it. About that time of life, apparently, the several attributes of strength, grace, will, courage, gallantry, generosity, etc., are placed in a different order of merit ; but none of these qualities can be spared from the woman's ideal of man at any moment of her life beyond seventeen. Goodness of course ; honour and truth of course : they are included in generosity. But power, power, power ! this and all that contributes to it is the adorable thing in man ; but especially command over other men, or over the brutes, or the more obvious forces of nature. Intellectual power of the abstract sort may be deeply respected, but neither inspires love nor secures it. Better the sword-play of Sergeant Troy than all the gifts of Bishop Berkeley and Sir Isaac Newton to boot.

This should make some millions of us unhappy who, with nothing but common cleverness and workaday good-nature to our backs, have no pretension to the heroic in stature, courage, gallantry, magnanimity, or anything else.   But again as to ideals, what is the use of them in a world like this, except as we strive to attain to them ourselves, and invest others with them to the utmost point of allowance ? And, as a matter of fact, this last is a benevolence which men and women do exchange between themselves unfailingly.   In these parts of the earth at any rate, the idealising of the one sex by the other is inborn and inveterate.   It may be absent in a few abortional minds ; it may be destroyed here and there by harrowing experience ; but in the nature of things to be a man is to idealise woman, and to be a woman is to idealise man.   The love of infant girls turns to their fathers, as is seen every day ; from their cradles boys look to their mothers most ; and even when heavy disappointments have broken up the illusions cast about now one and now another heart's delight, the original fund of idealism remains unexhausted.

Take it for all in all, this is the greatest blessing that imagination—finest and best of all faculties— bestows upon mankind.   Considering what we are in the general, it would be a sorry look-out for human happiness but for this mutual idealising of the sexes, which, first exalting the natural attributes of each, magnifies them when they appear in the beloved individual and feigns them when they do not.   Thus was Weaver Bottom clothed upon with ideality, to Titania's admiration ; and though we are not all manifestly beautiful or notoriously heroic, yet we are not all Bottoms either.

That, however, is a figure drawn from **poesy.** Is
a real-life illustration **of this blessed law needed?**
Then let us **take one** from the idealism of beauty,
which no doubt is **as strong** in the one sex as in the
other. In some dim light I catch sight of a face,
and say **to** myself, "What a splendidly beautiful
woman!" I look again, and she seems more beautiful
than before. Again, and now I see that it is the
face of a good-looking **boy;** whereupon the beauty
dwindles and is gone. Or a very plain woman comes
into view. **Gazing on her with** a feeling heart, I
wish the face a man's, **and set about** fancying what
it would be like above **a parson's** gown. Instantly
my feeling **heart** becomes more feeling still. *Now* I
see her ugliness, poor **thing!**

IDOL, IDOLISE

"**My** idol"; "love to idolatry";—extravagant
terms expressive of the passion which separates the
beloved object from the rest **of** mankind, admitting
neither equality, nor likeness, nor comparison.
Language of relatively modern use, and not recom-
mended.

Yet "idolise" **is not so wild** a word as some
others that frequently **occur in** love-letters. It is
literally justified, for example, when employed by
fond women who clothe the men of their hearts with
all the virtues they ever heard of, **and** worship in
them every merit that goodness honours or fashion
approves. That is idolatry in the proper sense of
the word; **and** though there is a vast deal of ex-

travagance in the thing expressed there is no harm
in it, or none that is generally complained of by
idolised persons themselves. " Bore," a vulgarism
which occasionally escapes the lips of husbands
honoured in this way beyond expectation, may be
safely regarded as the disguised utterance of complacency. But since none can forecast the future or
prescribe the course of change, it is but the merest
caution to refrain from exuberance in the language
of endearment and devotion. (See art. " Love-
letters.")

INELIGIBLE

In affairs of the heart, an adjective promoted to
the rank of noun substantive ; and in that relation a
word of fear to well-brought-up young ladies, especially in their first and second seasons. Its use
originated with anxious mothers, who employ it in a
purely arbitrary sense, and one that is often the
exact contrary of its signification to the minds of
their daughters. When this happens there is much
heartbreak in the family and many tears ; and
though in justice to a considerable number of mothers
it must be said that they have no patience with the
heartbreak and are annoyed to petrifaction by the
tears, in justice to others be it known that they
weep a little in secret too, simultaneously with their
daughters.

Some girls, no doubt, are so well brought up, and
so perfectly imbued with a traditional correctitude of
feeling on this subject, that they are never any

trouble.   But it is thought that these young ladies
are comparatively few ; they belong almost entirely
to the upper classes ; and it is difficult for middle-
class mothers to secure by ordinary tuition an acqui-
escence which is drawn from the surrounding atmosphere in long-established and well-endowed families.
This puts middle-class matrons at a disadvantage,
and their girls too.   If at about the time when her
little ones take their first dancing-lessons an anxious
mother could begin to inculcate the necessity of distinguishing between eligibles and ineligibles, shadow-
ing forth the substantial comforts and advantages of
consorting with the one and avoiding the other, the
lesson would be conveyed with the maximum of
success and the minimum of inconvenience.   Imparted early, it would sink unnoted in the infant mind,
as yet unprepared with any perversity of instinct to
combat it.   In brief, there would be all the difference
between the administration of a drug in small and im-
perceptible doses, and the sudden forcing of a full dose
with all the risk of convulsive effects.   But whatever
the mother's anxiety, this she cannot do.   It is
manifestly impossible to discuss with pinafore-girls
the differences between an eligible and an ineligible
parti.

But what, then, is the consequence ?   A mind
that might have been so gently infused with worldly
wisdom as to know not how it came, must have it
imparted so rudely, so coarsely, in such quantities,
and at such a period in the life of the recipient, that
her whole moral nature is in peril of disruption.
Eighteen is not a good age to receive lessons in
calculation and self-barter from maternal lips,

whether the young person be a willing or rebellious auditor.

That is on the one side. On the other, it is a grave truth, which young persons of the gentler sex especially should mark, that the world abounds in illusory and fraudulent eligibility. It is so in all things, from the choice of a religion to the cultivation of a taste. Young ladies should know that they are not always able to judge when the fascinations to which they are constitutionally subject are of the right sparkle or Brummagem impostures; and they should listen when they are told that one Major Dobbin is worth twenty Captain Osbornes. They should also understand that pennilessness is no recommendation, any more than feeble health or the cleverness that is self-consumed. The heart will choose, but the head should ratify; and whenever a woman has reason to believe that she is "all heart"—which is frequently the case—she cannot do wrong in supplying the obvious deficiency from amongst her friends. For her life she should do so whenever her own account to herself of her condition is that she is "completely fascinated."

INFATUATION

A term which is never taken on trust by the wise and gentle, so often is it applied in ignorance, impatience, envy, to a sincere affection well deserved. But that there are infatuates by the thousand we know from as many sad domestic histories. Some are properly so called because they are made fools

of ; others earn the name to the letter by making
fools of themselves. Of the latter the most curious
and pronounced type is the man whose sweetheart
or whose wife is so far from desiring his infatuation
that she would take five gray hairs to have it abated
and ten to get it under control. It may sometimes
amuse as well as sometimes annoy her ; but she does
not understand it, and would think the better of both
his intellects and his manhood were he to bring it
within reason or veil it more carefully from public
view.

Rare only by comparison, this gentleman belongs
to the softest of the soft order of infatuates, of whom
the greater number are undoubtedly assisted to their
unfortunate condition by strategic arts as well as
by involuntary seductions and voluptuosities. And
here, it may be observed, women play the strange
part of destroying their own ideal for their own
pleasure ; for the man who yields up his will to the
dupery of sexual fascination is barely respectable in
the eyes of any woman. She forgives the weakness
in her own sex readily enough ; but that is another
thing.

The soft infatuate comes to a bad end, weakening
down from point to point till he falls into a condition
of social and domestic imbecility. But it may be
said in his favour that he is rarely sensible of his
degraded state at any stage ;—as often as not,
indeed, he wonders to the last why he should have
been selected for so blest a life. But there is
another kind of infatuate who is far less happy.
This is the man who knowingly takes leave of his
wits the moment he comes in sight of his dubious

charmer, resuming them as soon as he is alone again to rage against the spells he can never resist and the folly he will never overcome. His condition is such that were she false before his eyes, laughing at him the while, he would indeed resolve to murder her on the instant, but the next he would have her in his arms. Conscious of an infatuation as low as this, men have been known to burst into tears at the thought of it five miles distant from the siren's abode, and with the roads open in every direction. It is a terrible fate, and usually drives its victims into the drunken and destructive kind of insanity called recklessness.

That women have their infatuations also is well seen. They take less harm, however, from what has been called the soft variety, since it is a grace in women to be yielding, solicitous, obedient. But as to the other kind of fascination, it is hardly doubted that they suffer from it as much as men ; though more in peace of mind and less in degradation of character.

JEALOUSY

LOVE has many torments, but of the whole number there is only one that is quite without a mingling of sweetness. This is jealousy; which is accountable for more agony of mind than any other emotion. All the other serpents that infest love's paradise have a little honey-bag beneath their fangs; jealousy is exceptional in that matter. Like greed, to which it bears a close resemblance, it is one of the original passions, and had a flourishing existence long before love was invented; meaning by that the love which this dictionary serves to expound. All the original passions are violent, and are expressed in ferocity when they rise to their highest: even the one that stood for love when as yet there was no such thing. Jealousy was all wrath till the tender passion of love grew up, and then became more tormenting for the tenderness. Now grief was added to wrath; and such grief that its tears, instead of solacing the heart they spring from, poison it. Nor had jealousy come to its worst

complexion yet. In due time imagination combined
with tenderness to madden jealousy, and keep it
amongst the blackest of human passions. The
jealous man is a prodigy of imagination, excelled by
none but here and there a jealous woman ; and
every new fancy is a new torture. It is characteristic of all the primal emotions that they are
capable of extraordinary increase by brooding.
Pity and some other gentle emotions do indeed rise
and expand when they are encouraged by thinking ;
but with no such volume and force as those that
were the first to move our hearts. The more savage
passions, being dwelt upon, rise to madness at an
awful rate of acceleration ; and since jealousy is most
apt in resorting to imagination for increase of its own
torment, none so quickly mounts to frenzy.

Jealousy takes three forms, or passes into three
phases. The first is fear that some one else will
carry off the loved one by superior attractions or
wicked wiles ; the second, suspicion that his or that
her love has been transferred to another ; the third,
suspicion become certainty. The first may originate
in mere crabbedness of temper. It may arise from
a native blend of envy, suspiciousness, untrustfulness,
which as often inflicts as suffers torture, and therefore deserves small commiseration. But it may have
quite another origin, and is then to be pitied however
fretful it may be. Jealousy at large is a constant
pain in the breast of many a girl whose worst faults
are that she is uncertain of her prettiness, knows herself in the common average for grace of movement
and line of limb, finds herself, in spite of every
resolve to the contrary, without the gift of winning

speech, and is of those (and this is about the worst, perhaps) who are either destitute of the wherewithal to go finely dressed or who "can't be made to look well in anything." Yet with all these disadvantages a young woman may be fond; and, what is more, she may have found a really beautiful lover, or one who has in him the unnamed charm that few women fail to discover and respond to. Then is her case a hard one. Impossible to say—especially if he be a cheery free-spoken man—what jealous fears may breed and wriggle like a knot of Egyptian vipers beneath the unbecoming bodice of her disappointing gown. And what is the cure for these jealousies? The only cure is years!—years alone; which is as much as to say the departure of youth and the slow approach of age.

The second or full-suspicion stage of jealousy is perhaps the most agonising of the three. It is worse than suspicion turned to certainty; for though in that case a storm rises in which all the fiercer passions join with grief to rend the sufferer, yet after a little while love and jealousy perish together in the violence of the tempest. The peace that ensues may be the peace of desolation, but it is peace, and it is often seen that new growths appear in desolated places. The jealousy in which suspicion is never quite confirmed; the jealousy that lingers now on some black proof and then beholds it lighten into doubt; the jealousy that is one day soothed with caresses which seem the merest blandishment of treachery the next —that is the worst of all. And yet there is reason to believe that it is sometimes wantonly inflicted, for the sake of sport.

The only known palliative of jealousy is not to brood upon suspicions. It is that which gives to trifles light as air the weight of perfect confirmation, and thus any little rootless cause of doubt may be nursed into a mighty pain. It is pretty well known that men brood more than women, though that is less a fault than a misfortune. A woman may speak of her jealousies and no harm done. She may even make charms of her griefs, which no man can do. From the hour that he becomes an accepted lover it behoves him to lock his tongue upon his jealousies, unless the outrage be open and palpable ; and then his expostulations must be made in quiet and to an audience strictly limited to the parties concerned. Jealousy is the most natural of passions ; it is known to be often blameless and always a torment ; but however blameless it may be, it is felt as something shameful by him who endures it, and is usually accounted ludicrous by the witnesses of his suffering. The jealous man can neither satisfy himself nor anybody else. If (with cause) his jealousy be great, he is laughably ridiculous ; if little and lightly borne, he is contemptibly ridiculous ; and it is no wonder to himself in either case that he should be so. Strange !—and yet the explanation may be found in any good psychological dictionary.

JILT

Formerly "jillet," says Mr. Skeat : diminutive of "jill," a flirt ; originating in Jill, or Gillian, a woman's name. But jilt is no longer the diminutive, it is rather the superlative of flirt.

Jilts may be compendiously if roughly described as *common* persons. They are always of inferior, usually of low capacity and character ; just as whole tribes and classes are who have yet to share in the general elevation of human nature. Jilts may all be brought under two heads, the trifling and the calculating ; but both are shallow—the one with a transparent, the other with a muddy shallowness. When of the light and trifling kind, their sensibilities are rudimentary, weak, weedy : when of the calculating kind, they are bluntly rudimentary or stunted. This observation applies not to one order of sensibilities alone, but to the whole range in every variety. Thus it has been found that while jilts of all descriptions make a poor, shuffling, prevaricating, swerving sort of wives, they also make bad mothers.

KISS

AN ancient name for what is ever new though ten thousand times repeated. In kindred forms, the word is found in many languages ; and but for some unknown and unimaginable reason would be found in all. With us it is a sacred word, in the sense that, except by the abandoned and insensible, it is never used commonly or lightly. Though framed in the barbaric youth of the world, it is the gentlest whisper of a word in whatever lingo we find it. " Kiss," "coss," " cus," " cys," " cussin,"—it cannot be spoken aloud, nor is it uttered without a consciousness of something shamefaced and yet sweetly reverential. It has been said that the word is never used lightly save by the abandoned and insensible ; but there are exceptions to the statement that heighten its significance. Though profligate women talk very daringly, it has been observed that they have a shyness of this word : probably for the same reason that they do not speak of their mothers.

The strangest thing about kissing is that there are

whole nations and peoples to whom it is quite unknown.   Sad as it may seem, incredible as it may
appear, millions of our fellow-creatures have lived
from infancy to age unkissing and unkissed.   As
babes, as sweethearts (or what answers to sweethearts),
as wives, husbands, fathers, mothers, not one kiss
given and none received.   To be sure, some of these
imperfectly-developed races have a practice of rub-
bing noses, but that is evidently a mere form of
greeting or expression of goodwill, like the shaking
of hands in Great Britain and the United States of
America.   No traveller tells of mothers running to
their babes to snuggle nose upon nose, or of lovers
stealing away into some neighbouring grove, there to
sit and say nothing between one little nose-rub and
another.   But the practice is *near* to kissing—so
near that we can but marvel yet more that the one
should be customary where the other is unknown.
That lovers should miss it !   Surely it was to be
expected, in their case at least, that on so near an
approach lip would be drawn to lip by the same
attraction that resides in the loadstone and other
material things.   The assumption must be that there
is a sensitiveness, a magnetism, of which these peoples
are ignorant as yet, though they may hope to attain
to it as they rise in the scale of humanity.

On this point the etymology of the word to kiss
throws a curious light.   According to the highest
authorities, "kiss" is allied to the Gothic "kustus,"
a proof, a test ; Latin "gustus," a taste.   The Gothic
"kustus" is from "kiusan," to choose.   From which
the etymologist's conclusion is that a kiss is "a taste,
or something choice."

Now inasmuch as to taste means to touch (and that seems to be its root-meaning), there can be no objection to the statement that a kiss is a taste. That it is "something choice" is generally true, no doubt ; but here the most learned of word-students seems to err—doubtless from unfamiliarity with the subject. Supposing him a man of limited and fortunate experience, it would be no disgrace to any student to take a misleading line from the etymology of " kissing " and describe it as " something choice." But that it is not always, and the fact that it is not seems to have been well understood when the word "kiss" was given to saluting with the lips. For the most accurate description of kissing is not " a taste, or something choice," but " a test and a *means* of choice " ; and that is why the word has the name we know it by.

A certain degree of advancement in sensitiveness is needed to make the test perhaps, but it is never safe to assume that you have found your counterpart till you have kissed. This is one of the mysteries of a mysterious matter. Strange to say, you may rejoice in a fond affection, be sure of your choice and delight in it, and at the first kiss find your rapture fall to "temperate" in a moment ; or even sink near to freezing-point. After longing to touch the dear lips with your own as if there could be no greater joy, you may do so with the consequence that next time you would as lief kiss your own glove or the label on the handiest folio on your book-shelves. This is an extreme experience, no doubt, but not extremely rare. A lighter degree of disappointment is by no means uncommon, and it suffices : here, indeed, is the secret of half the unhappy marriages. A young couple run to each other, embrace, kiss, and to both it is as when every petal of a rose falls to the ground in the plucking of it.

To be sure, some inkling of a natural lack of sympathy should be got from the mere clasping of each other's hands; but it often happens that communication that way is dull, or unobserved, or disregarded. It may be so even where there is perfect sympathy, the full revelation of which is withheld till it starts into intermingling flame at the first kiss. The first kiss has been much celebrated, and why but for the reason that this test and means of choice flashes from each to each the ascertainment of profoundly answering and profoundly joyful sympathies where they exist? And though a Shakespeare come again, no one will ever tell the wonders of its rapture when it does reveal and ratify not only a one-ness of the love that a child may feel and an angel acknowledge, but a one-ness of the soul of the body, so to speak: without which there can be no complete and lasting union.

Much more might be said of the philosophy of kissing. As to its practice, a pretty passage from the above-named poet may be quoted—

> When the sweet wind did gently kiss the trees,
> And they did make no noise.

LOVE

A GREAT book might be filled with apt, wise, and
beautiful sayings about love, culled from a thousand
poets, essayists, philosophers, divines. But there are
only two distinct views of it—the poet's and the
physiologist's; and the poet's is the right and
pleasant view, the physiologist's grubbing, muddy,
and as different from the truth as earth from the
flower that grows from it. There is a spiritual or
spiritualist account of the passion which tallies with
the physiologist's without being so smugly base.
According to one prophet of this transcendental
school, " The central force of physical and spiritual
life, sex-love, tears the whole mass of the globe's
habitants as with a destiny of unrest, destroys what
it creates, and bestialises what it transfigures." The
simple and the wise give no heed to these painful
unnecessary underground grubbings; taking love
for what it is in leaf and flower, the delight it yields
in flower and leaf, the wholesome perfume it dispreads
in every chamber of the mind, and the store of good
it hoards there.

And no wise man has said that anybody may judge of love and tell what it is. Whether the surprising fact will or will not be noticed in article "Misogyny" is at present undetermined; but whole nations are unable to give any account of love, except, mayhap, by the mouth of some extraordinary individual who remains silent in deference to public opinion. They are Eastern nations, these; peoples removed from barbarism by thousands of years, and yet in such ignorance of the sentiment which we of the Western world call love that when they hear of it they laugh, as at something too fantastic for manly comprehension. And this, be it known, is the reason why women are despised in those parts; for the women—(can it be believed?—believed, does it signify nothing?)—the women are as ignorant of love as the men.

Now we are not as those Orientals; but neither are we all so far from barbarism—no, not even our most cultivated—as to share the full knowledge of what love can be. So that when one says, "It is simply this," and another, "It is merely that," and a third laughs at fantasies and illusions which he is sure we ought to be ashamed of, they speak from half-developed sensibilities the imperfection of which is a misfortune for themselves. A Turk might know as much of love, or a Fair Circassian. They speak of it as they find it; so it is with them; but to others their conception of love is as much unlike as Pity is to pity in the court of an African king.

"But what, then, of the grievings, the disappointments, the distractions, the torments that we hear of as lurking under every bush in the lover's garden?

Love is delightful when it delights, of course; but how **much pain** goes to the pleasure?" A good deal, no doubt, in a general way. But there are miseries and miseries: all are not equally miserable. **As** it is written in article "Absence," the nature **of love** is such that its pains and its pleasures **are** often in embrace, and of all the many distresses to which it **is exposed there is but** one without some joy in it. **That goes** far for an answer. Tennyson said, and **nothing** that he ever wrote has been more commended **by** quotation, " 'Tis better to have loved and lost **than** never to have loved at all." It is a true saying, **but a mild** one and below the truth. Do we speak of innocent and noble love? Then better **is it to have** loved without possession even **for an hour,** and **not** only without possession but without hope, than never to have loved at all: and he **who** does **not understand that** may be assured that this is **a matter in which he cannot** be fully instructed. Yet he may **learn somewhat** by considering the lover's torments in their educational aspect, and as mere discipline. What is it to love?

> **It is to be** all made of sighs and tears ;
> **It is to be** all made of faith and service ;
> **It is to be** all made of fantasy,
> All made of passion and all made of wishes,
> All adoration, duty, and observance,
> All humbleness, all patience and impatience,
> **All** purity, all trial, all observance.

Why, can a man **be** made **all** this without being the better for it? And what **if he** suffer a little in the process, or even much? What miseries will not travellers encounter, by hunger and thirst, by frost and fire, to view a new country and discover a new butterfly! And when they return with a map in their pockets and a fever in the bones of them, how do they compare with him who has passed into the enchanted land where he may have suffered too, but where new eyes were given to him with which to view the whole earth and its glories; where a paradise was planted in his own breast; and where, being made all of fantasy, all of faith and service, all humbleness, all patience, all impatience, all purity, all trial, all observance, the best and the worst of him were schooled as if by hands divine.

But because this is a passion which, in the nature of things, is most romantic when it seizes upon youth, and because it declines into a matter for consideration as we grow older and wiser, and because its extravagances are better understood than its pregnant dreams and fruitful inspirations— (who remembers or who understands what was weaving in his brain when his brain was a child's?) —love must be laughed at as a youthful folly! When you hear the laugh, think of the seasons. Love is as much a youthful folly as the pushing of the leaf, the unfolding of the bud, the garlanding of every orchard-tree and hedgerow is Spring foolishness. Summer may call it so, remembering the hope, joy, promise that crowded every bough with blossom, reckless of east winds and ignorant that of ten thousand pretty blooms nine must wither and come to naught. Winter may call it so, thinking the same more painfully, and forgetful how much scantier its store would be but for the flush and stir of springtime. Both speak with an acceptable air of prudence, but the all-mother Nature could tell them that they might have wiser thoughts.

If there are madnesses in love, either believe that they are divine or that some disorder has crept in from a neighbouring passion. This is a very common accident ; indeed, there is only one sentiment which in all minds is clear of all faults, and that is pity. Quoting from an older philosopher, Montaigne says that " it is a hard matter for a man to be in love and in his senses at the same time." The saying is acceptable, but not without asking which of his senses the man is out of, and whether they are such as he may expect to take to heaven with him. Even the egotism of love, its exaction of the loved one's every thought and fancy, has its silver side. For love is not one of the original passions ; it came late into the human breast ; till it began there was neither faithfulness nor chastity ; and this egotism has had something to do in the establishment of both those virtues. But it is not lovely ; and when we see what it could reduce Keats to in absence from his commonplace Fanny—when we think of Hazlitt and *his* flame, remembering that these great men were no eccentrics, and that as it was with them so it has been with thousands more—we must needs endure the scoffer humbly. Not but what the deeper wisdom in these things—the poet's wisdom, such as may be found in the writings of Love's Laureate and Prime Philosopher, Coventry Patmore—can give us light and comfort. And maybe a word of prose might be found for the occasion ; but since this is a book of love in particulars, it would be bad architecture to thrust in a general essay. No more of love in the general, then, except to throw down the following useful observations.

The extravagances of love are explained by the fact that it is rarely in a mean. At a word it is in the skies, at a word it is cast down. Its delights transcend all delights, and what more poignant than its little miseries? It is rich and poor in a day; and when it is rich what wealth is there to covet?—when it is bereaved what else is there to lose? This, perhaps, is why a great sage of old pretended in a fable that Love was the child of Plenty (his father) and Poverty (his mother).

In some parts of Russia Jews will carefully impoverish their children, stunt their growth, deform them, that when they grow up they may not be taken for soldiers and sent away from home. Were a man to blind himself in imitation of this dreadful practice, so that he might never be caught in the entanglements of love, he would still be insecure. For the sound of a voice may give him sight again, or troop such rapturous visions in his mind as might as well have entered by his eyes. Therefore he must also block the channels of hearing, would he remain in comfort a free man. And then—why, then a touch may do it. Even the rustling of a gown may send a whisper to the heart that sets it all a-quake, and certainly an accidental meeting of hands will set it all a-flame. How useless, then, does precaution seem, and who shall measure and describe an influence like this?

Connect these last sentences with what is said elsewhere about a "soul of the body," which, like

the unseen star that sometimes figures in astronomical calculations, must be imagined to light us
through these mysteries. An " over-soul " has been
already invented, though we could do very well
without it. Our need is belief in the existence of
its opposite. The grand theme of half the literature
of the world has continents of darkness unless we
may conceive of a soul of the body, a spirit of the
flesh receptive and communicable. And when poets
and romance-writers tell of the mingling of souls
what else can their meaning point to ?

It is to the honour of a passion which is sometimes slighted that " minne " (" minne-singer ") was at
once love, memory, and the thought of the absent.
There could have been no mocking at love under
that name.

In an old Scandinavian ballad a warrior calls his
love "My dearest rest." Three grateful words, and
the most perfect crown of praise that ever woman
wore.

For ordinary domestic purposes it may be useful
to bring love into three descriptions, comparing them
with three different sorts of hearth-fires : the wood-
fire, the sea-coal fire, and the fire of anthracite. And
be it ever remembered that no fire burns bright
when the hearth is encumbered with ashes.

LOVE, FIRST

By their neighbours, who should know them
best, monkeys are believed to have a perfect faculty
of speech, but to be deterred from using it by some

strong precautionary instinct.   Whether as a survival or not, a similar shyness is instinctive in man.
Men talk abundantly—as some say, to conceal their
thoughts ; but certainly with no intention of revealing themselves.   Gales of trivial gossip sweep round
the world every day to one whisper of sincerity from
the depths of self.   Men are even shy of talking in
their own minds about the things that occupy them
most, though what these things are is well known :
love and money.   Does the money-grub ever debate
within himself what money is to him ?   Does he lay
open all his little tricks to get it, or what he would
do for it upon fair temptation ?   Not he.   He keeps
all this below the reach of words, and it is a grace
in him to do so ; though not so great a grace, or so
profitable for salvation, as frank converse with himself would be.

And so it is with the other grand occupation of
this mortal life.   Poets sing of it, novelists make
innumerable fables of it, dramatists array upon the
stage a thousand illustrations of its influence and
power ; and we read, and listen, and say nothing as
to what touches us most nearly.   Sometimes with
reason, oftener quite without, we are ashamed to con
in our secret minds the resemblance of the feigned
agonies, follies, indulgences, raptures of the stage
with those that we ourselves have known.   This is
less true of women than of men, no doubt ; but if
women think and dream more boldly than men,
their thoughts and dreams are far more rarely
discovered.

What love is to the general, therefore, or how
much life is influenced by the best and the worst

that goes under the name, can only be guessed.
But a pretty good guess of some things can be
made, and one of them is this. Could all the men
and women who were ever kept awake o' nights be
brought into the witness-box, they would agree that
there is no love like first-love. There are a few
dissentients from the opinion, but incomplete knowledge explains them away. Some natures are so
unfortunate that first-love will not thrive with them.
It is a poor, a lank, a weedy growth, of little bloom.
Its joys are feeble to disappointment ; and, indeed,
the only use of it seems to be to enrich the ground
it withers on and prepare it for a second love more
homely and robust. This is nothing but a tale of
native poverty, born incompetence ; and yet those
whose history it is are not without an inkling of
what first-love can be. That is what makes them
so uneasy when they learn that they are not their
sweetheart's first love, but the second. No doubt it
is true that jealousy starts up at the thought that he
(or she) ever had a willing mind for any other soul ;
but that is not the whole of the distress. There are
qualms as to whether a second love can be as sincere
as the first ; or if no disturbance arise on that
point (and it is not in sincerity that the one excels
the other as a matter of course), there is a feeling
even in minds that have been baulked of the experience that first-love comes in a freshness and
glory that is repeated never. Nor is it. We read
of love transferred, but that a first-love cannot be ;
which should be some comfort to the deserted maids
who study these pages. Some go so far as to say,
indeed, that the only true love is the first ; but this

is an excess of homage.   Another may be as true,
and even less of a mistake ; a third has been known
to follow and closely resemble the second ; but for
the loved they are not quite the same, and to the
lover they are very different.   First-love is more
than the awakening of a passion ; it is transition to
another state of being.   When it is born the man is
new made.   Were it Nature's plan that his perceptions, his ideals, his aspirations, his whole faculty for
seeing, being, doing, should take form and grow in
sleep, as it were, and then be started into life with
love, there would be no difference in what happens
to the young man when his heart takes fire at a
certain pair of eyes.   But as what does happen is
touched upon in article " Calf-love," it need not be
written here, though this is its proper place.

LOVE-LETTERS

It is often said that love is a selfish passion.
The saying is not a wise one.   It is extremely
superficial, and yet there is some countenance for it.
This appears by many things ; but especially when
we reflect, firstly, on the number of our fellow-
creatures who, being deep in love, are left alone as in a
wilderness ; secondly, on the worthlessness of their
lives in that condition but for the going and coming of
love-letters, like Elijah's ravens turned to doves ; and
thirdly, on the fact that not one of these sufferers
has a tear for the times when nobody could either
write or read a love-letter, except monks and nuns,
who rarely had any use for such things.   That the

world **should go very well** then seems impossible. No one will believe it who, himself in love, has been thirty-six hours out of sight of the beloved.

The truth seems to be that but for certain mitigations the world would *not* have gone on. Except for them that were away at the wars, there were no such absences as there are now. There were no such absences because there were no such distances. The **good** folk of one village looked no farther than the **next for their** sweethearts. **The** larger towns were little worlds apart, and the largest was not so large but that a word or a glance might be hoped for every day. No maze of heartless streets, no mass of strange unsympathetic men crowded the interspace "'twixt lovers parted," baffling the communication of a wish or a sigh. Little need of postmen then. **And** if there **were** no love-letters there were love-songs **to** answer **much the same purpose ;** as was partly the composers' intention, **perhaps. When** Robin heard some stranger maid sing, "**Think** naught but this, I love thee **well,**" he felt with little feigning that it was **his** own sweetheart's voice and was comforted. When Doll Milkmaid sang to herself afield, "Come, kiss me kindly, my heart's a-breaking," or, "Go, naughty man, I do defy thee," her ditty was what thousands and thousands of love-letters are exactly ; which may remain **a** mystery while we thank the **good** gods for the ease and comfort that songs have been, in their time, to the sorrowful generations of **man.**

All love-letters come into one or other of two grand divisions : those that are sent, **and** those that are not sent. Those of the second division outnumber the

others by far.   The Postmaster-General himself has
no idea of the multitude of love-letters confided to
his charge every day ; but what are they to the
number which, when they are written, are forthwith
committed to more ardent agencies of combustion
than themselves ?   The hand aches for the pen, and
no sooner has it than the heart opens as do the
sides of Etna.   We hasten ; we rush on ; we rush
into some excess, or what may seem so though it is
not.   A word escapes that doubt might dwell upon,
or that means too little, or may be thought to mean
too much.   Here we seem too cold, there too ardent,
too pressing, too complaining.   And there must be
no blotting, for a blot is concealment, and what, what,
what was written that must needs be erased so carefully ?   So all must be wrought over again, and most
likely for a seventh time before reluctance puts the
message beyond recall.

But these letters are intended for delivery, and
do get despatched in some shape at last.   It is
not so with others, the best and truest of all (and it
is these that Doll Milkmaid's song so much resembles), which are never meant to be sent.   The
poets sometimes tell us that they must either sing
or die.   It seems not unlikely ; for lovers are poets
too, and we know that they would perish by hundreds
did they not rise from their beds on moonlight nights
to write, and write, and write to the beloved, out of
the too great fulness of their hearts.   Doll would
not have her sweetheart think her heart a-breaking
for a kiss, but it is, and it would go very near
breaking indeed, mayhap, but for the relieving out-
burst in the cry of her song.   And so with many

another maid far above dairies.   Needs must to **pour forth, not to him, but to the shadow** of his **presence,** the love, the fears, **the** pride, the pain, the joy that cannot be contained, and must be spoken all out in the words it chooses for itself in its own passion. The letter ended **to** her heart's relief, she will not read it, but fulfils its destiny by burning it ; as with **the** hand of **a** priestess in those countries where prayers are written on sheets of paper and offered up in flame.

So perishes **the** best of all love-literature : the **least** adulterate, the most eloquent and sincere.   There **is** sincerity enough **in** the love-letters that are sent, and eloquence, and very often abandonment nearly complete ; but they cannot be **like** these.   **Neither** should they be.   The unsent letters should never be **sent, and there should be** little abandonment in those **that are.   It is true** that the eagerness of lovers to hear certain protestations is but one degree less tormenting than the hunger and thirst of castaway mariners ; but what **words** ever satisfied it ? Or what words the most ?   The passionate, the exclamatory, the high-wrought, the heaped ?   None of these ; for suspicion lodges in lovers' ears, and no measure **of** sincerity can insure such cries against doubt.   Love speaks not in syllables but in tones : in tones that make " yes " of " no," and of " a little " immensity.   It has no large language of its own, and never borrows but in a fever.   And though, to be sure, what **we** call " tone " cannot be imparted to written words, **do** we not **know of** a subtle spirit of communication that creeps into the smallest " How-d'-ye-do " message from certain hands ?   It creeps in

unless she is quite resolved to restrain it (and sometimes *though* she is), and it creeps out whether he
will or no.   When affection wanes, dies down, goes
out or goes afield, the recreant's letters may be in all
forms what they were at first, and yet something is
lost from his unchanged words of endearment that
changes them altogether.   The recipient is aware
that spite of " My darling " at the beginning and
" Your devoted " at the end, they are love-letters no
longer ; and she thinks, with tears, of certain timid
little scraps of notes that breathed love everlasting
in every formal line.

That love-letters should be ardent in expression,
assuring, unveiling—what more natural ?   They are
meant to be nothing else, and there is no wrong in that.
Too guarded, they would convey offence.   But quite
unguarded (this is counsel for ladies—the gentlemen
may shift for themselves), they are no' more love-
letters than when written in bright, sweet, generous,
tender sobriety, with permission to a flash here and
there of the flame uncontrollable.   And the risk of
complete abandonment !   That is seen when the
letters come back, as they sometimes will—by exchange.   What shame or what pain to read them
then, whether you betray or are betrayed ; or even
when, the false idol having revealed its worthlessness, vileness, baseness, you scan the adoring words
with which you threw yourself at its feet !

LOVELINESS

The best of women, when they send up their
petitions for their babes unborn, pray that he may
not only be strong but handsome ; or, if it must
needs be a girl, that she may be a beauty.   So
far off is the millennium still that the most excellent
mothers have not got farther than that; and yet
loveliness is known well enough for what it is, and
every Christian woman must feel at heart that to
pray for beauty instead of loveliness is passing the
Cross to kneel in a pagan temple.

Beauty is no more to be despised than thrones
of ivory and gold ; but loveliness is so much better
that it is the perfection of everything by an added
something which is like the living heart of love
itself.   If when the Venus of Milo had all her
limbs she had come to life one fine day, she
might have appeared supremely lovely as she is now
supremely beautiful ; but there is no knowing.   The
perfume of the rose speaks its loveliness but isn't
it ; and were every breath in a rose-bush bestowed
on the finest orchidaceous gaud from Borneo it would
be none the lovelier.   There is no such thing as
a lovely picture, though many are beautiful ; and
the more beautiful a picture is the more it astonishes,
which loveliness (take this for a mark that is egg-
full of meaning) never does.   Some books are
beautiful, only a few are lovely ; and not to withhold
an illustration of what may be an unfamiliar distinction, "Cranford" is lovely.   By whose hand
soever made, no house is lovely till it has been

lived in—no palace though inhabited a thousand years.

Yet the gaud from Borneo is a splendid rarity, and the palace is a palace, unique for miles round about, and there would be an end of the very Fashions if we were to give up the delight of being early in the field with an amazingly beautiful appearance. Beauty will still be prayed for, with a preference for the sort that astonishes most. It is in the bones of us— and especially in the one that was translated from Adam's anatomy—to think it a finer thing to conquer than to win : to wear a glorious rather than a suing grace. Yet let them be content that are lovely, for they have the best of it ; by how much, Mezzofanti could not have told in all his languages together. It is not only possible, it is common to be beautiful on an exchequer empty of goodness, contentment, love received, love bestowed, or anything that can be truly called life ; whereas loveliness includes all these things in the nature of it. Beauty goes in fear, loveliness in none. A breath may destroy the one at its fullest and brightest ; when there is dross beneath it will come through ; and there is nothing in a beautiful face, any more than in a beautiful flower, to slacken Time's effacing fingers or retard them. Lovely looks will alter too, but not so much and not so soon. For there is no dross beneath, or only as much as there should be for alloy ; and all the needed equipment of the lovely nature within—itself everlasting—is a pair of eyes to look out from clearly, and a mouth that speaks for it at all times, even when the lips are silent. There is no holiness of beauty, but there is

a beauty of holiness, and (bringing that last word
down within the limitations of human nature) the
name of it is Loveliness.

This, then, is the dower to pray for, especially as
it can be done with so much more decency than to
pray for beauty, which is as much as to pray for
riches or any other provocative of pride ; and even
though it be accompanied by a faulty nose or a
complexion too opaque, this is the gift of gifts for
man or woman, the happiest within and without,
the most endearing, the most enduring. It is better
to be a book like "Cranford" than a book like
"Vanity Fair." Though roses hang by every
cottage door, and are never put up at auction for
wealthy individuals to bid for, it is better to be
the rose ; and rather than any palace, it is better
to be a house made lovely by what alone can make
it so, the habitation of sweet thoughts and kindly
griefs and kindly joys.

And now says the gentle reader, a little out of
patience, "I understand that I am advised to be
humanly angelic, and to get me a pair of eyes and
a mouth appropriate to my new condition" ; and
this, indeed, is partly intended. But first the intention is another piece of advice : which is, to choose a
sweetheart where there is a good share of loveliness,
and let mere beauty go to them who are willing to
take the risk of it. This is counsel good for man
and woman alike : good ?—imperative ! As to the
rest, see art. "Beauty," concluding lines. There it
is said that loveliness may be somewhat commanded.
No one by taking thought can become beautiful, but
loveliness is of another nature. It must needs have

a vesture of comeliness, to appear; but that it can transfigure. It is even capable of transfiguring downright ugliness—if not with a continuing light, in summer-lightning lambencies; and if the face of the Second Murderer changed to something far more heavenly the instant he began to pity the Babes in the Wood, as we know it did, how can it be doubted that any pretty girl may take on lovely looks for a permanence with the habitual cherishing of a sweet will and none but considerate and kindly thoughts? And that can be *done*. The moralists and the d—l together have been infinitely successful in making it appear that only in evil things does habit become second nature. This is monstrous in the moralists; a hindrance to happiness, a limitation of loveliness, costing a vain expenditure of millions of money in washes, cosmetics, and other toilet apparatus alone.

LOVE-MAKING

It would be pedantic to insist that there can be no such thing as love-*making*, and what is worse, the pedantry would go astray into shallow waters. The argument that love cannot be made is closely shaved by the reply that both man and woman can be made to love. An affection so raised may lack the freshness of instant spontaneity; it may grow rather nearer to the ground, and harbour fewer of the soaring joys which at heaven's gate sing; but it is known to many as the true passion—sound, sweet, and lasting. And if we must needs be precise, what of the word "make" and its significances? Nowadays it means to form, frame, compose, and nothing different; but of old its meaning was less confined. "Match" and "mate" are stems from the same root; and both match and mate are words for comrade and companion. Down goes the glove, then, on behalf of the contention that love-making is love-mating; and for the first lance this shall serve—that in old songs and ballads "his make" stands for his mated love. "Mate" had not then superseded "make" as English for companion.

True, when we speak of love-making—("he made love to her at once," "they are love-making in the garden")—love-mating is not quite what we mean. That is what it *is*, but, following the only sense of "make" which is now acknowledged, making in some form is what we intend. And not without justification. Say that the two young people in the garden are making their love known to each other—which precisely states the fact—and love-making is the same thing with an ellipsis. Mr. Pedant will observe that they make love *to* each other, and that it is generally done in doing nothing. It is enough to go apart and be alone together. For all that they actually say they might as well be in the company of their friends half the time—indeed, nearly all; and yet at most stages of their experience nothing makes them more uneasy than to be together in the presence of others. This is generally accounted for by an embarrassing sense of shame peculiar to their situation. They would explain it themselves by that feeling, and no doubt it exists and is very disturbing. But below it lies another sensation, which

tells of baffled seekings and communications of
spirit between the two ; the interception of which
by aunt's presence, by uncle's presence, or even the
boy Tom's, is a very mystery of pain.   Alone
together, alien eyes withdrawn, nobody by, these
baffled seekings and communications flow sweetly
on without need of a word.   Each is sensible that
now the current is more and now less full ; now it
runs on in a tenor of gaiety, now in a bass of tenderness that must not long be dwelt upon ; and still
there is no need of a word.   No need, and yet
there may be talking, and the talking may be
about anything as long as it is trivial : the more
trivial it is the better it serves to chaperon the
speaking silences which are the real conversation.
(As to that matter, however, see article " Courtship.")
Nor is there any downright necessity for interchange
of looks.   Stolen glances there will be at every
minute—glances stolen by each when the other's
face is turned away ; but these are the common
food of love, and there is no communication of
feeling by them.   It is different, of course, when
eyes meet eyes with interchanging looks, but such
encounters are rare.   They are almost avoided.
Only now and then are they dared, the clash and
dazzle of meaning being so much.   Besides, when
they happen they are merely accidental to the conversation ; an addition, a gratuity, but not really
needed to sustain it.   For the silent colloquies that
lovers know are never so close, so deep, so confiding,
as when dusk falls on the love-making, and when it
is an added pleasure not to see each other clearly.

   There are more explicit passages in love-making,

and some more ardent ; but in Christian **countries**
its general course is as **thus** described ; or rather,
in countries where the passion has been purged of
grossness and becomes pure flame. Elsewhere love-
making seems to be carried on very much by music
and murder—a good **deal of the** last **or a** little of
both. The effect **of** music on the passions is not to
be measured **by beauty** of melody or cultivation of
ear. In half-barbarous lands **a** moaning chant, a
twanging of the guitar, will raise storms and languishings unsurpassed in **a** German beer-garden : and
then would a man enslave the fair, let him sally
forth and stab another man for love of her. In
more savage countries hearts are **won** in simpler
fashion, though much the same. **The** lover goes
head-hunting, and on his return silently but tenderly
leads his beloved to view his trophies in a basket.
We have amongst ourselves a survival **from** similar
kinds of love-making in a chastened preference for
military men. A **lower form of** the same feeling is
found in commercial circles, where commerce is
recognised as battle, warfare ; and it is not without
reward of smiles that Brown and Jones go to evening
parties with the scalps of Smith, Robinson, and Son
peeping from their waistcoats. But this is hardly
love.

LOVE-PLEDGES

More often called love-gifts, but without loss of
the meaning of " pledge," which is not only **gift** but
security, earnest, token **of** promise. A love-gift

is all these things.   Just as sweethearting is no
complete delight without love-letters, so there is no
complete surety without love-gifts.   Never has it
been otherwise.   It has always been thought that
there must be a gift, though it were no more than a
rush-ring.

Jewels were never unacceptable, probably ; but it
would seem that in ancient times love looked not
for gold in token of promise, and was rarely offered
it ; unless it were the half of a broken coin.   With
some the gift might be a kirtle ; with others, of
more gentility, a kerchief to lie in the bosom ;—and
yet the kirtle seems better, as witness Desdemona's
case.   Many poor ladies have been undone by the
gift of a handkerchief.   Scarves seem to have been
a more noble gift—gift from Her to Him in the
days of chivalry, and full of meaning as such.   Her
scarf was an accepted livery, and therefore twice a
bond : a bond of service and a bond of love.   Even
down to these times scarves are common insignia of
service and honour both.   This is their significance
on the breasts of aldermen.   Ribbons of the Order
of the Garter, the Golden Fleece, and the like, are
scarves arrived at the highest distinction ; and if it be
true, as the story is, that they are direct descendants
and representatives of the rope that soldiers used to
carry athwart their breasts to bind captives with,
how perfect a love-token was the scarf — given,
accepted, proudly worn and proudly seen !   After
the scarf, gloves, which again was good ; for what
does the glove represent but the hand, and the hand
the heart ?   Gloves are not chosen as love-gifts
nowadays.   Like handkerchiefs, a tenderness for

which lingered long in the navy, they have cheapened ; but when a man would steal from the lass he loves some token he dare not ask for, what does he covet most but her glove, her handkerchief, or a ribbon from her breast ? And to the last, what are more cherished than these trifles? Here again we see the wisdom of our ancestors. Or will it be said that by the time we come to rings and watches and bracelets we are no longer in the glamour that made the ribbon so precious, and that clings about it unceasingly ?

The arts of reading and writing have dwindled the significance of love-gifts. Once they stood for love-letters as well as love-gifts. They alone spoke for the absent or the dead ; as indeed they do still, with what poor solace there is in them. But it is to his or to her letters now that Absence and Bereavement turn. Yet there must be no misprising of love-gifts. They are a need, a grace, a propriety ; and whatever the first may be, it should be supplemented at the earliest convenience by a copy of that useful book, " The Lover's Lexicon," with a votive kiss on the " Constancy " page.

LOVERS' QUARRELS

Quarrel is a word of strong significance. Both in print and on the lips it suggests the complicated noises of two dogs in wrath with each other ; a resemblance worth remembering. Amongst the vulgar quarrel is called by various other names, of which one is " breeze." " Breeze " originally meant a cold wind, a bitter and a nipping wind ; but that signification having quite died out, it may be said with a good conscience that though " breeze " cannot possibly be substituted for the other word in the lover's vocabulary, lovers' quarrels are mostly like a breeze and should never be like anything else.

In heaven the atmosphere is such that its eternal calmness is an eternal joy ; but on earth it is otherwise. The atmosphere of our feverish lives is not so pure but that it will stagnate, and our natures are so imperfect that without movement, change, agitation, excitement, our spirits become turbid or evaporate to the lees. That is the way with most of us in the heyday of life ; and thus it is that even the rapturous calm of requited love may last too long in shallow minds, which will then be all the better for a breeze. They feel this themselves ; and upon any little doubt or disturbance will raise a quarrel, just as we may suppose Earth might if for years it had not seen the splendour of its own brightness and sweetness after a storm. Quarrels of this kind are veritable breezes in their effect ; and if they are not often repeated, if the blest moment of reconciliation is kept in view from the outset, they may be regarded as entirely beneficial. Incidentally, too, they are a sort of discipline, a kind of training for the rubs of married life : and to know how a man or a maid can love is not to know what either may be in anger. Besides, few young women can be satisfied that they have their rights without a little of the romance of love ; and no such romance is complete unless chequered by scenes of misunderstanding, coldness, tears, despair. And again, there is reason to believe that lovers' quarrels sometimes derive by obscure channels from that rage of love which Mr. Swinburne has celebrated—the literal desire to bite, the fury that threatens through close-set teeth to "eat you up." In that case the moment of reconciliation is never far off; but as to the rest, it is well to have a care.

True, it is not in novels only that women look "more beautiful than ever" when roused, and men more magnificent. But while in novels the number of persons so happily endowed is three out of four, in real life the proportion is one in six hundred. The other five hundred and ninety-nine look less beautiful than before, some ugly, and a few (without knowing it, of course) *shocking*. The looking-glass is nothing to go by, and here is proof of it. A woman who is really more beautiful in anger can never be sure of keeping it up. Superb for the first five minutes she may be, and then—flash!—a very different thing for a good half of the sixth. Among other pictures that dwell in fond hearts till they cease to beat, a portrait photographed in such a flash might often be found; but veiled, of course, like wicked or horrible pictures in public galleries.

Now when these things are considered, the hazard of entering upon lovers' quarrels for the romance or the excitement of it is evident enough; but since anger speaks by words as well as looks, there is another danger quite as great. In a moment some word may escape which the utterer would give years of life to recall, knowing recall to be impossible and that the wound of the word can never be healed. Who would carelessly run that risk,

however distant it may seem? When Coleridge
wrote, "To be wroth with one we love doth work
like madness in the brain," he did not speak of a
madness of remorse after the gust had passed,
though something of the kind steals into his meaning. He meant that, loosed against one we love, wrath
sweeps into madness with dreadful facility; and that
it often does. Whether Nature intends this swift
excess to be a warning, or whatever the mystery may
be, there it is, to the painful knowledge of many a
one. To be sure, lovers have so much respect for
love itself that they rarely quarrel bitterly, whatever
the provocation. Only the rudest minds are capable
of reviling and injury, even when the love is gone;
and that even such as these are capable of the sacri-
lege is the most dreadful revelation of the divorce
courts — hurting the mind more than the worst
infidelity.

It is agreed, then, that lovers' quarrels are neither
safe nor respectable when they are not of the nature
of a breeze—lively, fresh, re-animating; further, that
they are tolerable as satisfying the demand for a
little romance; and that it behoves every sincere and
tender heart to have a care lest the breeze should
rise to a storm and much that is precious be carried
away.

Item. — The association of "quarrel" with
"querulous," which means "full of complaints," may
be usefully remembered.

Item.—In a quarrel, beware above all things of
word or look that signifies disdain.

LOVE-TOKENS

" Love-tokens " is the common name for gifts bestowed in token of love ; but what is meant here are the signs that betoken love—the marks and indications by which the existence of the passion and its variations may be discovered.

Some writers are of opinion that either man or maid may fall in love without knowing it. In their novels, those handbooks to the heart, they often describe cases in which the heroine has found the object of a first and last devotion, but not to her knowledge. That she has undergone some mysterious change is not concealed from her. She is conscious of a feverishness, a restlessness, a readiness to flush and tremble at the sound of a footfall or the mention of a name ; but not till she asks herself in some fortunate moment, " Is this love ? " does she know what has happened. Young men, it seems, are less often ignorant of what has befallen them ; which adds to the difficulty of believing that a passion that enters the heart by eye and ear should be mistaken for a cold, or that the choice of eye and ear can be admitted unawares. For it is well known that young men are more insensible to the approach of love than young women,—have less thought of it and a duller apprehension.

Yet the novelists may be right ; and if so, behold another argument for establishing at Newnham and Girton a professorship of the Tender Emotions. At various stages in the course of our reading we have seen how useful such a chair would be at either college ; while as for its attractions, who can doubt them ? The fear is, perhaps, that the professor's lectures would be too attractive, drawing attention away too long and too far from severer studies. It might be so. But though his themes are too capable of personal application, though they invite to reveries which are neither scholastic nor comprehensive of the human race, they can be upheld as strictly philosophical. All have a place in the science of mind ; and it is but an added advantage if the study of them does the student's heart good as well as her head.

Besides, are not these themes discussed already ? Is it supposed to be all Greek and mathematics with the young ladies at Girton ? What ! in the college walks ?—in the soft evening hours ? No : and surely it were far better if their innocent way-ward speculations were instructed in a proper course. The Ethics of Disdain ; the Qualities of Fascination ; the Function of Habitude ; the Distinctions of Loveliness ; these and others like them are entirely psychological subjects, and, treated as such by the learned and gentle lecturer, would combine all the merits of the best of science and the best of sermons. They would interest, they would enlighten, they would warn and edify ; and they would serve in situations of momentous import where mathematics are at fault and Greek of small avail. The least of the student's advantages would be that she would bring a more alert percipience to the signs and presages of love, whether in herself or another ; and it is impossible to say how much of mutual happiness (which does not mean happiness

shared, but a much better thing, happiness interchanged—mine and thine, and thine for mine, and
mine in thine)—it is impossible to tell how much
of mutual happiness has been lost in this world for
want of a right understanding of the signs of love.
Should Julia, unobservant of the times and occasions
when they come on, mistake the flutterings in her
breast too long; if week after week it never occurs
to her to ask, " Is this love ? " when her sight with-
draws from everything about her for hours at a
stretch, when her feet know not that they touch the
ground, when the red rose burns upon her cheek
at night and the white lies dead there in the
morning—she may be carried off to Madeira before
she knows what the matter is, and so lose sight of
him for ever more.

This the delicate impartations of the Sensibilities
Lecturer would prevent ; while other and more
probable dangers would be diminished. If a young
woman can mistake the signs of love in herself, how
great the likelihood that she will misunderstand
them in the young man ! This is a much more
serious matter. Should she merely overlook his
symptoms, she may be thought cold and heartless
all too prematurely. Should she detect and yet
misunderstand them it may be altogether worse ;
for though the outward manifestations of love differ
in lads of different temperament, they are open to
unfortunate misconstruction, for the most part.
How shall perfect innocence distinguish between the
sheepishness of sheepishness and the sheepishness of
adolescent passion ? If the young man have a
foolish look and a stammering tongue, why must

she know that he is not a fool and that she is his only physician? When in the company of other young men—as it might be at a picnic or a ball—she sees him haggard, morose, holding himself aloof in gloomy isolation, what is to tell her that his mood is explained by a particular tenderness and not by habitual ill-humour? There is a light of nature that makes these things clear, no doubt, but not, according to the books, for everybody in every clime. Though in Juliet's country a Professor of the Tender Emotions would have much to expound, he would find no one in love for ten minutes who had yet to find it out, or who needed instruction to detect a lover at first sight. But we are not Italians. Here there is more dulness; for the thrice-blessed reason that the child lives longer in the woman.

One point would particularly engage the professor's attention when discoursing of love-tokens. It would be for him to inquire whether the quality of A's affection, the stability of B's, may be inferred from the symptoms disclosed. This is a most interesting matter for discussion, and entirely scientific. Temperament—which belongs to a distinct branch of physiologico-psychological study—has to be considered in every case. For each variety of young gentleman—the fair, the dark, the gay, the pensive, the studious, the soldierly, the commercial—has its own way of "taking on." Its love-looks wear a difference, and may glow with more or less of freedom and challenge as compared with the fund of affection within. The same scale must not be applied to the languishings or the audacities of

one and of another : the least may express the
most. In fine, the same signs in the lymphatic
young man, the sanguine young man, the bilious
young man may have different meanings or a very
different measure of significance. These variations
the professor would point out, assisted by typical
portraits from the hands of competent artists. He
would then take Mind into account, with special
reference to geniuses ; showing why none but the
most patient, most hardy, most humble-minded of
young women should listen to the heavenly addresses of these gentlemen. Lastly, he would warn
his class that after a certain age men acquire the
art of concealing or controlling their emotions.
They fall in love as thoroughly as heart can desire ;
but though the signs and tokens of their passion
are generally more agreeable than in the green
days of youth, they are less spontaneous and less
revealing.

MARRIAGE

MARRIAGE would be much less debated, a vast deal
of satire and many biting pleasantries against it
would be spared, but for one stupendous oversight.
There is enough discretion in the world to supply a
general understanding that we are not all born for
the studio, or to shine at harmonic meetings, or to
govern a parish, or even to govern ourselves as a
beginning for other undertakings. But marriage !—
we are all born with every fitness for that, it seems ;
and if it turn out that we are unhappy in the practice of it, why then marriage is a folly and a snare.
This is as if Gandish's failures were at liberty to
satirise the Fine Arts as a delusion.

The truth is that though marriage is wonderful
good discipline for many kinds of jades and rogues,
though many weaklings have been saved by it from
sinking and much indifferent honesty established in
tolerable courses, nor rogues, nor jades, nor fools are
worthy of marriage ; and how should they be, since
it is the sweetest and noblest companionship that man

can find ?   But because the number of such persons,
male and female, is extravagantly great, and because
marriage finds them out (small concealment for
character at the domestic hearth), and because grief
and resentment creep in upon discovery, to kill joy
and make division—*of course* there are many unhappy marriages.   Many ? — they abound beyond
all knowledge and suspicion.   Some are hidden by
generosity; some by pride, shame, pity ; and much of
bitter disappointment is put away for good and all
under cradles.   But if there be more unhappiness
in marriage than comes to light, so there is more
mending of misery in marriage by marriage itself.   For
illustration of this saying, see article " Habitude," and
mark what is sometimes confided to other sufferers
by married folk.   They can tell you that no sooner
were they housed than they were confounded by the
discovery of faults and incompatibilities — (which
surely were their own, and not to be laid upon
Marriage)—giving up all hope of happiness, and
even of complacency, almost from the wedding day.
But they were married, and lived on together ; and,
by the kindly virtue of that state, now one fault was
softened on this side, and now another gave way
upon that ; shame smoothed away a rudeness here,
there a naughty habit was expelled by gratitude for
forbearance ; kindness flowed in where rancour was
suppressed ; the reward of graciousness found them
out, bringing them day by day to a nearer con-
cinnity ; and so before long marriage made them
happy by civilising them.   But this was because
they were corrigible.   This was because they could
be mended, and the man was a man and the woman

a woman. With incorrigible hardness, selfishness, meanness, faithlessness, cruelty, marriage can do nothing except to couple two such natures out of harm's way—putting those who cannot live with vileness beyond risk of their companionship. And vileness to vileness seems to prosper well enough— often blending in an entire affection that asks no more of love.

And if the number of miserable marriages cannot be told, what of the happy ones? So many skeletons in closets, no doubt, but how many cupids behind curtains? If wretchedness will feign contentment, is joy to blab? It is the one joy that never blabs. Contentment is the whole of its pretension too; but just as the skeletons come forth to feast with Wretchedness when it dines at home, so when the doors are shut upon a happy pair, who is to tell of the little loves that come trooping out from their hiding-places at the click of the closing latch? They are secrets; secrets kept darker than the skeletons can be, and harbouring in thrice as many homes. Happy marriages are plentiful enough, they are equally shared all over the land, and nothing brings so much felicity. Once well matched and mated, conditions of life are neither here nor there if you are born into them and they are short of absolute penury. A little house and little in it; a great house full of fine things; in each a man and a woman " born for each other "—mates, comrades, lovers; and two pairs of human beings equally happy. If the rich home were bereaved, what but the poor one would be envied? When the poor one loses that which made it bright, what on earth can repair the loss? Happy marriages bring all who are blest by them into a garland of equality.

The happiest, be it noted, are those in which man and wife are chums. That is the estate to aim at. To be companions is not enough: an appreciable distance may be spied between two in companionship. To be mates and comrades is good —nothing better but one thing: to be chums. Chumminess —— (delightful word, and quite legitimate)—chumminess may be unattainable by persons marrying late, but not by frank and joyous youth; and these are some of the virtues of chumminess: It is to love what rain and warmth are to mustard and cress; it brings bosom to bosom with all the deep comfort of a hareskin waistcoat-piece in winter; it expels dubieties, disperses moodiness, imports cheeriness, confirms trust, inspires jollity, keeps bright the eye, light the heart, and prolongs youth in wonderful measure. It makes marriage perfect; as the deadliest of unions is union with some distant, cold, and polished person with the ugly name Prig.

But let no one despise imperfect happiness in marriage: take it, rejoice in it, what there is of it cannot be matched. The best of reasons can be offered for this counsel, as that half a loaf is better than no bread; and (to mount higher) that complete converse for mankind is unattainable out of the communion of a fairly happy marriage. Men talk with each other; women talk with each other; and men with women in the ordinary way of conversation. But in each case and all, much remains unsaid for want of the right listener. There are

spaces in the minds of both men and women which,
though they are not as desert as the moon, yield no
more sound till the born - for - each - other meet in
the sure confidences of marriage. A broad range
of converse and communication opens then which
otherwise is never entered on.

MARIAGE DE CONVENANCE

Since there is no English for this kind of
marriage, it is generally assumed to be foreign
altogether, and never to have found footing or
favour on wholesome English ground. But that is
a popular error. It is only fair to the French to
acknowledge that marriages *de convenance* were as
common as blackberries with us, and more unblush-
ing, for hundreds and hundreds of years. Indeed,
they are still common enough under the name of
Good Matches; nor can that designation be much
objected to, since no one understands the word
"match" in its proper sense, which imports equality
in companionship, fitness, right mating. But, speaking generally, there seems to have always been with
us an understanding that the parties should be
content with each other personally, upon an ex-
amining introduction. And so now, photographic
portraits are invariably exchanged in the conduct of
marriage-negotiations by matrimonial agencies, and
no Good Match is ever made public till it can be
said without contradiction that "they are devoted
to each other." In short, we are so far superior
to the *mariage de convenance* that (except in the

case of aged and infirm persons) marriage with no
pretence of love would be thought both hazardous
and indecent.   But again to do the French justice,
they view the matter with different eyes.   A maid,
they think, should not have the indecency to love
any man till after she is married to him ; and no
girl of France with true French sensibilities would
confess to an opposite opinion.   Young French
women have been known to weep with shame at the
rumour that they married for love, begging their
friends to lose no opportunity of contradicting so
calumnious a report.

It appears, then, that marriages *de convenance* are
one thing to the French, another to ourselves.
Each people brings to the question a sense of
outrage, but a contrary sense.   Now, considering the
delicacy of the subject, the explanation of that must
lie deep in character ; from which the lesson is that
our own dear daughters should be indulged as much
as may be with their heart's choice, according to
national predilections ; leaving our neighbours to
make the best of their logical peculiarities.

MEETING

That sensitive minds have more both of pleasure
and pain than dull ones is manifest ; but whether the
pleasure outweighs the pain, or the pain the pleasure,
can never be decided.   The healthier wisdom has it
that the advantage is with pleasure ; and since it is
certainly true that while the lover's joys are above
compare, there is some infusion of pleasure in his

worst of torments, we may suppose his super-sensitiveness not dissatisfied. Nor is it, in the general. And yet, contented as they are with fortune, all fond lovers forget the delights of meeting in the pain of parting—dwelling so little on the one in comparison with the other that it might be imputed to them for ingratitude but for one excuse. They only follow other folk in taking their permitted joys for rights and the withdrawal of them for wrongs.

But could they see themselves as the sympathetic eye beholds them when they meet and when they part, they would have more delight in the delight if no less sorrow in the sadness. As it is, when they meet they only see each other. The *ensemble* is lost to them. It is a pretty country lane and a summer morning ; or it is a bright still winter day, snow sparkling all along the boughs overhead, and lying here and there in the green tufts of the banks and the drift of fallen leaves. From one end of the lane the young man swings along, a full orchestra beneath his waistcoat making music to the beat of his heels on the frosty ground. She'll come—he knows she will, or there'd be a different tune ; and coming she is from the other end of the lane. *She* may not swing along—she must go sedately ; the consequence of which is that at every step her feet lift as if winged and then fall with a check, such as you may fancy Venus's doves experience at starting the divinity's car with the divinity's own impatience. She, too, has been conscious all the morning of rejoicing symphonies within—(stringed instruments, no drums and trumpets here)—but it has been

muted music with her for the last ten minutes ; and
her breast is a heaven of still expectancy by the
time he rounds a corner of the lane and they descry
each other.   That is the beginning of the meeting.
At first they advance at a quicker pace, being drawn
to it without consideration or consciousness ; and then
more slowly than before, for the pleasure of the view.
And the view ?   The view is straight ahead for
both, in opposite directions.   Each sees half of it.
The one her man of men—a picture of eagerness
clothed in tenderness from head to foot.   The other,
the whole world of women in a sweet epitome, giving herself to him anew by the beaming of her eyes,
the flush upon her cheeks, the smile, half raillery
and half caress, about her parted mouth.   A pretty
sight for either, on account of the particular applications and interpretations that each makes of his or
her half of it ; and as beautiful as any on earth for
one who (as it might be some ancient lexicographer
seeking matter for his pages) looks upon both, views
the whole scene, and beholds what they are too
confused to see.

And this is but an instance of ten thousand.   We
need not insist—love does not—upon country lanes
and summer morns or sparkling winter days.   The
only stipulation is for open air, since we must not
mention churches and the fortuity of the same pew.
A few yards of seashore will do, blow high, blow
low, so long as there is cover from the weather ; or
half an acre of wood ; or a bit of common (nothing
better); or the street itself on a Sunday morning,
when the windows all look inward and there are
very few folk about.   But for this dispensation, sad

would it be for how many thousand pairs of sweethearts in London alone! If we wish to make a
quantitative estimate of the joy there is in lovers
meeting, we must think of the multitudes of pretty
girls with sweethearts in the same case with him
who sang—

> Of all the days that are in the week,
>   I dearly love but one day ;
> And that's the one that comes between
>   The Saturday and Monday.

The weariful Monday, morrow of parting, uptake of
a whole week of absence ; the glad Saturday, with
only one night of sleep before we open our eyes and
it is Sunday again, and there is the pretty new frock
spread out on the chair, and the ribbons to match,
and the gloves in white paper, all ready, as if it were
a wedding-day. The sun shining through the
windows with the gentle radiance that it seems to
have nowhen else, she lies and thinks for awhile in a
mind to match ; and then out of bed at the spring
of a thought more blithe and stirring. Before the
church-bells begin to ring she is forth to meet him,
the whole body of her a song ; and though he is
but a carpenter lad, and she a milliner lass, and the
trysting-place a long solemn street, the meeting is
the same as that in the country lane, with only the
scene for difference.

Multiply by the thousand for every hour of every
waking day, and it will be seen that if love has
sorrows of which parting is reckoned among the
worst, there is a set-off in the joy of meeting which
neither lovers nor their bards take sufficient account

of.   One meeting, however, is never forgotten.
Songs innumerable have been set to the refrain,
" When first we met."   Every maid in her teens
has some confused presage of that meeting deep in
her bosom, and every old dame a minute remembrance.   It was thus and thus.   On a Tuesday.   A
late day in September ; and she was in her father's
garden gathering apples that had fallen in the night,
with her gown tucked up to drop them into ; and
he came along the path holding his hat on, for it
was still gusty ; and she being surprised, stood up
suddenly, and the apples fell out at a corner of her
gown, which was a Swiss cambric, sprigged ; and
then he stopped and looked, and then he went on
to the house without saying anything, and then, and
then———

MISOGAMY : MISOGYNY

There is an obvious convenience in taking both
these subjects into one article ; for though it is quite
possible to be a misogamist without hating women,
the misogynist must needs hate marriage as other
perturbed spirits holy water.

Misogynists, when genuine, are more often born
than made ; and the born misogynist is so strange
a freak of nature that he might be expected to carry
on the surface of him every mark of miscreation.
That albinos should be white-haired and pink-eyed
for no deeper cause than the lack of a little pigment
in the skin, while misogynists are able to go about
unremarked, except for a certain sourness of com-

plexion, is another proof of the incommensurate relation of things. But for their own declarations, it could not be said that women are ever men-haters, in the sense that some men are women-haters. They know the feeling, but not as one which it is impossible to get rid of. Nothing corresponding to misogyny is *born* in woman, though it may be implanted there by man's unkindness. The dictionaries have no name for such a thing.

That there are female misogamists or marriage-haters can hardly be doubted, though the evidence of their existence is mostly word of mouth. This statement applies to a vast deal of written testimony; for the letters of young ladies to each other are essentially oral. They are not from the pen but from the lips ; and when these letters are examined under the light of the writer's history, it is generally found that protestations of never, never, never marrying were little cries of alarm at the appearance of some young gentleman in the distance with a bristling "Your love or your life!" look about him. And most misogamists of the other sex are anything but desperadoes. Their hatred of marriage rests on the mildest considerations. They like their tobacco. There is no cold beef to be compared with the cold beef on a club-room sideboard. They have only three hundred a year and a profession. Jones's wife ran away last week, and Robinson's is not unlikely to do the same before the year is out. So runs the knightly tale. Mr. Stevenson put all in a sentence when he said, writing of this subject, " We are more afraid of life than our ancestors "; and yet he would have been more explicit had he gone on to say, " and we are less confident in the homage, the management and mastery of women." Cowardice is the right name for half the prevalent shrinking from marriage: cowardice in face of life, and that other miserable fearsomeness.

When misogamy proceeds from a born hatred of woman it is much less deplorable. In that case, it is foredoomed and imperative. The born misogynist can no more marry than some mysteriously sensitive persons can exist in the same room with a cat. Not that he would tolerate for a moment any account of himself which implied a weakness or a want. It is so ordained that every hunchback ranks himself with the most formidable of men ; as may be seen by his haughty bearing in presence of the fair. The misogynist, more unhappy, is more scornful still. There is a fierceness of superiority about him which calls up the figure of some Hebrew prophet of wrath, who, having said his say in vain, goes off to be silent in the wilderness. To show that he is not a woman-hater for want of human affections, he praises dogs and has one ever about him ; but who that views his crabbed and seeking visage as he fondles the animal, sees with a pitying heart that the affectation has no success. It is apparent on every side, indeed, that these unfortunates come into the world with some lesion of sensibility, some strange destitution of feeling, which for all their ferocious pride in it makes them unhappy. A cheerful misogynist has never yet been seen in these latitudes. They have a way of laughing sometimes, but their own mothers would say that even in their cradles they never smiled. And it is hard to believe them unaware of

the something denied ; for the mark of the misogynist is an inward-seeking look, very miserable
and uncontent.

MISUNDERSTANDINGS

Young lovers, like young turkeys, are peculiarly
subject to infantile disorders, which may be set
down in both cases to an inner tropical temperament,
at variance with all that is rayless and cold.   Both
require a warm and cosseting diet, and it is of the
first importance that the one should be guarded from
chills and the other from misunderstandings.

These are the lover's most insidious assailants.
They find entrance at every point of his changed
nature, and having entered in, they stir up such
jealous tumults in his breast—affection battling with
affection, feeling with feeling—that nothing can be
compared with them except England at the time of the
Wars of the Roses. To be in love is to be transformed
into a monster of apprehension, with six pairs of
eyes for all that the beloved may do, and six pairs
of ears for all that she may say ; each pair telling its
own story to the fears, the prides, and jealousies
within.   And these having grown into an extreme of
sensibility, they interpret what they are told with an
amazing predilection for the least delightful meanings.
The beloved one is equally alert, equally studious of
word and deed under the same magnifying glasses ;
and thus misunderstandings fetched from the re-
motest bounds of reason are added to the number
of those that indifference itself might stumble into.

And then the brooding that ensues !—the moodiness, the constrained looks, the wintry silences which are so likely to be themselves misunderstood with aggravated consequences. And now another phenomenon appears. Miles of distance palpable stretch in between two young people who are only thirty-six inches apart according to the standard yard at Westminster; and when in this state of things moments of Arctic frost are felt amidst the silences, the crisis has come. If neither the one nor the other will call across that bleak interspace, and call with love and tears, a long good-bye awaits them. But that is what usually happens. There is a look, a cry, the distance between the two shrinks in a moment to fractions of an inch by any measure, and some black doubt is known for a misunderstanding that would be quite ridiculous were it not so beautiful in discovery.

And now the cry is " O my dear, why didn't you speak ?"—a pretty reproach but unavailing. In all likelihood there will be another little misunderstanding next week. For, truth to tell, love is not only a delicate but a moody passion, especially in young hearts. Unsatisfied with cloudless felicities, it must needs have secret doubts to set them off. When joy is daily bread grief becomes a luxury. And the prideful sensitiveness which is so quick in taking injury is as naturally slow to ask for healing. Besides, it is often quite impossible to put question or complaint into words. The bat's cry is so shrill and small that it is inaudible to human ears, even when it speaks of the sharpest pain. The anguish that a lover six feet high will draw from an accidental

word is more exquisite than any mouse can feel ;
and yet when he thinks of telling it, and puts together
a few words for the purpose, he finds that the bat's
voice would be about the proper medium for his
plaint, so dwindled does the offence appear when
breathed in the ordinary baritone of forty inches
round the chest.   This is a perfect reason for silence,
rankle as it may ; and there is another reason not at
all ridiculous, in the fear that seeking relief may be
the infliction of pain.

From this it follows that candid cheery souls make
the happiest lovers, both in themselves and for those
they love.   Not that they obtain any special preference.   Gay, frank, open-hearted girls are commonly
suspected of shallowness ; they lack depth ; it is
feared that they are unprovided with the reserves of
tenderness in which the lover proposes to make his
bed.   On the other hand, most damsels prefer the
pale-browed, cogitative, poetical, moody youth, darkly
sensitive and passionate, who is precisely the man to
cultivate the most terrific misunderstandings.   Such
a lover brings variety, animation, *chiaroscuro* into
courtship, no doubt ; but he generally does so at the
cost of little miseries none too noble.   Many a
summer-day love has been done to death by the
merest midges of misunderstanding.

OBEDIENCE

To all appearance, this which is one of the first
of virtues will be last understood. Though the
world is growing old, though the excellence of every
other virtue is rising into knowledge, there is no
general apprehension yet of what obedience is. On
the contrary, as intelligence broadens (to misuse
once more a word which does not signify ability to
read and write) dulness to the meaning of obedience
thickens. Intelligence is a great thing, but it is no
foe to the satanic spirit in human nature; and by
this spirit obedience is so distorted and confounded with what it is not that it falls every day
into deeper disgrace. Fools, both male and female,
and especially a new generation which is both and
neither, rail against it with the sternest motives and
the meanest perceptions; blind to what is yet so
plain, that there is no creature on earth of whom
obedience is not required, none whom it does not
grace, none whom it does not inform with a majesty
of contentment which nothing else supplies.

In this place, however, obedience has but a narrow meaning,—one that seems to be very afflicting to high-school young ladies and the like, who, unwilling to deny themselves a sweetheart and the thought of marrying him some fine day, dread to become "a mere wife." But surely, with their reading, and their thinking, and their intellectual equality with man, they should know what obedience is ; and the knowledge should so enlarge their spirits as to leave them no longer fretful at the obedience mentioned in the marriage-service and not altogether unlooked for by their lovers. Rightly understood, what is it to them or to any well-conditioned woman? Let us hear the good and wise Jeremy Taylor on that point. He has it that the first duty of the wife is obedience: "which, because it is nowhere enjoined that the man should exact of her, but often commanded to her to pay, gives demonstration that it is a voluntary cession that is required ; such a cession as must be without coercion and violence on his part, but on fair inducement and reasonableness in the thing, and out of love and honour on her part. . . . The man's authority is love, and the woman's love is obedience. . . . A wife never can become equal but by obeying ; but so her power, while in minority, makes up the authority of the man integral, and becomes one government as themselves are one man."

Good sense, sweet kindliness, sound scripture, blameless metaphysics, all in a dozen lines. Yet exception will be taken to the concluding words, "as themselves are one man." This merging of the woman in the man is precisely what exasperates the

rebellious.   " Male and female created He them ! "
they cry, omitting to finish the quotation with, " and
called their name Adam."   There is a sort of woman,
backed by a sort of man, who will hear of no mergings,
though what she really means is that while she has
no confirmed objection to a partnership she revolts at
marriage.   Perhaps she does not understand it ; but
unless she have that in her which joyfully assents to
what Jeremy Taylor calls the first duty of a wife
(and might as well have called delight in her own
perfecting), she can never be married under any circumstances.   She may be legally united to some
other person of the male sex, but even though the
ceremony were performed by a bishop, and that
bishop her own godfather, she must not persuade
herself that she is a married woman.

OLD MAIDS

The gravest accusation that can be maintained
against women is that they are ungenerous to one
another.   Men think so, at any rate ; but, considering the inveterate idealising of either sex by the
other, perhaps they are wrong.   Yet it is a woful
perhaps, for if women are not commonly ungenerous
to each other—not too quick to perceive or too
willing to magnify the faults, the defects, the
absurdities of other women—it is clear that men
carry their ideals too high, and that the fair are
more open to reproach and ridicule than any male
creature believes who was not born with a touch of
misogyny.   Which alternative has most truth in it

no son of Adam can affect to decide. A confident judgment on that point is impossible to man ; but as long as certain observations strike his view he will still incline to think that the most charming women can be, and often are, mercilessly unkind to each other. It is for us they keep both their major and their minor generosities of allowance.

Were it not so, would it be possible for young, pretty, happy women to think scorn of old maids? Could they join in the fun when some low-minded but extremely clever fellow depicts a row of faded " wall-flowers " in a ballroom, or tricks out the old maid to be laughed at on the stage, or puts her to ridicule in some humorous history? But join in the fun they do—by yea and by nay! nine out of ten of them ; for what are the artist's cruelties but flattery to themselves, and, what his satire but homage to their youth, their beauty, and the good fortune achieved thereby? It is true that men laugh at such caricatures too ; but, to do them justice, it is only in a conventional way and in public company where it seems to be expected. And were they defended by counsel he would probably say that his clients never dreamed of making sport of old maids as old maids. What excites their ridicule is the persistent assumption of youthful charm where no such charms can be ; the beaming smiles forced from faded eyes, the languishings and friskings of a figure of fifty decked in the ribbons of fifteen. It would be further said that these antics are truly ridiculous in themselves, and that it is not forbidden to laugh at anything truly ridiculous. But in the height of the argument the learned gentleman and his clients would be feelingly aware that it is handsomer to let the poor ladies alone; that ridiculous old maids are but the weak ones, who—as an added misfortune—haven't it in them to live in the serene content of their more sensible sisters. And more, that the absurdities are always pathetic and the ridicule inhumane.

But what woman should take second thoughts to find this out? Every woman's thoughts are feelings, sympathies, intuitions; and how can they miss for a moment the pathetic in the ridiculous or the unkindness of the ridicule? And how do they fail to acknowledge what they cannot miss, since (to their own sensitive knowledge) but for better luck in face and fortune, or perhaps but for better management or inferior squeamishness, they might have been old maids too? It is ignoble. The fresh young lass, rejoicing in the comeliness of which she was unaware yesterday and newly awakened to the competitions of womanhood, she may laugh her little laugh of scornful triumph and be pardoned. But even this young lady would be none the worse were she apprised that her vanities are a survival from the sheerest barbarism, descending straight from the brute beginnings of us all. And by the time her heart is full grown (physiologists say that young women's hearts are still immature when the rest of them has come to perfect growth) she ought to need no teaching on that point. Everything is natural that is brutal; she is natural; but before she has passed her twentieth year her amusement at the " wall-flower's " patient humiliations may be expected to decline. In another year she should be learned enough to admit the reflection that most old maids were once as fresh and fair as herself, just as brilliant, just as joyful in the belief that the world was all their own. As to the rest of us, we have no excuse in committing her unkindly fault ; and when next the playwright or the public caricaturist goes about to make fun of old maids (some of whom may be ridiculous, though none are so because of their condition), let him remember how much pain his mockery may give to many a shrinking, inoffensive woman, whose loneliness may have secrets more worthy of respect than anything in his art.

OPPORTUNITY

The jumping of Baal-fires, May-pole dances, the worship of the mistletoe, are the most innocent but not the most enduring and significant relics of paganism. A man may be a good Christian and commit himself to all these things ; but not if he open his mind to belief in wandering Spirits of Evil, endowed with power to draw him into naughtiness unaware. Many drunkards, and a still greater number of drunkards' wives, complain of The Drink as if it were some wayward demon, commissioned from the Pit to seize upon any stray innocent and take away his brains. And so the soberest and most thoughtful—supposing them not to be philosophered out of human nature quite—have a lurking belief in a " devil of opportunity."

We are all familiar with the sensation of looking inward whenever we reflect on our mistakes and mis-

deeds ; **and it is** no news to self-investigators that
the glance **they turn in** upon themselves is invariably **tender.** Even **when** our self - regarding
looks are unshrinkingly judicial they **are** still com-
passionate : a hint—which we never take—that we
might look **with the** same kindness on the faults **of**
others **without** weakening to them and without any
loss **of virtue. But as** soon **as we** think of the
occasion **of our** wrong-doing **we cease** from intro-
spection, darting an angry glance outside ourselves,
as it were ; the English of which is that we are
searching for the Devil of Opportunity, to curse it as
the cause of our woe.   Thus an old **poet**—

Accursed opportunity,
That work'st our thoughts into desires, **desires**
To resolutions ; those being ripe and quickened
Thou giv'st them birth, and bring'st them forth to action.

But, changing a word **in the famous** exclamation
of Mrs. Jonathan Wild, " Why devil ? "   Might not
Opportunity be called angel with greater justice ?   If
the good reader will look back on the occasions when
opportunity has served and when it has snared him
(as **he** thinks) he will see that some rejoicing devil
in his own breast was the snarer.   Nine times in ten
the opportunity was innocent enough,—no more
demoniac **than an** art-embellished bread-knife, which
will cut a loaf or **a** throat as you choose to handle
it.   On the other side, what of **the** " blessed opportunities," the " precious opportunities " which are so
much oftener **known** than remembered, except those
that were flung away ?   If **the** devil brings the
others, **who sends** these ?   And while, as nobody

doubts, we are free to take the good opportunities into our lives, what compels us to embrace the evil ones? This also is for thoughts: when the Book is opened which records on one page all the opportunities of good that have fallen to God's several creatures, and on another page every opportunity alluring to wrong, there is no soul on earth but will find that the one do vastly outnumber the others. Further it will be seen that there are rows upon rows on the Benign page without a tick-mark to show that any notice was taken of them; while on the Malign side of the account great black crosses darken the margin, in proof of our much superior vision for opportunities of naughtiness.

N.B.—This little sermon is addressed to ladies and gentlemen both; and though it has no exclusive reference to love - making, stolen kisses, contrived accidents, devised interviews in powder-magazines, and the like incidentals, it may be useful to lovers as lovers. Particularly, they should take note of that Doomsday Book of Opportunities which they may not have heard of before.

PARTING

As pertinent to this subject, see article "Meeting"
for a remark akin to the lamentation of the divine
who, mourning over his hymn-book, complained that
the devil had all the best tunes.   Surely gladness is
better than grief, unless it be joy in evil things, and
what more innocent than the delight of lovers
meeting, what more sad than their farewells?   Yet
there are twenty songs of parting to one of greeting,
and they the best.   If this were a heathen land
there would be more conscience in the matter : more
thankfulness for the sweet in the bitter cup, more
avoidance of ingratitude to the gods in whose hands
is so much giving and withholding.

But even the word-makers lacked grace and insight when they contrived the vocabulary of meeting
and parting.   There should have been some equality
of poetic sense in these words, whereas there is none.
How mean a syllable is "meet"!   How meagre,
how measured and thin-lipped it is!   What voice
can give it melody — what tone convey between

the teeth of its two vowels the buxom joy of
love at the instant of encounter?   But " part " !—
a word of noble melancholy, that swells on the *p*,
bursts on the *ar*, and breaks like a wave on the *t*
with lingering sighs.   Look upon the mouth that
has just uttered it, and behold in the divorced and
silent lips eloquence made visible.

Here is a grievous disparity, in which parting
has all the advantage ; and it is a difference which
reappears when we compare the words that are given
to parting and meeting for their special use.   To the
one " farewell," " adieu," " goodbye"; to the other,
"How d'ye do ? ".   " How d'ye do ? " may be helped
out, of course, by borrowing from the common stock
of exclamation ; but so, if they need such aid, may
" farewell " and " goodbye."   Indeed, they generally
have in attendance on them a whole flight of pretty
and endearing vocables ; while in themselves how
superior they are !   Who will put " How d'ye do ? "
in comparison with either ?   Who will compare it
with " adieu," which is " goodbye " in the voice of
the dove ?   On English lips there is hardly a word
that fills with more of music and meaning than
" farewell " ; while as to " goodbye," give but the
occasion and " good " is a sob and " bye " the tear
that follows.

But though the bards of love are too niggard
in acknowledging the delights of lovers meeting,
the pain of parting finds but small relief in the
pathos of its own expression.   When Shakespeare
made his Juliet say that parting is " such sweet
sorrow," he wrote with his customary discretion.
For *parting* is not *parted ;* and thereby hangs a tale

which may thus be told. Parting means sharing, amongst other things ; and while Juliet and Romeo are together, saying " Good night, good night," till morning dawns, they are together ; and being together they see each other's grief, they view each other's pain, and therefore know the anguish of parting *shared ;* and that is the sweetness of it. The wrench comes at the moment when " parting " and " parted " may be uttered in one breath, though even then the sweetness lingers. It is when the break is complete and distance widens between these poor souls that their heaviest time begins.

There is no tender heart but must pity them, and yet plenty of solitary human creatures would be glad to inherit their miseries. They are but weeds, these sorrows, in a garden of joy — a garden, a great garden, while so many of us never had more than a few plants of contentment flowering in bow-pots, and have nothing now but a wheen brown leaves of what once was joy enclosed in a book. Besides, our distressful lovers know that in a few weeks or days their grief will bloom into expectations of pleasure renewed, with the pleasure itself to follow. This in the ordinary course of true love. But there is the parting for ever, on which we will not dwell : and another parting which some say is worse than all. This is when the sorrow is *not* shared ; when it is all the pain of one, who sees under the agitations of the other a gladness to be gone, an impatience to have it over and be done with it.

T

PASSION

A word that is none the better for the handling
it receives.   At first it meant suffering, which it
does still in a beautiful word of general use, " compassion" ; and as the dictionaries themselves remind
us, its original signification is preserved amongst
pious Christians by their Lord's Passion—the suffering and death of the Saviour.   But for this the word
would be obsolete in its old sense—remaining, however, for excellent uses.   From the sound of it, it is
the best word imaginable for the more ardent affections of the mind, such as anger, jealousy, grief,
hate, love ; and its use as a common term for them
is not likely to be lost.   But just as nobody would
think nowadays of calling any of these passions
an affection, so passion is being gradually made
to serve one range of meanings especially.   Its
general signification of ardour, vehemence, is more
and more commonly given to love.   Or no, not
quite to love ; not to that affection unless it have an
admixture of something else ; a sufficient admixture
of that something else ; more of it and more yet as
time goes on and novelists write and little bardies
sing.   When we come upon the word " passionate "
now, we know that a darksome ardency is intended :
no pale ichor at work, if you please, but hot blood
and black.   To say that a man or a woman has
strong passions is become perilously misleading
unless one passion alone is meant, and that one the
least mentionable.   In a book of synonyms printed
thirty years ago, when Literature still hoped to

thrive without offending Young Persons, **the words for** two of the great emotions were included amongst the equivalents of " passion ": one of them was " anger," **the vulgar synonym, the** other " **lust,"** the literary synonym.

It is plain, then, that the **once** innocent word at the head of this article **was** already going to the **dogs—had,** indeed, **been** on the road years before ; **and** since that time there have been such prose-and-**verse celebrations** of lurid dreams, purpling brows, quivering bosoms, swooning senses, languors hollow-**eyed,** kisses that sting, ditto with blood and foam, burnings, faintings, and similar delights, that " passion " has almost become a blush-word ; for **it is in** Passion's name that these violent **joys** are preached. **Yet we live in** very quiet times. **It is not as if this were** a full-blooded **and** robustious **age.** It certainly is not that, though **its** intellectual **persons** may be allowed the boast of being intense. **Of the** feigned Elizabethan lustihood there **is none** ; but there is **a vast deal of** stretching and straining of mental cordage, **in the** meaning of intensity. By God's providence, **however, it** will presently relax, and then we shall be at peace from the passion-mongers ; **who,** though they are entirely effeminate, are far from harmless. But alive or dead, their industry in **depraving a** noble and beautiful word is not to be forgiven.

PITY

" Ladies " (to this effect will the Girton Professor **of** the Tender Passion address her audience, when the chair is founded), "Ladies, it is a painful reflection that we may not indulge the sweetest and holiest of our emotions without thought, or rather without calculation. But when I speak thus of the sweetest and holiest of our emotions, I see by a tremor of surprise which pervades the class that I am misunderstood. I hasten to add, therefore, that I do not mean the Grand Passion, as it is sometimes designated ; for though love ranks high amongst the sweetest, it cannot be called the holiest of our affections. Your patience till I name the attribute to which your hearts will not deny that distinction. I mean Pity : but pity in relation to love.

"In that learned and most excellent work, 'The Lover's Lexicon,' there is a passage that would serve very well as a text for the remarks which I am about to offer for your consideration. Writing of another great and tender quality the author says, 'It is often seen that faithfulness is but a wanton sacrifice, though the faithful soul can never be persuaded of that ; and perhaps there is no call to mourn over a suffering virtue which never fails to find its own happiness in its worst distress.' That sentence may be usefully remembered when you give your mind up to the saying that 'pity is akin to love,' as one poet has it ; or as another, that 'pity melts the mind to love ;' or as a third—

> Of all the paths that lead to woman's love,
> Pity is the straightest.

I have said *when* you give your minds up to these saws ; but this you do already. You do not question them. It seems to you only natural that pity should

melt the heart to love. You even fancy it meritorious ; or if not that exactly, you think it a proof
of the greater sweetness of woman's nature that she
should so readily admit love by the door of pity.
The consequence of which is—I believe I speak of
many here present—that your minds are prepared
and open to these same persuasions of pity as soon as
you enter into the world ; and my purpose this
evening is to suggest that you may possibly find
that a misfortune.

"According to my rule, I do not proceed immediately to an exposition of my own views of the
subject in detail. These you shall have when we
meet again beneath these sylvan boughs, to discuss
the grave and interesting problems which, though
properly classed as psychological, have an importance
beyond all the sciences. At the moment, I content
myself with placing before you certain questions,
certain considerations, which you may profitably
debate in your own minds in the short interval that
will elapse before our next meeting. Think of them,
discuss them amongst yourselves, and you will be all
the better prepared to listen when I address you at
length on this most important theme.

"In the first place, you should consider what is
meant by pity in this relation. What does it
include ? How does it divide ? Is it safe to allow
pity of *any* sort to keep the gates of love ? On
reflection you will probably find that not one but
several kinds of pity lead to marriage ; and perhaps
to something very like love precedent to marriage.
There is pity for physical suffering, and for unde-
served hardship at the hands of a brutal world.

Loneliness is **understood**—(and **by none** better than **by** men themselves, **I would have you** to know)—to **set** up in your tender **bosoms a strong appeal to** love-engendering **pity.** Very well. What **I** have to say on those points **will** be said next week. **At some opportunity** meanwhile, take two sheets of paper **and write on the one,** 'He was lonely, and I pitied **him.' On the** other write, 'He was lonely, and I **loved him.'** Then place the sheets of paper side **by** side, **look at them, and** ask yourselves whether some-**thing that is both** fit and beautiful **in the one** does **not go rather lamely in the** other.

"**There is another pity** which is believed **to** operate with considerable effect—pity for the poor gentleman who **has been badly treated** by one of your own sex : **he** must be comforted by a kinder heart. **But** when **the poets sing of** the pity that **leads to love they** generally mean what is mostly meant : **that is to** say, the pity which a woman may **be** expected **to** feel for a man **who** loves her very **much but for** whom she has no affection at all. **Look into this a little.** Reflect on the qualities of **a love** which, finding requital denied, **is** content to **have its** own way through commiseration. Particu-larly inquire into **the** likelihood of **its** being durable. As **a** second and **perhaps inferior** branch of the matter, ask yourselves **how much of** gratified vanity combines with **a pity so excited,** and what the chances **are** that any remains of the feeling will exist six **months** after **marriage.** Put the question another **way and in these terms :** 'Pity having **played its part,** and the sense of gratified vanity being **exhausted, what will** my situation be if there

is any mistake about love growing out of pity?'—
meaning by love a genuine and lasting sentiment.
In pondering that question it will naturally occur to
you that if the affections of a man who is satisfied
with pity should happen to be transient, a time is
not unlikely to come when there will be no love at
all in his marriage, either on the one side or the
other. It does not follow from that state of things
that both will be utterly miserable, but there we
touch upon another part of the subject as a
whole.

"You should also entertain the question whether
pity ever does master to this extent any woman of
sound and wholesome instincts. At present, I say
neither yea nor nay to any of these questions: I
merely throw out the suggestion that such a woman
would be naturally convinced that she is to love
where she loves and not where she pities. On the
other hand, you are to remember this: pity may
well and warmly introduce a woman to habitudes
of love who would otherwise enter into marriage very
coldly—having no heart for it: a commoner case
than is generally supposed.

"That men sometimes practise on the belief that
'pity melts the heart to love,' affecting a vast deal
more suffering than they really endure, is a consideration well worth glancing at. But another
deserves greater attention from a point of view more
philosophical and less sentimental. It is almost
expected that pity should melt your hearts to love
when he who suffers suffers indeed. Your own impression is that it should naturally do so. And
why? Because you are women and not men.

There is no reciprocity in the case, you will observe : none offered, none desired, none endurable to you. A woman of common sensibility would almost die of shame at the thought of being married out of pity ; and what is more, she would think none the better of the man who pitied her : by which I mean that she would think none the better of him as a man. Ask yourselves how that comes about. Turn it over in your minds as an exercise in social ethics and psychology.

" To conclude, while you ponder these things, keep in memory the quotation with which I began these remarks, for it has a bearing on the practical side of the matter. Faithfulness, it is said, 'is often seen to be but a wanton sacrifice'——meaning a sacrifice of devotion to absolute unworthiness ; ' but perhaps there is no call to mourn over a suffering virtue which never fails to find its own happiness in its worst distress.' Now that is all very well for faithfulness —— the faithfulness presupposed. Founded deep in love and duty, it has its own sustaining joy in sacrifice, no doubt. Well, you bring the idea of self-sacrifice and its pleasure into your notions of the young woman who takes pity on a woe-worn lover and marries him. I warn you that there may be complete self-sacrifice without its pleasures. The sense of duty is naturally weak in such a case ; while as for the love that makes fidelity so sweet an obligation even to discovered worthlessness and wickedness, do you imagine that it naturally grows out of a feeling that is half of it gratified vanity— a feeling which, in fact, may never have been love at all, but only a likeness of it?

" And now——" etc., etc.   With a few words of benediction the lecture ends.

PRETTINESS

Prettiness is another example of the rise and fall of words, just as nations and families rise to distinction and sink into decay.   While Passion is put to the blush by the company it is forced to keep nowadays, Prettiness carries its dainty little head in the highest quarters with a grace more assured and a confidence more allowed.   And yet Passion is of the noblest descent ; it is dignified by associations most divine ; while as to Prettiness, the plain truth is that it was born a Fraud.   In every country where it appeared it was long known as deceit, trickery.   Prettiness was our forefathers' name for those qualities.   Rising in the social scale, it afterwards became the word for cunning, cleverness. From that point " prettiness " made a rapid advance, losing the last taint of its origin long ago.   It now stands for nothing that is not dainty and delightful.

And yet a certain duplicity attends it still ; though not to its own blame, and (so constant is the luck of prettiness) much to its advancement.   What prettiness in a woman is we all know, and know that it is something that falls short of beauty.   Not to speak of other countries where English is the mother-tongue, England abounds with beautiful women, and yet more with pretty ones ; but there is a standing difference between the sexes as to which are the one and which the other. Does a man say of some charming creature, "That is a beautiful woman," she must be beautiful indeed, or every other woman about him will answer, "She is certainly very pretty." Or should he say of another, "How pretty she is!" his taste is at once corrected by an offer of agreement to consider her good-looking. This is all to the advantage of prettiness, which gradually rises to a higher place by these comparisons. And thus does it continue to prosper by insincerity; though its own associations with deceit are all abolished.

Yet that prettiness is often tricksy is true enough, to the vindication of etymology and the pleasure of mankind. For however winning it may be, the tricksiness is without guile; which is no longer natural to prettiness in any sort. Whatever its kind, —whether the sedate, the twinkling, or the cheerful open-eyed frank variety,—it is never without a touch of the child-like. Though some of the cleverest-looking women in the world are the pretty ones, it is still true that the nature of prettiness is to wear the grace of childhood. Thus it is that many pretty old women look as if their years of life had been all Spring: a Spring that must change and fade, but never rising to the large sobriety of Summer as beauty does, thence to descend through Autumn's solemnity. It is a sufficient gift, prettiness, corresponding when compared with worldly goods to an ample though modest competence. Its home-associations are with an ivy-grown cottage, a man-and-a-boy garden, a stable of two stalls, and a paddock with three Guernsey cows in it. In point

of looks, it supplies the ideal of what women should
be if they could all be put on an equality of personal attraction.   An equal distribution of loveliness
were too much to dream of.   A general dispensation of beauty offends imagination almost as much
as a world all millionaires.   Better a population of
pretty women in their thousand diversities, with
every one her match in a comely man.

PROPOSAL

Since declaration of love and proposal of marriage are so much the same thing, the word at the
head of this page can hardly be left out of a Lover's
Dictionary.   But yet it is a mechanical word—
formal, adjunctive, with scarcely more claim to
inclusion than "trousseau," which is not to be admitted.

In the right order of things there is no ceremony
of "declaration."   Spontaneous love declares itself
without words, and is in full traffic of interchange
before a syllable of acknowledgment has passed the
lips of either party.   It is necessary to say something,
to be sure; but not, as would appear from the
works of novelists and play-writers, to make known
the existence of a passion and solicit the happiness
of requital.   "May I presume, Miss Emily, that you
are not quite unaware ——," "Miss Goodenough,
you must long have observed ——," such forms of
address would be a ridiculous and rather painful
surprise to the ear of any young damsel who shared
the heyday of a frank affection ; and shy as it may

look, first-love is rarely otherwise than frank. No,
it is necessary to say something, but not that sort of
thing nor for that purpose. The necessity has
quite a different origin. It arises from a craving to
hear and to speak the language of endearment.
This is a craving which becomes almost insupport-
able after a little while, and the utterance of one
familiar word will not only break the ice for it, but is
quite enough of formal declaration at the same time.
The lad is spurred into the boldness of saying, one
fine day, "Mary, dearest," and there is the whole of
the novelist's rigmarole in four syllables, the choicest
that could be picked from the language in a month's
study. All is over so far as he is concerned. As
for the lady, she need not say anything. It is
enough for her to flush as she must, lean toward
him a little by the same compulsion, or put a hand
forth toward whichever of his own happens to be
nearest. Now there is an end of that matter.
Whatever word-of-mouth expression is necessary to
constitute Engagement (a word that never falls
sweetly upon sensitive ears), is supplied from either
side by casual exclamations, incidental adjectives,
and the like; and if by and by these unpurposed
ratifications are topped by an exchange of vows, believe that lovers' oaths express the fears, the solicitudes natural to love, rather than any design to fix
a matrimonial obligation.

Now proposal comes in as part of the business
arrangements—right, and seemly as well as absolutely unavoidable, but pure business; and it would
save a world of confusion and perturbation if some
near friend of the young man's were permitted by

custom to lay the state of affairs before the lady's
father and seek his sanction. Moreover, it would
be done much better so ; and since there can be no
doubt of that, we see at once that in coming to
" proposal," we cross the borders of sentiment and
enter the region of affairs.

It is true that formal proposals are often made to
the Divine Object herself in the most genuine love-
affairs, and when mutual inclination has been mutually
ascertained already. They are yet more frequent,
perhaps, when the lady's mind is a doubt to her
lover and to herself. But in either case proposal is
of the nature of an *operation*, and therefore barely
pertinent to the design of this Work.

PRUDE

At various periods down to the fourth or fifth
decade of the present century prudes were heard of
a good deal ; nowadays they are rarely mentioned,
and are obviously passing out of existence. It might
be expected that, in the nature of things, women
" over nice and scrupulous and with false affectations "
(as prudes were described by an essayist of the
18th century, when they seem to have flourished
in troublesome quantity) would be pretty numerous
in every generation ; but there is no appearance of
any such persons at the present day. How may so
strange an evanition be explained ? There are
scrupulous women in every parish, and plenty of
" nice " ones in all meanings of the word. Are we,
then, so favoured that the nice of our day are never

over-nice, nor the scrupulous too exact? Is it that no false affectations mar the age—that the free are frankly free, seeing no reason to be otherwise, and that the modest and precise are content to live to themselves, undisturbed by the laxity of others and indifferent to the luxury of censure?

In answering these questions it is necessary to recollect that there is no agreement on the meaning of prudishness. It was one thing in the mind of Esmonde's Beatrix, another in the mind of Lady Castlewood, and not quite the same in Esmonde's own. Above all be it remembered that "prude" is the one retort and sole kick-up of immodesty against pure-mindedness. And here again we are helped a little by looking to the relationships of the word. Origin-ally, "prude," "preude," was no term of mockery or reproach, but stood soberly in Old French for the good and chaste; and as it stands in our dictionaries to-day "prude" is own sister to "prowess,"—bravery, valiancy. Thus informed, fancy may figure to itself a valiant and as it were a knightly modesty, assured, open-eyed, quick to detect offence, and not slow to confront it reprovingly; and as soon as this picture rises into view the use of the name "prude" in its newer signification is explained. The prude was a reprover; the reprover was sometimes over-nice, for the pleasure of being censorious and self-edifying; and therefore when the next epidemic of licentious-ness broke out, it became both easy and convenient to make prudishness and affectation synonymous in common talk. By this ingenious stroke modesty was abashed. From that hour its valiancy declined. Withdrawn into unprotesting silence (which was always more congenial than rebuke), it has now **no** more **to** say. Since it has no more to say, mock modesty conceives **that** it may as well be **silent** too. That, however, **is** not saying enough. **The** mock **modest** have naturally gone over to the **other** side, where they are far more comfortable and equally free from reproach. And thus it is that **prudes** are never heard **of** nowadays.

RAKE

SOME words carry their primal meanings on the face of them, so that the most ignorant get a glimpse of it. "Rake" is one of these words, when it stands for "a loose, disorderly, vicious, wild, gay, thoughtless fellow," as Johnson described the *roué* of his time. Had the wild, gay, thoughtless fellow been called a rake after the farm-yard implement—which also goes through a deal of muck—it would have been quite natural; yet nobody takes the word in that sense altogether, although "rakehell" was the first form of the word, afterwards shortened to rake. But "rakehell" was a corruption of "rakel," Old English for rash, which is not our meaning for rake either, or only a small part of it. When we learn, however, that "raker" meant running about in a hasty, dashing, restless way, we see that the popular understanding of the word and the thing is entirely accurate. The meaning brought in by the muck-rake is allowable but accidental.

To rake was once a fashion; but though it is

never out of all repute, raking has no vogue at the
present day, and is only practised for such violent
delights as eating lobsters in low company at two
o'clock in the morning. The looseness that Johnson
speaks of is flat—no small beer is flatter; the vice,
bloodless; while as to the wildness, the gaiety, and
even the thoughtlessness, they are quite, quite gone.
It was possible to love a rake while those qualities
lasted in him, for they implied a certain generosity
and aboundingness of heart and life. On that account
it was that few women could find it in them to
condemn a rake sincerely; that he was particularly
dear to his maiden aunts; and that he had a fascination for young women which they could but confess
to their pillows. Then-a-days it was possible for the
saying, "Married rakes make the best of husbands,"
to gain faith and currency. But without the vigour,
the wildness and thoughtlessness, what romance can
be made of such rakes as ours, with their lobster-salad
orgies and negotiated intrigue? And what could
be done with them reformed? There is an answer
to these questions, perhaps, in the fact that the saying
which commended married rakes was dropped about
fifty years ago and has never been uttered since. It
then became outworn. By that time a certain type of
man had disappeared—a wild and wastrel generation
with some sterling qualities, to be succeeded by a
tame, furtive, hang-dog variety with none.

The poet's declaration that "every woman is at
heart a rake" shall not be discussed; but it may be
said for her sex that if they are rakes enough to
lament the degeneration of rakishness it is a right
womanly sentiment, and capable of vindication as

U

such till Doomsday.   Yet women are gainers by the change to this extent.   It was a perilous saying, "A married rake makes the best of husbands"; and whether from a certain Eden-born sympathy with rakes, whether through instinctive motives of conquest, competition, compassion, reclamation, it led many a maid into the worst of marriages.   But there is no glamour about the rake's successor.   No false glory conceals him ; and, except in its literal sense, no mistake can be made in taking him in marriage.

RAPTURE

A grammarian would be right in saying that to be rapt and to be in a rapture are the same things ; but we who have voyaged and travelled through the whole round of the emotions know there is a difference. With this difference poets are perfectly familiar. Geniuses like Wordsworth are rapt for hours together ; that is to say, lost in the scattered, wool-gathering state of mind which is not thinking, but is to thought what the wandering bees of a hive would be to honey-making if they roved without intention and took their spoil from the flowers in merely alighting on them. The poetry-making begins when the thoughts swarm home, to distil and parcel out their sweets in verse, as bees their treasure in the comb.   If the grammarian insisted on it, there would be no denying that while this process is going on the poet is still rapt ; for that he is, but in quite another sense.   No longer flying all abroad, his mind concentres on itself, and in doing so rises from time to time into a rapture.

And he would tell you that being in a rapture and
being rapt **are** as different as the sea leaping and
flashing in the sunshine **of a** June morning, and
Windermere under the stars on a stilly night.

This is exactly what the **lover would say of his**
own sensations. The raptures of **love were** entirely
denied to Young John, **the** unfortunate lover in
" Little **Dorrit," but** who **more** rapt than he, sitting
amidst the linen in his mother's garden on washing-
day and " fancying it's groves " ?   Sauntering, as
where the willow waves—repose, as on a bank in the
woods, or on a stile, or in a window-seat—are all but
compulsory in these moods of mind, when even the
happiest lovers look most melancholy **and are** most
absent : rapt, out of themselves, their thoughts converted into dreams and all gone wandering.   **The**
Philistine word for these moods, whether they appear
in poets **or lovers, is "mooning"; and it** may be
accepted **as** quite **appropriate on account** of the
stillness and brooding vacancy **of moonlight.**   **But**
there **is no** brooding and **no vacancy in** rapture, of
which the most complete embodiment that ever has
been or ever will be found is the rising of the lark in
the morning sky.   It is to a bird, and to a bird that
makes its home in plough-furrows and by grassy tufts
on the ground, **that** the perfect voice of joy has been
given.   We " who are the best of things " should
never have known that rapture was capable **of** expression but for this little creature, who has **a** stave
for every change and turn ; **as** when he reiterates the
long-drawn note that speaks of rapture rising into
pain.   **There** is Shelley's rhapsodising to be sure ;
but that does not come into everybody's reading, and

to no reader does it mean half as much as the lark's
song to the simplest country maid with a sweetheart
of her own.   And it will mean yet more to her if she
has ever seen a lark in a cage ; for his wings never
cease to beat while he sings in his dark and narrow
prison, and if there be no beating of wings in her
breast when her joy swells into its unheard song there
is something very like it.

There is an ecstasy of love, and rapture is often
mistaken for it.   Though they are generally confounded, they are not the same thing exactly.
Ecstasy is a rapture of the spirit ; rapture is an
ecstasy of what the good reader has been asked to
recognise as " the soul of the body."   If he has wisdom
enough to trust his own sensations, he will agree that
rapture is the soul of the body rising into song ; a
song, be it observed, which is all of the joys of earth,
its loveliness and its affections.

RESERVE

When the Girton Lecturer takes this subject in
hand she will find it necessary to proceed with
great caution ; for she must deprecate as well as
commend, and it is not easy to draw sharp lines of
distinction between a righteous reserve and one that
is neither wise nor fortunate.

Discipline has many uses ; the cultivation of
reserve, restraint, is one of them ; and reserve is
not only a virtue but a grace.   This is true, the
Lecturer will say, whether we speak of reserve in
thought and feeling or of carriage and conduct.

But, like other virtues, it begins to take a different
character, like other graces it loses grace, when it is
worn as a garment.   An obviously defensive reserve
in social intercourse has little charm, but there is
an offensive or challenging reserve which has less.
Save for the circumstance that the old tavern sign
of " The Hog in Armour" is rarely seen nowadays,
it might be usefully likened to this kind of reserve,
which is not uncommon.

Without condescending to resemblances of that
description, the Lecturer will lead her young ladies
to consider whether reserve in thought and feeling
may not also take an unfortunate character.   She
will remind them that reserve is not insensibility.
Insensibility can neither receive nor render.   Reserve
implies accessibility to emotion—the existence of
affections and sensibilities however secret or con-
trolled.   And reserve being the concealing and controlling power, it is obviously within the dominion of
will.   It is possible to choose the more or less of
reserve, including that called natural ; which is the
great point to remember.   We do hear of " inveterate
reserve " as we hear of inveterate jealousy, envy, and
other things ; but the strongest inclination to concealment is never unaccompanied by a sense of
voluntary choice.

It appears, therefore, when we have got a right
comprehension of this quality, understanding that
it is neither fortunate nor meritorious in all relations, that we are not powerless to make the best of
it.   There is a common belief, however, that reserve
is always good ; at the least it is thought to be judicious.   But it is not even that, sometimes.   Modesty

is grounded in natural reserve. Delicacy is a something made up of contributions from every virtue,
every grace ; but what blends and binds the whole
is the spirit of reserve. Without that spirit there
can be little of either modesty or delicacy, as may be
seen from the manners of the time. How fine a
quality reserve can be is shown by these examples ;
but when it is practised as a considered and system-
atic concealment of feeling it takes a doubtful character. It is one thing to wear your heart upon your
sleeve, another to keep it under bolt and bar, with
every kind affection tethered close between its more
or less infrequent spells of measured liberty. Yet
wives who are fond enough will use this restraint,—
some because they are persuaded that it is womanly ;
some as a matter of prudence, or as a point of management in the higher domestic economies ; some
because it pleases them as a kind of preciosity ;
and many for all these reasons combined. But
unless a wife be strangely wed, she might do better
than plan her new life upon them. They have the
sanction of much wise-looking precept, no doubt, but
of none that is very noble : and in most cases the
best that can be hoped from their observance is
the cold tranquillity of " Greenland's icy mountains."
There is too much frigidity, too much sterility, in this
kind of reserve. Kept in ice, the affections take the
habits of certain arctic creatures—dwindling and
losing colour ; and there is always a danger that,
instead of being maintained in glowing vigour, the
affections of the human being on the other side of
the hearth will fall into a similar decline.

　　Reserve, by all means : the same that makes for

modesty, the same that binds the bouquet (" Delicacy " hight) which justice, generosity, sweetness, candour, tenderness, compassion, and other fine qualities each contribute a spray to, and which should lie in every woman's bosom.   But of the more deliberate and attorney sort it is well to beware.   There should be a reserve *like* it, but more like that in the Bank of England, where, besides plenty of currency to meet every ordinary demand at sight, there is a cellar-full for emergencies—all ready to come up, bright, fresh, smiling, sterling.

RESPECT

Meaning to be kind, women will sometimes clothe the rejection of a lover with assurances of profound respect.   They should never do so, unless he happens to be an elderly gentleman ;—no, nor then.   He will read into the word an irony which no good-hearted young creature can ever intend.   To withhold such an assurance in the case of youthful suitors is a mere counsel of humanity.   Admiration itself, if that can be conscientiously offered in lieu of a responsive heart, is but poor porridge ; yet there is warmth in it, while at its best respect is a dish of consolation cold.   And meek is the man who will sup from it.   Flaming young lovers start at its presentation, as at an indignity.   Youthful as they may be, they know by instinct what observation will afterwards confirm, that love can and does exist without respect ; while respect is with some a restraint on love, with others a makeshift for it, with

others its very negation., Expound the riddle as
we may, when an enamoured swain reads in the
fatal *billet* that he is deeply respected though his
love can never be returned, he takes the respect for
a reason why love is impossible ; and it is not certain
but that the lady is conscious of a similar understanding of the matter. He would feel more hope of a
different answer on some future day if she could do
away with a little of that profound respect ; while
were his case her own——! Imagine the impossible ; fancy her in receipt of a communication
from the man of her heart, informing her that he
cannot requite her affection but that she may be
assured of his deepest respect !

Be it agreed, then, that " respect " is a word for
other uses. Of course the thing must exist in every
happy and assured affection ; but even then it is
more acceptable under an *alias*, such as confidence,
faith, belief, admiration.

SENSIBILITY, SENTIMENT

SENSIBILITY may be described as feeling at a high
stage of refinement—receptive, susceptible, responsive. Obviously, therefore, there is much to commend it ; and at various times in the history of this
country it has had a considerable run. Attractive
not only from intrinsic merit, but also from its
inseparably-attendant graces, it no sooner gains a
footing amongst the polite than it becomes a
fashion ; and as nothing of its kind is easier of
cultivation than sensibility, the fashion speedily becomes general. And this is its bane. It is too
capable of cultivation. Under hot-house treatment
(which it always receives, unfortunately—cannot be
preserved from, according to experience) it soon
takes the rankest, the sickliest growths, and is then
banished from morals and manners in disgust. The
last invasion of sensibility came to an end in England about fifty years ago ; or, as some say, it then
took another shape, finding an opening for itself in
public affairs. It certainly has no existence now in

its native regions. Neither sensibility nor sentiment in its weaker and more imaginative forms is discernible in the manners, the conversation, or the poetic and romantic literature of the time ; which might be considered a gain if the banishment of those attendant graces had not been followed by the cultivation of barbarism in literature and rudeness in manners.

At no time, however, can sentiment and sensibility be banished from love affairs. There they belong, not as appurtenant, but in the body and soul of them. It is impossible to be in love without sensibility, and hardly without being sentimental ; and this is why that, falling in love, the most savage men and the least gentle women are tamed to sweetness and civility in all their walks and ways. But here, too, there is a tendency to cultivation— resort to the hot-house. Young men are especially subject to an apprehension that they do not love as others love unless they feel their sensibilities a torment, nor can look the lover in the lady's eyes without an air of sentimental gloom. A little brooding, as of the hen upon her nest (but it is not so pretty a sight), will produce torments enough from any young man's sensibilities; so that for the matter of that, he is soon satisfied of the depth of his affection and that it is duly tragic. And being of that cast of mind, it is easy for him to look more melancholy than the moon, and darker than her engulfing clouds, simply by taking thought. A week will do it, but what then? To be sure, his tortures are pleasant in the after-taste, and, when they are at their worst, place him at a conscious height in the

realm of romance.   Moreover, it is not to be denied
that his tragedy brow, his pining cheek, the dreamy
or the darksome boding in his eye, make a pretty
reflection in the looking - glass, and add, perhaps,
to the graces which his lady knows him by.   But
he should understand betimes that it is not a
grace that lasts.   After a while it fatigues.   That
which seemed poetic takes a common look, and
what was hugged as a compliment is resented as
unkind.   It is felt to be eclipse of sunshine by
a sort of moody egotism ; and as that is exactly
what it is, let the young man beware who
this day has " met his fate," and order himself
cheerfully.   He will have exercise enough for his
sensibilities in the natural order of things without
contriving more ; while as for sentiment, that is best
and most wholesome which is allowed to grow as
the daisies grow: as they please, and not very
high.

If no address to persons of the other sex is made
they will not take offence.   It is only because they
manage their sensibilities much more wisely than
men, and because their sentiment, though sometimes
tearful beyond forgiveness, is sweeter and brighter
in the general.   Possibly the explanation of the
difference may be that they have no mind to veil a
pretty face with clouds, or choose only those that
are all silver lining.   If so, it is a creditable explanation.

SPOUSE

Many words take a physical aspect to the fancy.
Though their meanings do not point to any such
qualities, there are tall words, dwarfish words, lean
words and stout, pallid words and ruddy, sombre
words, smiling words, words with Roman noses, with
padded chests, with a variety of other features of
which the eye alone takes cognisance in a general
way.   It is the sound of such words in the mouth,
and their aspect as they squat, strut, couch, crawl, or
stand a-tiptoe on paper that give to them their
visual distinctions.   And just as the expression of a
face is changed in a distorting-glass, so may some
words be by the transposition, addition, or subtraction
of a letter.   Give an additional vowel to "captivate,"
for example, and you have a lively word for a whole
underworld of fascinations heretofore inexpressible:
"captiviate."   Captain Arthur captivates ; his man,
the elegant Mr. Jenkin, captiviates.

 "Spouse" is of the order of words above described.
Say "spouse," and whether a man or woman be
meant you have before you a much more definite and
characteristic picture than that which would rise in
your mind did you say wife or husband.   Husbands
and wives are of many varieties ; you can have only
a general idea of them, but from that a conception
of gravity, carefulness, rainy-day preoccupation is
rarely absent.   "Spouse" gives you at once a
definite picture with none of these marks upon it.
"My spouse" is a round, well-conditioned, homely
man ; a comfortable, cheery man, good to live

with at all hours ; a man who begins the day
like a sunny morning, and ends it with the
cosy radiance of a sea-coal fire in winter. And *his*
spouse ?—no difference to be mentioned except the
accident of sex. Just as "sweetheart" is without
any change of significance whether it be said of
man or maid, so it is with "spouse." The word
brings maid and man into a union of identity ; and
it is to be observed that spouses are generally made
of people who begin by being sweethearts. They
are, in fact, married sweethearts ; as is partly expressed in the name they choose to give each other.
It is not a name that any one is supposed to use
seriously, but there is a deal in it that is worth living
up to.

SWEETHEART

The prettiest, honestest, wholesomest word of all its
kind ; the one most full of meanings ; and its meanings as clear as a brook, as sweet as the thyme on
the banks of the brook, and all in a winding, low,
incessant harmony like the honey-making bees in
the thyme. For music, for significance, for fitness,
for completion, when else did two such syllables
come together ? First you have *sweetness*, which is
a dulcet quality in one meaning, gentleness and
purity in another ; then you have *heart*, which is
courage, boldness, fervour, and kindness and tenderness too. Here in the one word is the maid, there in
the other is the man ; and the two, when joined, are
so well and appropriately made one that " sweetheart "

is a name of equal application to Darby and Joan.
It is not so with "lover"—a much inferior word,
belonging to the same common stock as "piper,"
"tinker," "tailor," and other terms of mere mechanic
structure, which cannot be applied to women without
a sense of awkwardness and impropriety. "Her lover,
Alfred Smith," is well enough, but "His lover, Emily
Price," is so much beyond endurance that the phrase
is never heard. Yet by the treacherous aid of
literary folk this smooth insidious half-word has
taken so tyrannical a hold that it must needs be
accepted and employed on every dignified occasion,
even in the first of Lovers' Dictionaries.

There is the comfort of knowing, however, that
"sweetheart" still reigns under the rose; which is
the right ensign of its dominion and might itself
have been called Sweetheart. Choosing what pretty
terms we please in talking with ourselves or our
other selves, "lover" may be serenely left to literary
uses. It is convenient to have some such hack-word
for the harlotries of print and the scramble of general
conversation. "Lover," too, is always the more
appropriate word when suspicion, or mystery, or
moodiness, or suicide, or murder, or match-making is
in the case. "Sweetheart" has small association
with the murk and morbidness of tropical love—none
with sensational affectations on the one hand, nor, on
the other, with matrimonial transactions and negotiated pairing. It is all for what the word itself is,
and, both to heart and ear, it equally spells sincerity,
spontaneity, simplicity, security, contentment as in
the vales and orchard-grounds of happiness.

"'Sweet,'" says an old writer, himself in the

lexicographical line—"'Sweet' expresses the pleasant perceptions of almost every sense. Sugar is sweet, but it hath not the same sweetness as music, nor hath music the sweetness of the rose, and a sweet prospect differs from all." True : but " sweetheart " *sums* all. Every delight of the senses breathes in the utterance of the word, with other pleasures which are deemed of higher worth by moralists and divines. To speak it places between the lips a little parcel of sugar-sweetness (see its name under letter K) which for excellence beats all that could be expressed from a hogshead of the best Barbadoes. More than the sweetness of music is remembered in the rustling of a gown, the calling of a name, the sound of a voice, even when it spoke the prose of common talk. " Her speech is graced with sweeter sound Than in another's song is found," says Waller. Though music hath not the sweetness of the rose, sweetheart has, precisely ; while as for "a sweet prospect," go to the rock-head by the church above Festiniog's vale, and even there you will see no sweeter prospect than comes into view when "sweetheart" brings up a vision of your Mary in a morning gown.

Long, then, may this pretty word remain unhackneyed, even at the cost of being thought a kitchen term by professors of refinement and taste.

TEMPTATION

IT would be needless to include this word in our list were it not the habit of mankind to neglect its half perceptions unless they happen to be entirely agreeable. Should some flattering truth, some pleasing discovery peep into our minds, it is taken by the hand at once and entertained with the largest liberality ; but whenever a troublesome doubt looks in, we turn away till its questioning face has passed the window. Thus, most of us have frequent glimpses of the fact that the very spirit of temptation has crept into the word ; but we never look twice, for that might be the beginning of an exercise in morals and possibly restraint on inclination.

Is that a hard saying ? Then let us illustrate by one that we are familiar with. " 'Tis human to err " is a very old saw, ten thousand times repeated in our own day, with drawn solemnities of visage betokening a mournful sense of human imperfection. All our woe told in four little words—three if you go back to the Latin—but yet with so much com-

fort in them that, from serving as a memento of
weakness and admonition to charity, they have
become a sort of horse-block from which to mount
into naughtiness.

> Then gently scan your brother man,
>   Still gentler sister woman ;
> Though they may gang a kennin' wrang,
>   To step aside is human.

"It is ! it is but human !" sighs the tempted one,
her voice melting on the word ; and so, with another
sigh, leaps to some forbidden joy.

And thus it is with temptation. To be tempted
is to be drawn away from what is known to be
right into what is felt to be wrong ; and therefore
temptation should be a word of fear. But the
tenderness, the self-compassion that has filtered into
"human," so that it has almost become an expression for weakness sweetly forgivable, has found its
way into "temptation." The word has been so
abused that instead of being nothing else than a
warning of danger and a call to resistance, it is
nearly as much a plea for wrongdoing and an
excuse for surrender. That is what is meant by the
spirit of temptation having crept into the word.
Such are its acceptations among the gentle souls
who sigh over one naughtiness and another as "so
very human" that temptation is desired wherever
there is a mind for loose indulgences. "Lead me
not where I shall be tried, for my strength may
fail" : that was the prayer under the old and right
meaning of "temptation." But now it has another
meaning besides, and another prayer runs upon it :

X

" Lead me into temptation, for then I shall be pitied and excused."

Now the land through which this lexicon is a guide has its own laws, but no magistracy and no police, except such as sits in the hearts and marches in the thoughts of its inhabitants. Therefore all honest folk who pass through that country are careful to exclude the soft alluring sense of temptation. They know it to be treasonable in the first degree ; and treasonable, not to one or two laws out of many, but to the whole body of obligation. Remembering that the whole body of law and obligation rests on trust alone, all the more heedful are these honest folk in their faithfulness ; and who would be less loyal for want of thinking what temptation really is ? No reader of this book for certain. There is not one but is too sensible and kindly. They turn the matter in their minds—(as many as need do so)—and see that where love and trust are engaged "to step aside" may be human in one sense and yet quite inhuman in another. They comprehend that here we are in a country where small transgressions may inflict a world of pain, and that the plea of temptation is nought. Temptation ? Temptation is trial ; trial of strength, honour, trustworthiness. What of the sword which, breaking to pieces in the smith's hands, cries out, " Ah, me ! my melancholy fate ! That I should have been so unfortunately tried ! "

TENDRESSE

It is a reproach to the language that it has no word for a state of mind which millions of those who speak it are sensible of generation after generation. And not only is it a reproach to the language, but a reflection on the character of the people. For what *tendresse* stands for, when we borrow the word, is a gentle, sweet, and modest feeling distinct from every other ; and to have no name for it suggests that it is a sentiment with which we have small acquaintance. We cannot say "a tenderness" : "she has a tenderness for him," "he has a tenderness for her." Though often used as an equivalent, "regard" or "great regard" is not to the purpose : it conveys neither the delicacy nor the depth of the nameless feeling. And what an expression is "sneaking kindness," our nearest approach to the word desired ! "Sneaking kindness" !—a hang-dog phrase. "Creeping kindness" would be better ; and yet there is comfort in the thought that "sneak" was not always intended to bear the vile signification it now carries, but had the meaning of "hankering after." We may believe, if we please, that a sneaking kindness is hankering kindness ; and even substitute the one expression for the other without offence to "sneaking." Nor should that word be banished altogether. It has its uses. Amongst the various degrees and manifestations of the tender passion there is a kindness both sneaking and hankering, and, like everything else, it should have its own distinctive name.

For this other feeling—as innocent as new-born babes of all that sneaking implies, and nearly as unconscious of hankering — let us boldly take *tendresse* and make an English noun of it without further ado. We have been shy of it too long. French though it be, it is not more French than a thousand other words reminted at less need ; while as for the whisper of sentimentalism that breathes through its gentle syllables, there it is in place.

That it is so is conclusive evidence that tendresse should not be confounded with affection ; yet that imperfect name is often given to it, partly for want of a better, and partly because tendresse, like affection, is something less than love. The truth is that both are less, but in exactly different ways : the difference being that of substance and spirit. Affection, which takes more embodiment than love, is without sentiment entirely. What we mean by " a tendresse " is more ethereal than the love-passion itself, and has more of sentiment in its fine and tenuous composition : so that—what shall we say ? Affection is the bread, love is the wine, tendresse the perfume of the wine : more than the perfume, perhaps, but the comparison will serve.

To make another, there is a tendresse of one kind like the dawn, of another like evening. The first steals into the hearts of timid maids, to linger there in a beautiful half-light which is to be seen in the eyes of them. But after a while the light grows, the morning haze that held so many mysteries lifts away, and, as if by magic, she is in the full sunshine of an acknowledged passion. Yet though, while it lasts, this unformed forming sentiment has nearly all the characteristics of tendresse, it lacks the one that is most distinguishing. There is no meridian for the feeling which is henceforth to bear that name. Tendresse never attains to noon-tide heat and glow, and is almost in dread of fervour as something in which it might exhale. Youth never knows it in this character, but only in the other, which dies with youth not unseldom. Many a maid has gone to her grave with that half-light in her heart ; though whether to pity such an one the more for that or not who will choose? Im-possible to pity her the less, is the better answer. It is after youth has gone—long gone, perhaps—that a tendresse for some one will creep into timid bosoms, never daring to be more, but cherished for what it is with pathetic fondness and unfailing con-stancy. Nor is it always concealed. Since it must have a little sympathy, it is often allowed to appear as tender friendship ; and if it be so accepted and responded to, happiness enough.

Men know little of this feeling as one that is complete and sufficient. Tender friendships of course they know, but not this other sentiment, or very rarely. It is otherwise with the spindle sex. There are many women in the world who, shrinking from the passion of love because of an extreme sensitive-ness, see their youth go by without it ; but that not being well either, for all too sensitive souls, they find a twilight heaven of contentment in the luck of a half-known, half-concealed tendresse. Many an old maid could tell that story.

VOICE

IN the state of being called love there are pleasures as violent as the clashing of two worlds to make one of perfect ray ; and others so gentle, so subtle, and yet so appealing to the senses, that there is nothing to compare them with. The delight of hearing the voice of a certain Someone must be reckoned amongst these delicate pleasures ; meaning by that the first sound of it after absence ; or when it is heard unexpectedly — coming in at a window, mayhap ; or with closed eyes ; or in any sweet and sudden situation such as all happy lovers can remember.

The words to which this music is set are almost a matter of indifference, though not quite. " Good morning, Rover," coming as a surprise, will equal Tennyson's most lovely line, and yet it is impossible for any school of criticism to make more of " Good morning, Rover," than an address to a dog in friendly conversational tones. But there is one song which, when breathed in this same music, makes so ravish-

ing a melody that it can hardly be endured. And
yet the canticle is but brief—seldom more than three
syllables long, and often only two ; but these are the
links of the listener's name. There are times when,
as they chime on her lover's lips, every nerve in
her thrills to the sound ; and then for the hundredth
part of a second her senses faint away. And this
mysterious effect will return with the mere remembrance of it.

It may be imagined that a rushing, crowding sense
of the joy of possession accounts for these strange
overcomings ; and there is enough in the explanation
to cover many a case. But what if estrangement be no
bar to them ?—and a cloud of witnesses, more or less
unhappy, can say that it is not. Estrangement is no
bar, nor even indifference to everything but the voice
itself. There are those who can affirm that they have
been shaken from head to foot by the sound of a voice
proceeding from some neighbouring figure whose
face they could not see ; and such was the effect
on them that some were plunged at once into an
unchangeable affection all happiness, and some
into a bondage that could not be much else than
misery. For with a liberal offset of good creatures as
sweet of nature as their voices are, it is the story of
the sirens : the sirens transferred to theatres, ball-
rooms, opera-house lobbies, park promenades, and
other fashionable assemblies. And there is this to
be said, that if the originals may be judged by
their successors, the voice so fatal to Mediterranean
mariners of old was a low, soft, vibrating contralto,
answering to the dreamy middle-tones of violoncellos;
and its music is the same whether it fall from the

lips of perfect loveliness or the most manifest *beauté du diable*. There are differences between true beauty and the beauty of the devil that may always be marked ; but the siren voice is the same and undistinguishable when it speaks from one breast and when from another. In both cases it is beautiful beyond compare ; and the magic of it is an enchanting invitation to trust, and a yet more entrancing promise of repose.

Though there are no tales of whiskered sirens and mustachio'd loreleis to bear out the statement, it may be said without fear that if the influence of voice on the sensibilities of the one sex is great, it is an influence more widely felt by the other. Reasons might be given for supposing that it would be so, and so it is. Further we may believe that amongst men, as amongst women, the worst have this seductive charm in as much perfection as the best. Warning may be drawn from what it utters—from unguarded words attended by unguarded looks ; but the voice itself falls on the listener's ear with the same irresistible appeal when the speaker is false and when he is true. For in either case it is entirely an appeal to sense, whatever they may think who are moved by it ; and some are moved by it profoundly though they are too innocent to know that what responds is the animal, or, perhaps, what we have called the soul of the body of this flesh. From which it will be seen that these are cautionary remarks, and bear a moral.

VOWS

   When lovers' follies have been laughed away, satire will make **an end of lovers' vows.** Till then they will neither **cease nor** diminish. **As** many as ever will be vain and perishing, though, for all that, no treacheries ; for a love **may** be born to live scarce **longer than a day-fly, and** yet be all aglow at its meridian, **and quite** unconscious then of night so **near.** And as many false vows there will be; and such as are made without guile though only to be broken **without a care.** Sir John Suckling's, for example, where he sings so wickedly——

> Dost see how unregarded now
>   That piece of beauty passes ?
> There was a time when I did vow
>   To that alone : **but mark** the fate of faces !

That all true lovers will **send up** to heaven their burning **vows, even** though **they are** laughed at **more** and **more, may** be **safely** prophesied ; for it is **no** matter **of** choice with them. They must. **They are under** compulsion of an ardour which **cannot be** content with Yea, and indeed, and be-lieve me !

> When the blood burns, how prodigal the soul
> Lends the tongue vows,

says wise Polonius. And when the blood burns, these vows leap out like flames unbidden and un-asked, from the mere fury of the fire within. But that is not the whole secret of lovers' vows. If in the heyday of young love there seems **to** be a

passion for vowing, ascribe it partly to these brave
heats, but for the rest to quite another cause.   Not
only do lovers tremble lest they should lose the
treasure bestowed on them, and therefore never tire
of hearing the sweet oaths by which it is given
beyond recall, but considering what tales are told
of wretched misunderstandings, mysterious estrange-
ments, hearts grown cold or won away by demon
tempters irresistible ; and considering how little it
would matter whether Paradise were lost a second
time by its Adam or its Eve—young lovers are in
haste to bind *themselves ;* and do so by more oaths
than are ever interchanged.   It is she who most
often takes these secret vows.   For once that she
swears to him, thrice will she make a Bible of her
pillow, and, with far more devotion than he has been
witness of or ever can be, vow herself his till death
and after.   Since so many of these oaths of fear are
uttered in the heart and never pass the lips, we
have here a squinting sidelight on an oft-repeated
passage in Shakespeare : the passage where it
is said that the vows that men have broke outnumber all that " woman ever spoke."   And if per-
juries are to be weighed as well as counted, no vows
are so hazardous as these that are made in silence
and darkness, and are meant for no human ear but
the votary's own.   None are so deep and deliberate ;
and the most delicate creatures will couch them in
words to tremble at.   But are they any the more
binding ?   There is little reason to think so, and
much to decide that it is better to forbear than be
forsworn.

WED, WEDLOCK

WHAT is it to be wed? The answer is ready in millions of pretty mouths. To be wed is to be firmly united with another; to be insunderably joined with another, so that the two are one. The idea of welding enters into the word; it is to bring in the meaning of an inseparable union that we say a man is wedded to his opinions or what not. If any further answer be required, there is the word "wedlock" to supply it:—Wedlock; to be locked in union.

And so it shall be. "Wed" shall still have these significations, supported by these associations; but in point of fact they are not the right and proper ones. The historians and antiquarians of the language are in quite a different tale. They make out that to wed is to pledge, to engage, wherefore the word was used for betrothal first and afterwards for marriage; so that when the bridegroom says at the altar, "With this ring I thee wed," his words are an oath of promise, and the ring is a pledge or gage of fulfilment.

"Gage" is an allied term, and so, it seems, is "wage" or "wages"; which makes "wed" a more appropriate word than any in his own language, probably, for Jacob's marriage with the daughters of Laban. And then (but this again is not so well) there is a close relationship of meaning between "wed" and "wager"; that is to say, a bet. Of course, when you have "gage" it is not easy to keep "wager" out; but it is an unfortunate offshoot, and gives too much countenance to the mocking spirits whose cry is that marriage is all a lottery.

But what, then, as to "wedlock"? Why, here, it seems, we are out still more. "Wed" we now understand; next we are to learn that "lock," in this connection, has nothing to do with fastening, but really and truly means "lark." It will be immediately supposed that the bird is meant; that, however, is not the case. The dreadful truth appears to be that "lark" is intended in the vulgar sense of fun, sport, frolic: in short, wedlock is a wed- or wedding-lark. As some may doubt this statement, reference is made to Mr. Skeat, a great authority on the history and meaning of our language, whose works are published at the Oxford University Press warehouse in Paternoster Row. It is something that "lark" (spelled "lâc" in Anglo-Saxon, and pronounced lāāk) is "also a gift in token of pleasure; a gift to a bride." The fastidious will incur no serious rebuke, probably, if they reject the one meaning and hold by the other.

WIFE

In the list of words made out for this lexicon, the last three were Wife, Wile, Worship. But worship?—what of worship, except that besides being an exaggeration of a noble sentiment (as worshipping is in love affairs), there is a touch of baseness in it? And have we not said enough of worship, by implication, under the head " Adore "? Away with Worship !

But that being struck out, what word is this to stand as the last chapter in the lexicon of love? " Wile " is the word ; deceit, craft, artifice ; a worm of a word. And what of the wits who, finding " Abhorrence " on the first page, smartly turn to the last and there discover " Wile "? It were hardly Christian to tempt them so. Away with Wile, then — the better riddance as an ending because there is nothing conclusive in the word itself or what it represents. And then — why then we halt upon " Wife " : which is in accordance with the endings of all agreeable books about the master passion.

Even by some women marriage seems to be doubted, so melancholy is the age ; and yet we may believe that there is not a woman in Christendom who does not dote upon the name of " wife." It carries a spell which the rebellious themselves acknowledge. Say what they may about the trammel, the subjection, the treatment as " toys " and mere child-bearing creatures to which marriage reduces them, " wife " is a word their hearts will not harden to. As often as it is repeated it enters there with troops of tender associations that cannot be denied, and with a sense of sanctity, dignity, worshipfulness yet more irresistible. How should that be if marriage is so offensive and dispiriting? But this is a question they do not ask themselves; the answer would confute them.

And wives should be the better pleased with the name they bear when they learn that it originally stood for "woman." In "ale-wife," "fish-wife," it keeps that meaning still; and in such expressions as 'an old wife's tale." Wife is woman; and when we see how soon after marriage some pretty girlish creature will bloom into womanhood complete, it might almost be fancied that Nature herself is pleased with the identity and takes pains to make it good. But if, on the hint of that metamorphosis, we ask ourselves at what age between eighteen and eighty the word sits on a woman most becomingly, what answer shall we give? At every age it has its most perfect fitness; at every age its own beauty and adornment. It brings summer into the spring of "sweet seventeen," and when it is said of some old dame whose sons are gray men, maybe, she is clothed at once with summer memories. And at what time does the word sound most pleasantly in a woman's ear? To think of a young wife in her first estate is to say, "It must be then." But why not in the meridian of life,—love confirmed, confidence secure, trust established, her sheaves about her, so to speak; her right and title won and gratefully acknowledged? Or why not when she is an old woman, the heyday long over, and her life and her love little more than a tale that is told? When her good man says, "dear wife," as they sit together by the hearth-side, can it ever have been a sweeter word to hear?

Of course, and as we have seen plainly, if a woman is not a woman she cannot be a wife. And inasmuch as she is not a woman she cannot be a wife: all that can be said for her is that she is partly the one thing as she is partly the other. And is a shrew a woman? Is a scold a woman? —or a slut, perchance? Only in a measure, and very possibly in nothing but appearance. Therefore none of the foregoing remarks have reference to such persons. We speak of true women and true wives: and were the satirists, cynics, misogamists, misogynists and the like permitted to enclose all females who are not of that description in sacks and sink them in the sea, the number of women in the world when all was done would confound them.

THE END

Printed by R. & R. CLARK, *Edinburgh*